A Trip to Jericho

A Hal Westwood Restoration Mystery

SUMMER 1664

by Jemima Norton

TUDOR GATE PRESS

LARGE PRINT EDITION

ISBN: 0-9740949-2-7

Large Print Edition

You'll find information on the other books in this series at:
www.halwestwood.com

For ordering information visit:
www.tudorgatepress.com

This book is dedicated to:

Irene

A TRIP TO JERICHO

JUNE 1664

THE WESTWOODS OF WESTWOOD HALL

Hal Westwood	24	*owner of Westwood Hall*
Francis Westwood	61	*courtier, Hal's father*
Hetta Westwood	14	*Hal's sister*
Harry Westwood	3	*Hal & Libby's son*
Jacqueline Westwood	25	*Hal's stepmother*
Katherine Westwood	39	*Hal's aunt*
Libby Westwood	22	*Hal's wife, Justin's sister*
Ned Westwood	18	*Hal's brother*
Marie	35	*Jacqueline's maid*
Thomas	28	*manservant*
Delia	17	*laundry maid*
Tilda	19	*maidservant*

THE ARMSTRONGS

SOON OF ELMLEY PARK

Mary Armstrong	25	*Hal's elder sister*
Guy Armstrong	27	*Mary's husband*
Cecily Armstrong	15	
		Ned's betrothed, sister to Guy
Margery Kingscott	59	*Hal's aunt*

The Kingscott Family   *kin of the Westwoods*

Glossary

OED- Oxford English Dictionary

an ordinary   a public meal regularly provided at a fixed price in a tavern   *OED 1589*

brandywijn   ardent spirit distilled from wine or grapes   *OED 1657*

brought to bed colloquial term for having given birth

buck water   water and alkaline lye to boil linen in   *OED 1598*

conclave   any close assembly   *OED 1568*

confinement   the act of being in childbed, delivery   *OED 1646*

court cupboard a moveable cupboard to display plate   *OED 1592*

doxy   a paramour, a prostitute   *OED 1530*

drab　　　　　a slatternly woman, a strumpet

OED 1530

ell　　　　　a measurement of length,

45 inches in England　　　*OED OE*

fellow feeling　sympathy　　　　　*OED 1613*

flibbertigibbet　a gossip, a flighty woman　　*OED 1549*

hypocras/hippocras

a cordial drink made from wine flavoured with spices.　　*OED ME*

greensick　　　an anaemic disease which mostly affects young women at puberty giving a pale greenish complexion.

OED 1583

"Go to Jericho" the equivelent of go to the devil

Penguin Dictionary of Historical Slang, 1635

Glossary

jointure a sole estate limited to the wife to take effect on the death of a husband.

OED 1451

kennel surface drain of a street, the gutter

OED 1582

lawn a fine linen resembling cambric

OED ME

long gallery a long narrow corridor *OED 1541*

mace-bearers a staff of office resembling a club borne before certain officials

OED 1440

midden dunghill *OED ME*

a moonling an absent minded person *OED 1613*

petit point tent stitch in embroidery *OED 1621*

posy a bunch of flowers *OED 1573*

screens passage

a partition of wood or stone, pierced by one or more doors which divides a room into two *OED 1460*

short commons

rations, daily fare that is insufficient

OED 1540

stout-enough fellow one who can be relied upon

tenements a single room let in a larger house

OED 1593,

thunderstruck struck with amazement or terror

OED 1613

English Feast Day
Twelfth Night *January 6*
Feast of the Magi, the Epiphany

English Cross-Quarter Days
Candlemas *February 2*
Feast of the Purification of the Virgin Mary
Lammas Day *August 1*
An Old English Quarter Day

English Quarter Days
The dates when tenancies begin,
payments of rents are due and servants are hired:
Lady Day
March 25, Feast of the Annunciation
Mid-Summer Day
June 24th, Feast of St. John the Baptist
Michaelmas
September 29th, Feast of St Michael & all the Angels
Christmastide
December 25th, Feast of the Nativity

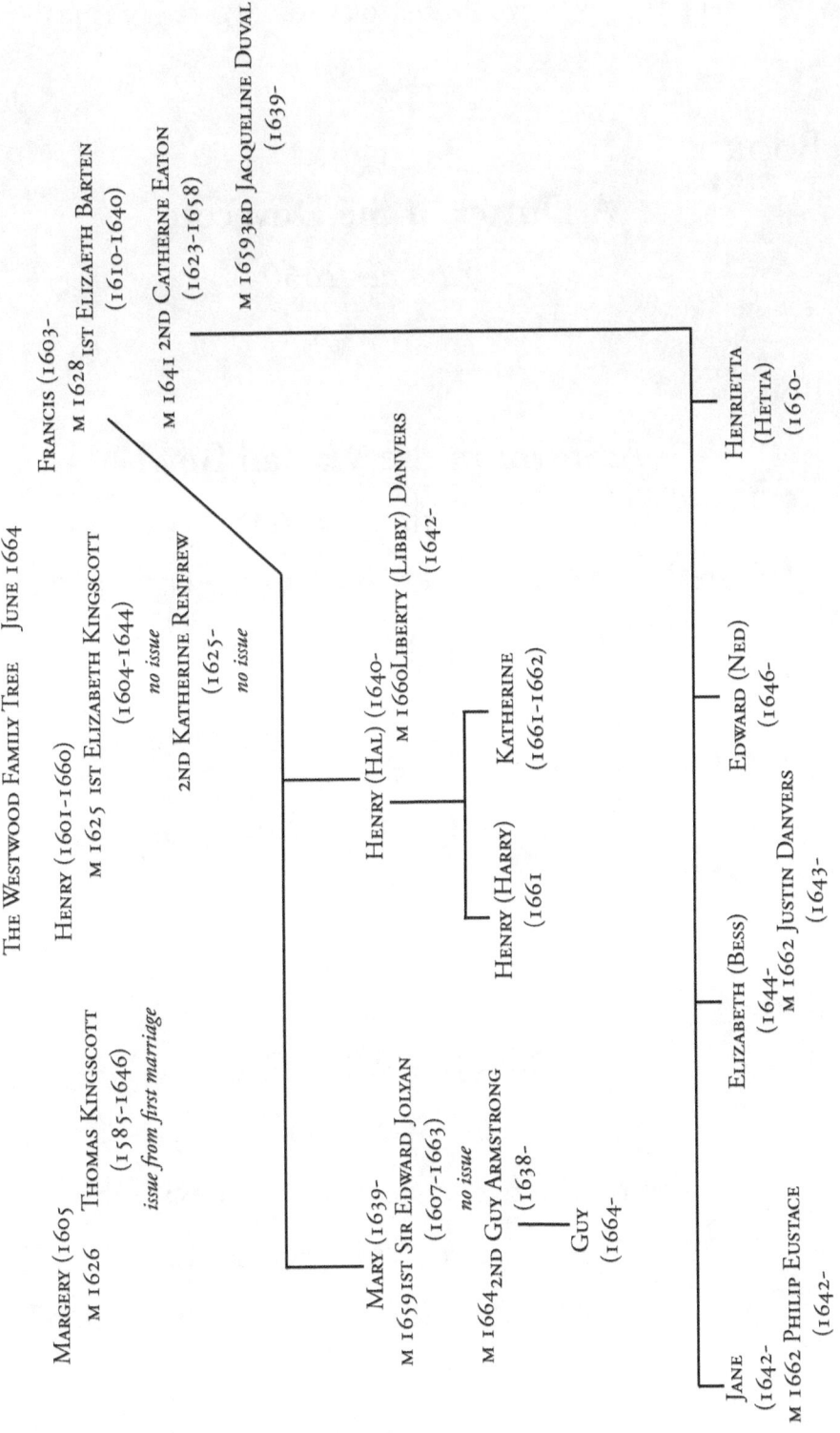

THE WESTWOOD FAMILY TREE   JUNE 1664

MARGERY (1605
M 1626 THOMAS KINGSCOTT
(1585-1646)
issue from first marriage

HENRY (1601-1660)
M 1625 1ST ELIZABETH KINGSCOTT
(1604-1644)
no issue
2ND KATHERINE RENFREW
(1625-
no issue

FRANCIS (1603-
M 1628 1ST ELIZAETH BARTEN
(1610-1640)
M 1641 2ND CATHERNE EATON
(1623-1658)

M 1659 3RD JACQUELINE DUVAL
(1639-

MARY (1639-
M 1659 1ST SIR EDWARD JOLYAN
(1607-1663)
no issue
M 1664 2ND GUY ARMSTRONG
(1638-

GUY
(1664-

HENRY (HAL) (1640-
M 1660 LIBERTY (LIBBY) DANVERS
(1642-

HENRY (HARRY)
(1661

KATHERINE
(1661-1662)

JANE
(1642-
M 1662 PHILIP EUSTACE
(1642-

ELIZABETH (BESS)
(1644-
M 1662 JUSTIN DANVERS
(1643-

EDWARD (NED)
(1646-

HENRIETTA
(HETTA)
(1650-

THE HAL WESTWOOD RESTORATION MYSTERY SERIES

❧

Chapter One

Hal Westwood paused, glancing rapidly about the courtyard. He was a stone throw from Lincoln Inn, but a hundred miles from it in spirit. His heart sank abruptly and he pushed his way through the squalor to the house, where a lop-sided sign proclaimed: Steene and Johnson, Attorneys at Law.

The entrance was dank, narrow, and the room he entered only a little better, having a stained flag floor, dark panelling and the distinct odour of rot. A bent, balding man looked up from a desk, blinking as he took in the prosperous air of his master's latest visitor, seeing a tall, handsome, dark young man; well dressed, although not in the excessive fashion of the court, with an air of one well-used to command in his eyes.

"Mr Danvers?" he asked. "Can you tell me where I'll find Mr Justin Danvers?"

"Danvers?" replied the man, his high opinion of the visitor falling abruptly. "He is working in the chamber above, but surely a gentleman like yourself would rather see our principal Mr Johnson? Or, if you could come back tomorrow, perhaps even Mr Steene himself might oblige."

"No, I thank you," replied Hal pleasantly. "My business is with Mr Danvers, and is purely personal."

"Danvers is not permitted personal callers," said the chief clerk flatly. "He's not a partner, you know. Indeed 'tis only the goodness of Mr Steene's heart which—"

"Yes, I do know," interrupted Hal sharply, "and if Mr Danvers isn't permitted personal callers, I'll seek his professional advice. Pray, tell him I am come."

The clerk sniffed audibly, "I'm not an errand boy," he muttered. "He is in the first chamber to the left, at the head of the stairs."

Hal's eyes lingered reprovingly on the man's pinched face for a few seconds, in a manner which, those who had occasion to come before the Bench these past few years, had reason to remember. Like them, he squirmed mentally, and hastened to open the door for Hal, bowing in an obsequious manner.

"At the top of the stairs, sir!" he said quickly. "Take

care of that stair. Rats have eaten part of it."

Hal mounted the stairs, observing the rat holes grimly, feeling the heat rising with him in the narrow space. The door stood open wide at the head, and the windows likewise, in the room beyond, but no breath of air came to relieve his heated brow.

"Hal?" Justin Danvers brought to the doorway by the footsteps, stared in amazement. "Hal! Is it truly you?"

"Justin—at last!" Hal grasped his hand. "By heaven, you've led me a merry dance across London! I'd have never believed anyone could disappear so effectively."

"It was relatively easy," returned Justin, his eyes wary as he recollected himself, after his surprise. "Once one gives up all pretence to gentility, life is easily anonymous."

Hal, entering the chamber in his wake, turned to look at him as the full light of the summer's afternoon fell upon his young face, and he was shocked. Gone was the confident young fellow of last Christmas-tide at Sidworth Castle. Instead, a hollow-eyed, thin-faced man, with lank hair, and shoulders bent with care, looked back at him.

"Justin, are you ill?" Hal asked in concern.

"I've had the fever," he conceded. "There's a mite of it

about, and plague, too, so they say."

"But you are so thin, and pale," Hal said in shock.

"Aye, lack of food does that,"retorted Justin, "and sixteen hour days working in this place." He laughed bitterly, and coughed in a disquieting manner, as if it were habitual.

"Sixteen hours a day?" Hal asked in dismay.

"I start at six and finish, on average, at ten," he replied wearily. "What can I do for you? Please sit."

Hal took the unsteady chair gingerly. "Bess, she is well? Where is she?"

"She is not far from here, in Rankin's Court," said Justin, his face stony. "She is well enough," he hesitated, then added: "She expects our child in the autumn."

"Bess is to have a child!"cried Hal, then glancing about him added, "Here?"

"Where else is there?" Justin asked impatiently. "Many are born in the city you know."

"Aye," said Hal grimly, "and a few even survive! Come home, Justin."

Justin's jaw set. "This is my home," he said waving his hand in the direction of the sooty rooftops.

"No," Hal shook his head, "this is nobody's home. This is the mouth of hell, and only your stubborn stupidity keeps you here! Why didn't you come to us when you fell out with your father? Why run off in that dramatic fashion, leaving Libby mad with worry?"

"I had no right to lay my troubles on your doorstep. You no more approved the match than your father," he replied.

"You lie, Justin," Hal said hotly. "I swore to give you my support at Sidworth Castle."

"Aye, when you were drunk," retorted Justin flushing. "After Mary had given you herbs to sooth your shoulder, and Armstrong fed you enough wine to mellow your censorious disapproval of their affairs."

"I admitted I'd been wrong," snapped Hal. "Did I not say so before all of you? Did we not plan how to get my father to agree to both yours, and Ned's marriages?"

"Yes! We planned it and it went awry on my father's meanness," he replied bitterly.

"He's dead, you know, Justin," said Hal, in more gentle tones, as he recollected his errand.

"Yes, I know," said Justin. "Old man Steene told me. One of his cronies told him—and all about the marriage my father made before that!"

Hal nodded, casting his feathered hat to the table, and unbuttoning his coat. "No doubt, you found that as difficult to believe, as we did," he said evenly.

"Difficult to believe?" Justin echoed, with a bitter laugh. "Aye, I did, at first I was thunderstruck. Then, when I thought about it more, I understood. He was hoping for another son, so he could completely cut me out."

"And he may yet do so," said Hal crossing his booted feet. "Mistress Johanna is with child."

"So I understand," he said bitterly. "There's no fool like an old fool!"

Hal smiled faintly, "How old was your father, Justin?"

Justin shrugged, "Fifty, fifty two, why?"

"My father has recently attained his sixtieth year, yet he still speaks hopefully of another son."

"He may speak hopefully, but 'tis many years since he sired a child. Hetta is fifteen and Jacqueline has never had a pregnancy, has she? Tell me, is it true, as they say, my father's widow is a trollop?"

"One couldn't call her a trollop, Justin," said Hal, "not in all fairness! She is, to all intents, a respectable widow. Not exactly a gentlewoman, but nothing, truly, to blush for, I assure you. Indeed, even Libby agrees, she appears good-hearted enough and certainly made it her business to keep your father happy whilst he lived."

"Only he didn't live very long," said Justin. "What is

wrong with her?" he added shrewdly.

"Do you know, I couldn't say," cried Hal, sounding surprised. "I mean, she is all I've said, and yet—and yet something's not right! She's not bad, I don't think, and certainly not simple. If anything, she's rather sharp; in a cunning sort of way. Yet still, she's not right. She makes me uneasy."

"Do you mean she's—she's mad?" asked Justin, looking dismayed.

"No, no, not at all! I don't mean that, I mean she— she is a bit of a mystery. She lacks something—scruples, I suppose. Yes, that's what makes me uneasy. I think she'll stop at nothing."

"Nothing, do—do you mean—murder?" asked Justin quickly.

"No, no, I don't," said Hal. "Such a thought never occurred—well hardly. Only it was rather odd, but I suppose I just dismissed her as a designing sort of female."

"I knew that as soon as I heard of her, and had it confirmed when I saw the will!" replied Justin dryly.

"Yes, that was odd!" agreed Hal unhappily. "You see your father came out to Westwood from his home at Adamsholme, towards the end of January, just before he married, to tell Libby of the new will he'd made out. In it he said he'd left Mistress Johanna an adequate jointure, even though she'd had no dowry. He left everything else to Libby—house, business, money—trusting to her good sense to see everything properly bestowed. We took it as meaning that he wanted Libby to see Mistress Johanna wanted for nothing, and I privately believe he was asking her to make everything right with you for him, if you should not be reconciled. But then, when he did die, this new, totally different will appeared, which, it seems, he signed in the few days he was ill. He sent for a notary, and signed it there and then."

"So it is completely legal?" sighed Justin.

"I fear so," said Hal. "I do believe in his weakened state, he may have been coerced into signing it. You must understand, neither Libby, nor I were sent for, even though he was ill for some days. But what I can't understand is this: why didn't she take everything in that case? Why still leave the house and business to Libby, in trust to the child, if it were a boy?"

"Because that way, she'll get it all. And we'd not think of contesting it. If she'd been greedy, we most certainly would have done so, but now, if the child is a girl, or still-born, she'll have a handsome fortune to walk away with, which she will probably get anyway!"

"So, why didn't you come home to contest it? It's taken me three months to track you down," said Hal.

"Come home, to what?" Justin demanded. "To become my sister's pensioner?"

"You arrogant fool!" cried Hal angrily. "You know Libby better than that! She needs you. Your stepmother has this rascally rogue, her 'cousin,' she says—her lover, is nearer my guess—and he's playing ducks and drakes with the business your clever brain made ten times more successful!"

Justin's head came up at that. "How is it Johanna is still there?" he asked.

"Because who else would run the business? Libby herself?" asked Hal. "No, she's waiting for me to find the fittest person—her brother."

"I'm sorry, I have employment," Justin replied with some arrogance.

"Aye, I can see how delightful it is," said Hal, his tone cutting as he rose to his feet. "Where will I find Bess?"

Justin rose also. "She is—she is unsettled in her mind, at this time, Hal. I pray you won't distress her."

"I distress her?" he replied coldly. "What mean you, Justin? Do you fear I'll try to keep her in squalor and poverty in this city for my own vainglorious ends, rather than bring her to safety and security, in the heart of her family in the country?"

Justin hunched a shoulder. "She's in Rankin's Court, across the square," he snapped.

Hal stood up. "I calculate I've had thirty minutes of your time. Whom do I pay? You—or the clerk below?"

"I'll deal with it," snapped Justin.

"Indeed you'll not," returned Hal coldly. "If you can take nothing from me, I'll take nothing—not even bad advice—from you. Good afternoon."

⚜

Chapter Two

Hal crossed the open field, his face grim. Justin's directions had filled him with foreboding, and so it proved. The squalor of the lawyer's office was nothing to this place. He hurried on, conscious of the groups of men, either idling their time away at dice, or bent on more dubious errands. He cut diagonally across the open space to the houses that lined it.

He felt safer once the buildings enclosed him, yet hardly knew why. The tenements had a grim, grinning, closed look about them, and the streets were littered with all manner of refuse, some even human, he thought, as he saw small children squatting over the kennel playing, whilst rats ran unhindered from midden to rubbish heap.

He spied the house, and was approaching it when the sounds of an altercation came to his ears. Loud shrieks, which somehow didn't have the ring of truth, followed by a coarse, rough voice and then a gentler, higher tone. With an oath, he ran up two steps and entered the open doorway of a large hall. Bess was there, broom in her hand, with two women, dressed in cheap finery and tawdry silks, standing over her in a menacing manner.

"What is going on here?" Hal demanded, with all the natural authority of a justice of the peace.

"This strumpet attacked my daughter," cried the taller of the women, the many plumes of her hat nodding. "Threatened and attacked her she did, her with her high and mighty airs and graces!"

"Hal!" Bess, who had shrunk back a little in the doorway in dismay at the diatribe, turned to him in patent relief.

"Oh, know him do we, my fine lady," sneered the woman. "And you no better than you ought to be, I dare say! This ain't your clever lawyer husband, is it? No! I swear he's your lover and the father of that brat under your petticoat."

"Oh hush, Mrs Redman," cried Bess blushing. "This is my brother, my elder brother, Hal." She held out her arms to him and received his kiss.

"Heavens, Bess! How far gone are you?" Hal exclaimed.

"Never you mind that, what about my daughter?" Mistress Redman demanded. "Threatened and abused she's been. I want compensation!"

"The only compensation you are likely to receive, my good woman, is seven days in Bridewell for being drunk and disorderly," said Hal firmly. "As for your daughter, a fit mother wouldn't let her get in that disgusting condition! How old is she—eleven, twelve?"

"She's fifteen, Hal, and I did threaten to slap her if she vomited in the hall again," said Bess wearily. "You can't imagine how difficult it is to keep it clean."

"I imagine it's impossible," he replied austerely. "Get gone, woman, and look to your daughter. Try to keep her at least off the brandywijn!"

"Lord have you, it ain't brandywijn," the woman cried indignantly. "Christ no, I'd not waste strong drink on her, not now she's breeding! Oh aye, 'taint only me lady as is in the family way! Deb here is pregnant, too, and what's more the father is a lord! There now, what do you think of that! My Deb a fine lady, with a carriage of her own!"

"I think I'll see pigs in the sky first," said Hal, with a half-laugh. "Is that your chamber, Bess? Then let's inside, where hopefully the air is less foul."

He followed his sister into a large room, hastily shutting the door on the loudly complaining pair. He paused to glance swiftly about him, his eyes incredulous and dismayed, coming to rest finally on his sister's pale face.

"What in God's name are you doing here?" he cried angrily.

"Living," she replied wearily. "Just living, like hundreds of other poor families in the city."

"Aye, and most of them in this house, I'll swear!" he retorted furiously. "Bess, this won't do. You must come home!"

"This is my home," she replied with simple dignity, propping her broom in the corner of the room. "I'm sorry it cannot hope to meet with your standards, but we cannot afford to be so dainty! Do pray, take that chair. Justin has been at some pains to make it sound. It may not look elegant, but it should take the weight of even a man as wealthy as you!"

Hal coloured at her sarcasm, for Bess had not used to be anything other than gentle. "I am not a particularly wealthy man," he snapped. "If you are referring to Libby holding her father's house and business, that is in trust, until the sex of Mistress Johanna's child is known.

Then we hold it in trust, if it should be a girl, for Justin, whose it is by right. We'll not gain by a penny until the child is born, and then, not touch a penny until Justin comes to sort out the muddle."

Bess stared, her mouth dropping open a little, "But it's left to Libby, Justin said so! If it's not a boy, or anything happens to Johanna and the baby, it's all Libby's by law! Libby has the house and the business, and that wretched female all the money, and you—as Libby's husband—can dispose of it as you see fit."

"That is the law," he agreed. "And it would seem nothing can be done about it, but Libby controls the business. If Mistress Johanna produces a boy, then Libby will require her brother to run the business for her until the child comes of age, and if Mistress Johanna doesn't produce a boy, then we are agreed, Libby and I, we'll make the business over to Justin, whose it is by right. Would you and Justin not have done the same if the roles had been reversed? Besides, what need have we of a house and business in Adamsholme, when we've Westwood to take care of? No, the old will shall be adhered to, for we are convinced there was some foul play along the way from Mistress Johanna."

"The will is legal. Justin said so," said Bess dully.

"I am aware of that. Not being a simpleton, I took advice," he replied tartly. "But I'm pretty sure it's not what Philip Danvers wanted. Much of what happened at his death would, I am sure, bear investigation, but even supposing we could find proof of Mistress Danvers coercing the old man, I doubt we could overturn the will, and certainly not until we know the sex of her child. Even then, if it should be a boy, a sound man will be required to stop the foolish woman ruining the business. Justin, as Danvers's eldest—if not only—son must take over."

"Oh Hal!" she cried, tears filling her eyes. "If only it could be so! If only we could leave this place and come home."

"Of course it can be so," he said firmly, eyeing her wet eyes with distinct feelings of disquiet. "You have but to say the word, Bess, and I'll call up a coach, and we can all be gone from this place!"

She bit her lip, tears sliding under her lids and glistening on her cheeks. She sank to the battered, but spotlessly clean table, as if her legs would no longer hold her, dropping her head into her hands.

"I cannot," she whispered in anguish. "Oh, I dare not. Justin would be so angry."

Hal came to pat her shoulder. "There, there, don't cry," he soothed. "As for Justin being angry, what utter nonsense! I tell you I am angry, to see my sister reduced to this!"

She looked up, her fine hair spilling from its restraining coil. "Oh, Hal don't," she sobbed, "it's not so bad!"

"Bad!" he echoed. "It's appalling! We never lived in a hovel like this, no, not even when things were at their worst during the war, when we were exiled in France!"

A watery chuckle escaped Bess. "That's because father never paid for our lodgings," she wailed.

"That's true enough," said Hal, after a stunned moment of reflection. His lips began to quiver, "I—I can recollect him saying it now, 'if we aren't going to pay, we may as well have the very best!' God, how it used to worry me!"

"Me, too," she agreed, joining him in a half-laugh. "I much prefer honest poverty!"

He glanced about again, disbelief on his face. "And I'd prefer you had some home comforts for your confinement. When shall that be?"

"In September," she replied. "Or early October."

"Wed on Christmas Eve, it could hardly be earlier I hope," he said severely.

"Libby was delivered of a little boy, on the first day of May," he added.

"Another boy! Oh, I had forgot she was with child, in all my own troubles! She is well? The babe is well?"

"No, it was a difficult birth," he said, with a sigh. "The baby died. He came early, a result, I think, of her father's troubles and his demise. Nor has Libby's recovery—hampered as it was by grief and anxiety for you and Justin—been as swift as I'd have liked to see."

"Oh, I do so miss her," sighed Bess. "I am sorry that she has such grief, and she is far from well! Mary said nothing of it, when she wrote last."

"You have been in communication with Mary?" he cried, shocked. "Whilst I scoured London looking for you, our sister Mary knew where you were?"

"Yes," she faltered, "but Justin swore her to secrecy. She wrote to say she'd been delivered a son the first week of May. She sounds deliriously happy," she added, hoping to avert his anger.

Hal looked put out. "So I gathered, from a similar missive," he replied austerely. "How a woman, not three months a widow, can be happy engaging in a second marriage, is beyond me."

"Well, Guy said he was determined his son would

not be illegitimate, and Mary agreed on the whole that there was going to be scandal and gossip anyway. It's not as if she cared for Sir Edward anyway, in fact, you said at the time that he was a pig of a man," Bess retorted with some spirit.

"What I may have said is neither here nor there," he snapped. "Sir Edward, as Mary's legal husband, was due a little respect, I feel."

"Yes, I think Mary felt that once she'd begun to show quite definitely with her baby, any respect for Sir Edward's name was rather compromised," murmured Bess, looking distressed at his severity.

Hal grunted, his face grim, as he reviewed the conduct of his elder sister.

"Have you heard the latest of Jane's husband?" Bess asked tentatively, hoping to give his thoughts fresh direction.

Hal bit back a groan, asking anxiously, "What has Philip Eustace done now?"

" 'Tis said he is dying," said Bess earnestly. "That he has the consumption, and won't last the year out. What a lucky deliverance for Jane, if it is so!"

Hal blinked, but didn't argue. "Has he seen a physician?" he asked quickly.

"So Mary said. He's seen several, but they all agree!"

"An unpleasant end to an unpleasant fellow," sighed Hal. "Poor Jane."

"How so?" Bess asked quickly. "She, like Mary, will be better off without her husband."

"I sincerely hope Jane hasn't so far forgotten her position, as to be pregnant by her lover," Hal returned coldly.

"No, I don't think that would be possible," said Bess, with a reflective frown. "Phillip Eustace keeps her so close, you know. The only men she ever meets are his friends, who have no liking for women at all."

Hal sighed, and then brightened, as he thought of something. "At least there can be no objection to Henrietta's proposed bridegroom, he is her age and a nice young lad, to my mind."

"Yes," agreed Bess doubtfully, "but don't you think they are both a mite young? Hetta is not yet fifteen, you know."

"Yes, I do know, she has lived with us at Westwood, these past three months," he said in a stately manner. "Her betrothed, William Shearsby, is a month short of his sixteenth birthday, a little young perhaps for matrimony, but it is an excellent match. I've met the boy and spoken to him on many occasions. There is nothing at all wrong with his character."

"On balance, I suppose one of us had to be lucky in a marriage of my father's making," she replied candidly. "What does Ned think of this young paragon?"

A slow grin spread across Hal's face, making him look much younger and much more handsome. "When Ned has a moment to direct his thoughts away from his sweet Cecily, it will be a miracle, but he has hunted with Will, and thought him a stout-enough fellow."

Bess chuckled, "Yes, I can hear him saying it! So, he does still hunt, does he? He's not totally bewitched by his Cecily?"

"On the rare occasions he cannot find an excuse for visiting Mary and Guy, or having them come to us, he does still hunt," he agreed, laughing. "What a boy he is!"

"Yes, Ned, who so distained all females and all emotions, to fall so hard!" She laughed again and tears filled her eyes anew, as she realised how much she missed her family.

"'Tis always those who protest so much who get it bad," he agreed. "But sweet Cecily is a dear girl. I like her enormously, and she thinks Ned is wonderful."

"Not only Ned," Bess smiled up at him. "She told me

you were her hero, too."

Hal looked uncomfortable. "She was probably jesting. She's a great girl for jest."

"No, she wasn't jesting, she's too innocent for that. She sincerely hero-worships you, after all, you did save her life."

"No, I just got to her first," replied Hal, in some embarrassment. "It could equally have been Guy, or Ned, or Justin who effected her rescue from that poor mad woman. I was just lucky to be first." He glanced up as the door opened again to admit Justin, looking hot and slightly harassed.

"I came home early," he announced, a shade belligerently.

Bess jumped to her feet in dismay. "Oh Justin, I've not cooked your meal yet! I'd quite forgot in talking to Hal."

"Stay, shall we not all go out to an inn?" suggested Hal. "I am staying at the Golden Lion at Charing Cross, but that is surely too far. Is there not a decent tavern nearer?"

"There's the Pope's Head in Chancery Lane," said Justin doubtfully. "I've never been there, but Johnson, the clerk, says they do a good ordinary."

Although both Bess and Justin were a little reluctant, Hal insisted, and an hour later found them in that very inn, dining on a chine of beef with oysters and some pullets as a side dish. Hal, guessing they fared ill these past months, pressed them to the food and plied Justin amiably with wine, but he, however, was not taken in by it.

"No, no more, Hal," he said, as Hal went to fill his goblet again. "We have yet to get home, and I don't want to disgrace myself."

"Tisk," said Hal, "we'll call a hackney coach."

"No coachman will go to Rankin's Court," laughed Bess, her cheeks delicately flushed by the wine and her eyes bright at the sight of all the good food.

"Not unless he wants his throat cut," agreed Justin, removing a dish of strawberries from Bess's reach. "Nay then, sweetheart, do you want our baby to have a strawberry mark?"

Hal laughed. "If that's the case, our little Harry should have been born with scales, for I vow Libby ate fish that entire spring."

"Fish?" Justin asked in astonishment. "Libby dislikes fish."

"Aye, so she does again now," agreed Hal. "But from

Easter, until she was delivered, she ate fish every day. Trout, herring, sprat and eel, she ate them all. Indeed we all ate them, for fish was there every day, so that now, I've no great liking for it myself."

Justin laughed and then sobered, saying gently, "It's no good Hal, don't you see, nothing is changed. My father vowed when we quarrelled over my marriage that he'd not leave me a penny, and neither he did!"

"Quite so," agreed Hal. "Libby and I were there when he wrote a new will at the end of January, and he was still in a fury, on the face of it. He vowed he'd not leave you a penny, and he was a man of his word! But that's why he left everything to Libby at that date. He told her plainly he'd done so because if he were to die before you'd seen sense and swallowed your stiff-necked pride, she was to seek you out and get you to make sense of the damned muddle. Those were his very words, Justin," he added as his brother-in-law stiffened.

"If that's the case, I don't see how I can return," snapped Justin. "I'll never admit my actions were wrong."

"You don't have to," cried Hal in exasperation. "Your father is dead, and probably turning in his grave, at the mess Mistress Johanna and her 'cousin' Dwyer are making of a sound business. It's my guess your father was secretly relieved to think he could trust his daughter to undo the injustice of his stupid obstinacy!"

Justin was silent. The obstinacy hadn't only been on the side of the old man. He'd inherited more than a fair share of it, too. He'd also been intolerably hurt by his father's reaction to his marriage to Bess. In the heady days leading up to Twelfth Night, which had constituted their honeymoon, he'd come to believe in her family's assurances that all would be well. The first blow had been expected. Francis Westwood's fury at Bess's marriage and the withholding of her dowry had been as Hal had predicted, when he'd written to inform his father of the facts and advised him to accept what he couldn't change.

But Justin's father's tantrum on their arrival at Adamsholme had been totally unexpected and their stay but brief. They had merely had time to exchange a few hasty, furious words over Bess's lack of dowry, and then off on the stage coach, on their way to London short of money, with nowhere to stay, and no future prospects but drudgery. It still angered him that the old man's temper had reduced his lovely Bess to their present poverty, and that his own intemperate folly and obstinacy, had been a contributing factor. He now had a chance, it would seem, to rectify some part of it—and even if his own inclination was still to hold out against his father's wishes—did he have any right to resist, and continue to injure the two women he loved?

"What sort of mess?" he demanded abruptly.

"I am no man of law, I cannot say," replied Hal. "But the local talk is of bad advice and dissatisfied customers. That Shillingforth—Adamsholme's old lawyer and your father's rival—is happy for the first time in ten years."

"Shillingforth? Why, surely he was about to retire?" cried Justin.

"Yes, so it was rumoured, but your father's death meant he had fresh business. He's dug up a nephew, a great lumpkin of a lad, still wet about the ears, but even if he has loutish feet, he at least has the advantage of being honest. Which is more than can be said for Mistress Johanna's 'cousin' Robin Dwyer!"

Hal continued, "Added to that, as I explained to Bess earlier, I have grave doubts about your father's will. It most certainly wasn't the one he signed just after you two quarrelled. In the first will, almost everything went to Libby. Then Mistress Johanna really seemed to get her claws into your father. I believe she made marriage her object from the very first. I tell you, I've never seen a man so bewildered as your father. Yes, he was plainly flattered by her attention, and I suppose, still resentful enough to marry her to show you a thing or two. But to my knowledge, there was never a suggestion of him altering his will so totally in her favour. I must confess I was amazed when that rascally fellow, Dwyer, read it to me. I knew by then Mistress Johanna was expecting a child, and some provision had to be made for it, but it came as a shock to learn that your father only made the will out just after the marriage, and then died within the week."

"But it is legal," Justin repeated dully.

"I believe so. I took it to a Mr Brewer in Gloucester, a lawyer recommended to me by one of my colleagues. He said he could find no fault in it. It may be legal, but it certainly isn't ethical."

"The law has little regard for ethics," replied Justin, slipping an arm about Bess, who, unused to the warmth, wine and good food, was on the verge of sleep. He drew her head protectively onto his thin shoulder.

"Very well," he said after another lengthy silence, during which Hal mentally held his breath, "I'll come back, but—"

Hal raised his glass. He was amazed at his own

success, but made haste to conceal it. "Yes?" he asked, his tone neutral.

"I'll accept no charity," Justin replied, his face austere. "I'll take on the business and run it as Libby wishes, but in return for a salary."

"You can argue the details out with Libby over the next few months, until we know whether it's a boy or a girl," cried Hal, unable now to keep a note of triumph from his voice. "Just as long as I get Bess back where she belongs, in safety and comfort, away from any further danger."

"I don't know that the risk is so great," said Justin defensively.

"I'm not prepared to take any risk," said Hal. "I've seen a red cross on a door in Fenchurch Street!"

"There are cases of the plague every year, they say. As the heat rises, so do the number of victims of the plague."

"Indeed," replied Hal grimly. "I'm not happy with any plague and would see you safe in Gloucestershire."

⚜

Chapter Three

In spite of Hal's efforts and desire to be gone from London as soon as possible, Justin, in allowing his brother-in-law to persuade them to a night's lodgings with him at the Golden Lion, still insisted on returning to his office the next morning. Hal's concerns where not without foundation, as the heat in the city grew and a few more cases of plague were reported.

Hal accompanied Bess back to their lodgings later that morning, and by dint of bribing a stout coachman, hastily helped her pack the very few personal possessions they had, and so got her quickly away. Pausing only to take up Justin, who had finished his outstanding work and tendered his resignation, they drove off to Charing Cross where they changed to a travelling coach. Hal's groom had been sent ahead with news of their coming, so his coach could meet them at Oxford next day.

The journey was accomplished in easy stages in defer-
ence to Bess's condition, for the swaying of the coach
made her feel queasy and the jolting of it from the rock-
hard ruts in the road told on them all. Neither did they
enjoy the thick dust that the continued hot weather
threw up in their wake, and they arrived on both eve-
nings, weary, sore and covered in a fine layer of grime.

Libby came hurrying to meet them upon their arrival
at Westwood, anxiety along with the welcome in her
eyes, for Hal had penned a letter to her for his groom
to carry, and this had left her in no doubt as to their
condition.

"Bess! Justin! Oh, I am glad you are come," she em-
braced both, making no comment on Justin's thinness.

He, however, did not show a similar reticence, "Libby?" He held her firmly, scanning her pale face, "My
dear, are you well?"

"Yes, yes, of course, or I shall be, now that you and
Bess are safe,"she cried, laughing a little. "Come Bess,
I've had them prepare a bath for you. Oh, you must
have been jolted to pieces in that coach!"

"I am weary and sore, although Hal's coach is infinitely
more comfortable than the hired one," agreed Bess. "Where
is little Harry? Oh, Libby, I am so sorry about the baby."

"Harry is long abed, you shall see him on the morrow when you are rested. As for my little one, yes, we are greatly grieved, but it was the Lord's will. Do not worry, you shall see your pet Harry in the morning. You will not believe how he has grown. Haste you to your chamber; I'll have Maria bring you some hypocras. Hal, you'll attend on Justin?"

⚜

In less than an hour's time, all were assembled at the supper table. Hal and Libby, Aunt Kate, Bess and Justin, Ned and Hetta.

"Oh, it's quite like old times to have you all back home, and to see the table filling up!" Aunt Kate sighed. "But I am so glad you are returned, Hal, so that I can go to Margery. I had not wanted to leave Libby alone, but Margery writes, begging that I go to help them at Kingscott."

"Do you miss Aunt Margery, ma'am?" asked Bess, who felt Westwood infinitely improved by her removal.

"Well, do you know, yes I do," she said with a smile. "I suppose I miss having someone of a similar age to talk to mostly, but yes, I do miss her company. However, I didn't begrudge her to her poor stepson. I imagine Tom Kingscott must need her help greatly at this time, what with his wife dying as she did in the spring, and now his son, James, taken so tragically, too. How poor Tom is managing, I cannot think."

"Yes," said Bess frowning. "How dreadful for Cousin Tom. He must be shocked to lose his son in that way. And James was a good horseman, too. But, there is an heir, is there not, Aunt? Indeed, do you not go on a visit there to see him soon?"

"Yes, another Henry, it does make for confusion!" Aunt Kate smiled ruefully. "Poor little lad, he is but three years old, like little Harry. He must miss his father. However, Tom's daughter-in-law Lydia is expecting another child, about the same time as you are, my dear. I shall go to them tomorrow. But, do not fear, we'll both come back for Hetta's wedding next week. Although, Tom will not, of course, or poor Lydia, who is due any day."

"Oh, poor lady, to have to face that alone without the support of her husband," said Bess with feeling.

"She'll have the support of Aunt Margery and Aunt Kate, which is probably a lot more use to her than that of a man," remarked Hal. "I know I always feel so very inadequate at a birth, and so very much in the way."

"It will be of much comfort to her. Aunt Margery is a godsend in a crisis and dear Aunt Kate is just wonderful," said Libby, for her husband's aunts had come over the years to replace her own long-dead mother, and she now had a very real affection—even for the vinegar-tongued Aunt Margery. "I know I could not have managed any of my confinements without the help and support of either of our aunts."

"You have such a sweet nature, Libby dear," murmured Aunt Kate. "But Bess, you haven't said, how is your health?"

"Why, Aunt, I am exceedingly healthy, am I not, Justin?" she replied, a little too quickly. "I was sickly at first, but now I am in excellent health and spirits!"

Kate smiled and nodded in agreement, thinking privately that Bess needed her cheeks to fill out and her eyes to lose the black marks from around them, but compared to her husband, she did look healthy. "Tell me is it so? Is there much sickness in London?"

"There is some," agreed Bess. "I saw red crosses on doors as we left," she shivered suddenly, "poor souls."

"And you, Justin?" Kate asked gently. "You, I think, need my honey syrup for your cough."

"No, ma'am." He glanced up, his thin face firm, "I

need a few solid meals inside me and to sleep for a week. My cough will then soon disappear." He hesitated, as there was a shocked silence then added: "I hope you intend to pay me a living wage, Libby."

"I shall pay you your worth, Justin," she replied calmly, having decided with Hal to defer discussion of the matter until such time as everyone should be rested.

Justin smiled faintly. "Short commons again, Bess, we'd best apply to our wealthy kin for aid." There was a certain bitter edge to his voice.

"We expect our other guests to begin to arrive soon for Hetta's wedding," said Ned, exchanging a glance with Hal. "So Cecily will be here by the end of the week. She's coming with Mary and Guy."

Bess nodded, "I can't wait to see her, or Mary and her new baby."

"An infant prodigy, if Armstrong is to be believed," said Hal dryly.

"Every baby is a miracle, Hal," said Libby, wistfully.

"By the by, Hal, did you know Guy is going to look at Elmley Park when he's here?" asked Ned, making haste to change the subject.

"Elmley Park?" Hal asked, glad of the diversion. "Why, in heaven's name?"

"He's thinking of buying it," said Ned, shrugging. "Mary never liked the country around Sidworth Castle and now that Sir Walter Soames is dead, and his son Geoffrey is Lord of Sidworth, they find it rather uncomfortable living so close. Geoffrey Soames has neither the manners nor wit to keep quiet about last Christmastide's events, and now Guy has made so much money in his venture with Justin's father, he can afford to buy what he wants."

"Is it true that Geoffrey Soames has put out Tom Featherstone from the living?" Hal asked.

"Yes, and Guy has taken him in. Which is why, by my guess, he is intent on this move. His sister Fanny and ten stepchildren, he can just about tolerate, he says, but not Tom Featherstone's chagrin over all that happened. That, and Mary wants to be nearer us, here at Westwood," said Ned with a grin.

"I know he thinks nothing's too good for Mary, but surely he'll not leave the family home on one of her whims?" Hal sounded scandalised.

"I don't think it is their family home," said Ned, "Mary was telling me it came from Guy's mother's family, and that her great uncle had won it in a game of dice or some such thing! Guy and his mother moved there, when they were put out by Parliament, from their own home at Theresby. Apparently it was falling to pieces then, and until now, Guy's never had a penny to spend repairing it. Mary says it's in a worse state than Sidworth Castle."

"Yes, I can imagine she would," remarked Hal. "As you say, she never liked the place. And Guy truly thinks on looking at Elmley Park?"

"When does your bridegroom arrive, Hetta?" asked Bess of the girl who sat silently, as her brothers continued to discuss the relative merits of rival properties.

"He comes to visit most days," Hetta replied, her face breaking into a smile. "We wait only for father to arrive, for the wedding to go forward."

"Father is coming here?" Bess cried, in a panic.

"Yes," said Hal. "How could you think he would not? You don't have to meet him if you don't wish, but I think it might be for the best, don't you?"

"Most probably," agreed Justin. "After all, you'll not want to grudge him his gloat, Bess. He said I'd amount to nothing, and so I have. If only you'd listened to him, you'd be living at court now."

"If she'd listened to Francis, she'd be dead!" said Aunt Kate. "Haven't you heard the latest news? Margery's letter was full of it. Jack Petherbridge's wife Eleanor is dead. She was a Somersby, you know. Her mother is a friend of Margery's."

"Dead?" asked Justin, as Bess turned pale.

"Aye, and there is talk," said Aunt Kate. "Jacqueline says nothing else is spoken of at Court, and but for the fact that Jack Petherbridge's father has the ear of Lord Sedley—and he's a rogue if ever there was one—and that Jack's the godson of—now who was it? I cannot for the life of me remember—but somebody of note at Whitehall—well, but for that, they say he'd be in Bridewell!"

"How did she die?" asked Justin gravely.

"She took sick after eating a dish of mussels," said Kate. "Of course, I know mussels can be a dangerous thing to eat, but it seemed others ate from the dish and didn't die. But she, Eleanor, had irritated Jack Petherbridge only the day before, by refusing to sign over all her properties, and of course, the following day she had signed!" Kate sighed, "He must be a very wicked fellow!"

"I think we all knew that," agreed Hal. "Let us be thankful Bess wasn't tied to him, and it's not her death we are talking of. More than one suspicious death is enough for any family!"

On this happy thought, supper continued. Justin remained a little distant, but Bess was happily back amongst her family, joining in with the conversation more than had previously been her want, as if she had time to make up for.

❧

Justin stood thinking of this early next morning, as he drank off a mug of ale. He was resolute in quashing his feelings of guilt, for better or worse they had agreed, and so far, for Bess, things had been worse and he'd been to blame. Yet, if they hadn't been married secretly, perhaps she wouldn't be alive today.

"Justin?" Libby entered the hall, her basket over her arm. "Why, I quite thought I'd be the first from my bed."

"No," he said, turning to look at her. "No, I couldn't sleep. Would you believe it? The first chance I've had since Christmas not to have to leave my bed before dawn, and I was wide awake before cock-crow."

She smiled and linked her arm though his. "Well, I'm glad in a way, because I want to talk to you. Come help me pick my herbs."

"Herbs?" he asked, opening the door for her.

"Yes, some for strewing, and others to make up Hetta's bridal posy. They must be dried now to be included."

He smiled faintly at her air of assertion, thinking how quickly she'd become the perfect country house-wife. "Are you happy, Libby?" he asked on an impulse, as they stepped out into the fragrant garden.

"Happy?" she looked up at him quickly. "Yes, yes I am! Of course I am happy! I mean, obviously I am not without worries, and there's always the sadness for my baby, not to mention the death of our dear father, but yes, I am happy."

"Good," he said. "Good, I'm glad."

"You are not?" she asked gently.

His smile was a grimace, "I suppose I am disappoint-ed," he confessed. "Things haven't fallen out as I hoped, or expected."

"But you still have Bess," she reminded him.

"Yes, I thank God daily that I have my darling Bess," he agreed fervently.

"Even though your marriage has cost you so dear?" she began to snip the early sprigs of lavender, but darted him a sharp look as she spoke.

"Yes, for don't you see, without Bess, everything else would have been rather hollow anyway. It's just that—"

"Just?" she prompted, as he took the bundle from her.

"Oh, I don't know," he sighed. "I suppose I hate

being worsted by anyone. It was *my* money, Libby, and *my* business! I'd worked damned hard for the past seven years for it. From the time I could add a column, I'd done the accounts—well, you remember how it was!"

"Indeed I do," she agreed warmly, "and I find it very difficult to forgive father for his actions. Mind, I don't think he'd have continued quite so obdurate, if it hadn't been for Johanna."

"No," he agreed. "I was amazed at that turn of events. He'd been a widower for twenty years, near enough! I never expected him to remarry after all this time."

"From what I gathered, it was a very determined campaign," said Libby. "She chased him, and he was flattered."

"Do you think the child is his?" asked Justin, idly picking the tops off the lavender and putting it in the basket.

Libby looked shocked. "I'd never even considered another possibility," she said. "You mean you think—"

"I just think it's all so convenient," he said bitterly. "He met her in January, married her by Candlemas, and she's with child immediately!"

"Yes, I suppose it is rather," she agreed. "Oh, how very wicked, surely she'd not dare!"

"It wouldn't be the first time, would it, that an old

man has been fooled in such a way?" he said glumly.

"But Justin, if that is so, why, you are doubly cheated!" Libby cried indignantly. "If the child is his, there is some justification, but if it isn't—oh, this is dreadful!"

"Now, now don't get in a pucker," he soothed. "It may indeed be that the child is our half-sibling, but I must confess, I'd like to be sure."

"How can you?" she asked. "Only Johanna will know for certain."

He shrugged his shoulders. "When does she expect the child?"

"I don't know, sometime in autumn, I do believe," she said blankly.

He nodded. "Well, we shall see," he said. "We shall see! Now, to discuss our affairs. Hal says you want me to run the business for you, when the child is born. Indeed, from now on, for you are the child's trustee."

"No," she replied firmly. "I want you to take the business from me, if the child is a girl."

He shook his head, "I can't do that my dear. 'Twas left to you."

"It shouldn't have been," she said quickly. "It was pure spite. It's yours by right and I want you to have it."

"No, I won't take it," he said bluntly. "It wasn't left to

me and I won't have it. But I will run it for you, if you wish."

"Don't be silly, Justin, how can I employ you?" she cried.

"Very easily," he replied. "And make no mistake, Libby, if you persist in this, I shall go back to London, and leave you to muddle through!"

"Justin, you wouldn't!" she cried aghast.

"Well, no, most probably not," he agreed, "but I won't be moved on this, Libby, so stop it."

She was silent a space, absently trimming the tops of a crop of chives, then she said, "How shall you manage it? Johanna will object immediately. She did at once, when Hal first went to see her. She said her cousin was more than capable of running the business, and that's what father had wanted."

"If that's what father had wanted he'd have left it to her," he replied. "As for the awkwardness, I intend to leave it all to Hal. It's his business, not mine, after all."

"She has the right to remain in the house for a while, you know," she said, her face filled with doubt as she acknowledged this.

"Yes, so I gathered," he replied. "We'll just have to hope we all manage to get on, won't we?"

Libby opened her eyes wide. "It's not likely. Of course,

she could elect to buy a house with some of the money."

"I doubt that she will, however," he said sardonically. "What think you of Hal's idea, that the will is dubious?"

Libby sighed and came to sit on a stone bench in the morning sunlight. "It's like you said, Justin, all so very convenient! You and father quarrelled—when? Just after Twelfth Night and within a week, he'd met this Johanna. He told me about her when Hal and I went over to see him. Hal tried to remonstrate him over his attitude to your wedding."

"I never knew that," he said. "Hal went with you?"

"Yes, and came the nearest he ever did to quarrelling with father, too. He actually called him a bloody fool, Justin—to let someone as good as you go, for his own stubbornness. Father was not pleased. He called Hal an impudent young jackanapes, but he apologised almost immediately! Then he was full of this 'daughter of a cousin of cousin Nancy', who'd come to stay. Mistress Johanna said she still thought I lived at home, but I didn't believe that. Anyway, he'd found her lodgings with Mistress Tripp, and said she was looking for work, as her husband had just died."

"She soon found employment, didn't she?" asked Justin grimly.

Libby sighed, "I couldn't believe it when he wrote, only ten days later, to announce his wedding," she agreed. "Hal and I went to see him again, for Hal was so concerned that your quarrel had not blown over, and we met Johanna that day."

"What did you think of her?" asked Justin curiously.

Libby hesitated. "I—I didn't like her," she said slowly. "Yet, I don't know why, except that she plainly admired Hal," she added waspishly.

He laughed. "Surely you must be used to that, Libby, Hal being so very handsome."

"Naturally, I see and fully comprehend that admiration for him, yes," she agreed with dignity. "But, somehow, I don't know, some females are able to express it less offensively than others. Take the Armstrong sisters—well Fanny is married now—but at Christmas when we first met, it was plain both she and Cecily admired Hal's good looks initially, but neither alluded to them or ever made him—or I—uncomfortable by that admiration."

"They are both well brought-up young ladies, of course," agreed Justin, with the glimmer of a smile. "Johanna plainly, is not."

"No, and yet, there is something there. She's—she's

not a—a trollop, like Jacqueline," she said roundly.

"My dear, should you call your husband's stepmother by such a name?" he asked, gently smiling.

"I speak as I find," she replied. "Jacqueline is a trollop."

"Yes, yes indeed," he agreed hastily. "And our stepmother is not a trollop?"

"No, at least she may be, but not from conviction," said Libby. "I mean—oh, I don't know what I mean, you'll have to judge for yourself when you see her."

"I shall look forward to it," he said politely. "Shall we go back to the house, and discuss this further with Hal?"

"Yes, we must do so," she replied. "For already the day is beginning, and I fear it will be a long one."

"Are you recovered enough for all this, Libby?" he asked, anxiously scanning her face. "You are still very pale."

"I am well enough," she replied. "I've only lost a child. 'Tis a common enough occurrence."

"It would be better for all concerned if it doesn't become too common," he said grimly.

"I know only too well I am failing in my duty," she replied, "and that one heir is insufficient."

"Never say Hal says so!" cried Justin angrily.

"Hal, no," her face softened. "No, Hal says that save for our pain, it doesn't matter. That we are young and have plenty of time to get more children."

"Well then," he said gently, as they walked back toward the house.

"I feel I am failing him," she said softly. "I know he wants more boys. Harry isn't strong."

"Harry's a lot better, don't fret," he soothed, as they passed by the stables. "All children have these childhood illnesses! Good heavens, I can't believe how quiet it is, now that the pigeons and old Jonas are gone!"

"Yes, Hal kept them whilst Jonas was ill. He lived with his daughter in the village, you know, and could still see them every day. But when he died last January, well, Hal thought they were rather more trouble than they were worth."

"Yet, I miss them," said Justin glancing up at the old dovecote. "That's one of my first memories of this place, the doves whirling at the slightest noise!"

"Yes," she agreed, "I feel we've lost something, but Aunt Kate's cat used to catch them once Jonas wasn't there. And that made such a mess with the feathers, so in the end, Hal said it just wouldn't do."

Justin nodded, glancing to her doubtfully. "Are you

sure you are happy, Libby? I know you grieve for father and your baby—but you and Hal, you are happy?"

She smiled up at him, puzzlement in her face, "I daresay I'm as happy as I have any right to be! What is the matter with you today? You're so solemn, I think you've forgotten how to laugh or smile in London."

"Aye," he agreed. "I expect I have."

"Was it grim, Justin?" she couldn't keep the anxiety from her voice as they entered the house.

"Yes, it was grim," he replied, handing her the basket, and turning away as if he didn't care to think of it.

"Hal said he didn't think you got enough to eat, and that you were working yourself into an early grave," she said, observing the breakfast set at ready with satisfaction.

"We'd been so protected before, Libby," he said. "Cushioned by comfort, easily knowing where the next meal was coming from, not afraid of getting sick! To be poor, really poor, is terrifying."

She shuddered. "Yes, it must be, but you've left that behind now, Justin. You are safe back here. I'll fatten you up these next few days, and you need never want for anything again."

"Bess need never want for anything again," he amended. "Provided, that is, you pay me a decent wage."

"I've told you, Justin, I'll pay you your worth, and you are worth a fortune to me."

❧

Chapter Four

Johanna's eyes dwelt on the faces of the two men sitting opposite. Justin had enough likeness to her late husband to catch her attention initially, but Hal Westwood held it. She'd met him several times now, but never before without his mouse of a wife, and she couldn't deny that she was drawn to him. Why, she wasn't sure, for he made no pretence of wanting to be on good terms with her.

It could well be it was this aloofness she found so very intriguing, for he was remote, she knew that. Remote, elegant, fashionably dressed and so coolly arrogant, he represented everything she'd ever wanted. What wouldn't she give to be an intimate of his, to see those dark eyes light up at the sight of her, to see his finely-moulded lips break into a smile as she came into a room, for him to take her hand and kiss it with suppressed passion, rather than coolly nod as he had done.

"So you see, Mistress Danvers, as my wife's agent in this matter, I wish my brother-in-law to run the business for her."

Johanna managed a limpid smile. "So we meet at last, stepson," she said with spurious warmth. "I cannot tell you how it affects me, to see one who so resembles my poor Philip."

Justin raised his brows, "I am flattered, madam," he said ironically.

"Naturally, I understand, Mr Westwood, how you want to put in your own man. Blood, as they say, is thicker than water, is it not?" she said with an ingratiating smile.

"So I am given to believe, ma'am," said Hal coolly.

"It would be so silly for us to quarrel," she said, with an air of candour. "For are we not all related here, if not by blood, by ties of marriage?" She clapped her hands coyly. "You are both my stepsons, in effect. Is that not so foolish? Me, a mother to two such handsome gentlemen."

"Foolishness certainly played its part in this scheme," agreed Justin.

She flashed him an unloving glance, and sighed. "You think so, Justin, do you? Ah, but I am not so sure!"

Then, as Hal began another of his carefully rehearsed statements, she interrupted impulsively. "You must allow me a fellow-feeling. I am sure you'll allow me that much, will you not, Mr Westwood? Or perhaps I should, as your stepmother, call you Hal?"

"I think perhaps, as I am also your landlord, we should retain some formality," replied Hal coldly.

Her smile became fixed. "No doubt you are correct, however you'll permit me to finish, I trust?" Again he nodded coldly, and a feeling of thwarted rage swept over her. "I, too, have a feeling for my kin, as you're reputed to Mr Westwood. My dearest husband reposed the greatest trust in my cousin, Robin Dwyer. I should not like him to lose his employment."

"The greatest trust," echoed Justin dryly. "For all the six weeks of his acquaintance, madam?"

"Trust is not a matter of time, Justin," she replied with a careful smile. "Philip knew he could trust Robin, the moment he set eyes on him. Ah, but he was a saddened, desperate man then, and so glad to have the assistance of a capable, younger man."

"If he hadn't been such a stubborn fool, he could have continued with the help of his son," said Hal, who had no patience with her nonsense and artificial sighs.

"Now, Hal," she scolded. "I won't take offence, for as I say, we are all family, but really, such disrespect."

"Quite," said Justin pointedly, "but before you speak, Hal, I have no objection to this Robin Dwyer. I shall need some assistance."

Hal met his eyes, his own showing faint surprise, but he nodded, knowing Justin too well to dispute the matter with him. If he wanted to keep the man on, it would be for some good reason. "Very well, provided it is made clear he works for you, Justin. You are to take control."

"I am not so sure he'll consent to that," said Johanna indignantly. "Really Hal, you should bear in mind he has obliged you these past three months, without a word of complaint."

"I wasn't aware he had any," replied Hal. His eyes flicked over her face coldly and he found himself wondering how it was that she was so very commonplace. She should have been quite lovely, her features were regular, her skin clear, her eyes blue and her dark hair shiny and curling, and yet there was something in the over all cast of her face which spoiled it.

Perhaps it was the sharp expression of her eyes, or mayhap the too-full curve of her lips, he wasn't sure. Either way, he didn't admire her at all, and wondered what exactly his father-in-law had seen in her.

"Well, he's not one to complain, but things are placed very awkwardly for us, you'll agree." She said, with a return to her air of candour. "I am left well provided-for, yes, but this home I have come to love, this haven, where I at least felt safe from the rigours of the world, is no longer mine! Left to Libby, who has that great house at Westwood, and others I'm sure, and the business too! Unless this dear babe is a son, as I'm sure it will be, of course. This greatly embarrasses me, for I promised Robin employment, if only he'd take pity on poor dear Philip and come to his assistance. Now I am to tell Robin, another has been put in above him, and a younger man."

"Therein lies the folly, ma'am, in promising something without your gift," said Hal unmoved. "How fortunate that you have been so very adequately provided for, as to make the purchase of your own home well within your means."

"As for that, I have tenure, you know, for as long as it takes me to find a new home," she replied quickly.

"Indeed you do, ma'am," agreed Hal. "It is something I should be happy to assist you in. I can't see it taking much longer than, shall we say, three months?"

"No fixed time limit was given," she replied petulantly. "Philip was anxious I should not be hurried from my home in my condition."

"I can fully appreciate his sentiment, ma'am, for I am most anxious to see my sister settled in her new home before the birth of her child," said Hal. "That is at Michaelmas, three months hence. In the meantime, as this is fortunately a commodious house, you will have no objection, I am certain, to their joining you."

"Joining us here? Why, when you have such a great house at Westwood?" Johanna stared, looking greatly put out.

"True, Westwood is a large house, but hardly a convenient one for Justin, who must be close to his employment," replied Hal.

"Justin? Justin won't mind travelling. Why, it can be no more than six or eight miles to Westwood from here and you can't say you haven't room enough, for don't all Adamsholme know about the great works going on at Westwood!" Johanna cried incensed.

"The great works?" repeated Hal, rather dismayed.

"The building works going on. All Adamsholme knows about it. We get a week by week account of the progress of the building," she retorted.

"The restoration of the building, ma'am," Hal replied unhappily.

"Indeed, is that what you call it? We all marvel at the increasing size of it! Westwood Palace, we call it, now!"

"It is no larger now than it was before the war, Mistress Danvers," Hal replied, an edge to his voice. "I am merely making good the damage of the Parliamentarian soldiers and their cannon."

"I've heard tell the cost of the glass alone would keep the poor of Adamsholme in bread for a month," she replied slyly.

"True, as part of the west wing was so very badly damaged we are taking the opportunity to enlarge some of the windows, thus ensuring—"

"I'm sure my dear husband would be only too pleased to see his fortune laid out in such a manner," she interrupted. "Dear Philip was so proud of the connection between him and the Westwood family. Such a pity he so seldom got across the threshold of his daughter's home."

"My father refused many invitations to Westwood, madam," interrupted Justin, as Hal looked confounded. "Both Mr Westwood and Libby constantly asked him to join them at Christmas, indeed, at any time he cared to visit."

"Yes, but of course, it isn't easy to visit a house when one isn't sure of one's standing. Dear Philip was always adamant he wouldn't intrude upon his daughter's new family. Only I know how it cut him to the quick, that he so seldom saw his grandchild," she replied sadly.

"My father saw his grandchild as often as any other grandparent," said Justin, seeing what she was about. "I don't recall him ever expressing a desire to visit Westwood, or see his Harry more than he did."

"No, well, he'd hardly confide in you, would he?" Johanna snapped at Justin, angry that he had stepped into the firing line, thus letting Hal off the hook.

"I fail to see why he wouldn't tell me," Justin snapped back. "Until last Christmas, I was with him every day. We were the closest of companions."

"Aye, until last Christmas, when you abandoned him!" She turned on him fully now. "How do you know which way his thoughts turned, left alone and childless as he was by your imprudent marriage?"

"But not for long!" Justin was now incensed and his suppressed fury spilled out. "By heaven, I don't suppose you could believe your luck, could you? What happened? A cousin of Cousin Nancy, who you met at Cousin Dorothy's house at Christmas, and followed him to Adamsholme by Twelfth Night, and were wed by Candlemas? Is that how it happened?"

"I was there to help him in his grief," she replied pulling herself up to her full height.

"Help him in his grief and add fuel to the flame of his anger! And wormed your way into his affection—"

Hal interrupted hastily, as battle lines were clearly drawn, and the contestants forgot all else but their hatred of each other. "I really don't think this sort of mud-slinging is going to help. Justin, be calm. We came here today to treat with Mistress Danvers, to discuss matters and to try to achieve a compromise!"

"Compromise?" Justin laughed aloud.

"Mistress Danvers," Hal turned to her. "Mistress Danvers, this really will not do. Come, you must both stop this unseemly quarrel! Justin, you know we agreed that it was essential we compromised."

"I am more than willing to compromise, Mr Westwood." Johanna got control of her temper, annoyed with herself for showing it before him. "If you'll recollect, all I said was that I was surprised that your sister wouldn't be staying with you at Westwood, and pointed out that sharing a house with her would be difficult, as I don't know her," she protested. "We might not agree!"

"A matter soon remedied," said Hal. "She is, after all, your stepdaughter by marriage, and Bess is the most placid of creatures. As you have said, we are all family here."

"Indeed?," she cried, her eyes flashing again as he tumbled into her trap. "And yet some of us are clearly not seen as such, are we? Surely, if you truly believed that we were all family, I wouldn't have been so insulted as to be left out of the guests for your sister's wedding."

Hal stared at her, fascinated. The idea that he should invite her to a wedding in his family had never occurred to him. On his marriage to Libby, it had been tacitly assumed by both himself and the elder Mr Danvers, that there would be no mixing socially.

True, Justin soon became intimate with his sister's family, but Justin, like Libby, had been carefully educated and was plainly superior to the position he held. His father had never aspired to mixing with his social superiors, and yet this was plainly what this woman expected. Irritation flickered over his face at the thought of Libby's reaction, then he realised it might make things easier for Bess. Breaking in on Justin's stammered excuse of her widowhood, he smiled, exposing her to the full warmth of his charm.

"Had the invitations gone out for Hetta's wedding, no doubt you could feel yourself insulted, ma'am," he said smoothly, "but you see we are waiting on my father's word as to when he shall come, and so we haven't issued any invitations. The family is just gathering and when he sends word, it shall all be arranged."

Johanna, a little dazzled by his smile, closed her mouth with a little snap. "Oh, I see, but of course, Sir Francis Westwood, having the ear of the king, so to speak, cannot get away, I can quite understand! Oh, yes, that explains everything. So, when should I come?"

Hal, whose thoughts had been diverted, glanced back to her, only concealing his horror in time. "Come to us at Westwood?" he asked. "Oh, well, Libby didn't want to put too much of a strain upon you, you know, not in your condition, and so recently bereaved. She thought you might well prefer just to come for the wedding itself."

"A much better idea all round," said Justin quickly. "With the house so full of those who must come far greater distances, and Libby still not fully recovered from her lying-in."

Johanna cast him a look of scorn. "My poor Philip has been dead quite three months now, Hal," she said

coyly. "Time enough to come out of complete seclu-
sion, and as for this"—she patted her smooth stomach—"why, Robin said only this morning, that I am at
the stage of pregnancy which is so infinitely becoming,
and I've never felt better in my life, I must confess. No,
Hal, you don't need to fear for me. I shall make an effort. I find that is the way to banish melancholy. I will
come to Westwood almost immediately. Indeed, it is
time I put aside my selfish feelings, and hurried to assist poor Libby, if she is still not recovered. I know how
Philip used to worry about her in that great house, with
all the responsibility!"

"As to that, ma'am, she has my aunts to assist her, and
my sisters," said Hal taken aback. "I don't believe she
lacks anything."

"Well, she'd hardly tell you if she did, would she,
Hal?" she said, with an artificial laugh. "Oh, you husbands, you just don't see how a woman suffers. Libby
has never truly been in health and spirits, so Philip said,
since the death of her little daughter, and now she's lost
another child. I may not be her true mother, but I can
at least do my poor best for her, now she has no parents
of her own."

Hal, who had gone pale at this casual reference to the

deaths of his and Libby's children, said sharply, "I can assure you ma'am, none entered more fully into Libby's grief than I, who shared it! As for feeling the loss of her mother, indeed, she said only a few months ago that she had no recollection of her own mother, but that my Aunt Kate had come to mean as much to her."

"Well, of course, Hal, we all make the best of every circumstance we can," she replied. "I know how bravely Libby has met every daunting task set her. Philip greatly admired her determination in becoming one of your family. He said she was braver than any man he knew, in going into the lion's den of Westwood Hall. It can't have been easy for her, poor girl, there is always so much prejudice against a new bride, and she cannot always count on the support of her husband."

Hal's eyes flashed. "Libby has never complained of lack of support from me, ma'am," he snapped.

"No, indeed, have we not just said that Libby never complains," she said smiling, pleased to have pierced his cool exterior.

"No more has she ever complained to me," said Justin, as Hal looked thunderstruck.

"Well, of course not, my dear boy," she laughed, although her eyes were as cold as pebbles at the bottom of a stream. "There are many things never said to young men. They so seldom understand. Philip knew what she suffered, and worried greatly about her. Yes, I have been very remiss; I see that now, to stay here, safe in my dear, dear house, nursing my grief. I shall come to Libby as soon as I possibly may, and thank you, dear Hal, for reminding me of my duty! No, you mustn't think I mind your little hint. I tell you I am grateful for it! Yes, I shall be with you at Westwood just as soon as all can be made ready. How fortunate that we have so solid a fellow as Robin to leave here to run things, Justin, whilst we enjoy ourselves!"

"How the devil did that all happen?" demanded Hal as they mounted their horses and rode out of the town. "I thought we'd gone there to get rid of her!"

"So you have," grinned Justin. "She's moving out of my house and into Westwood."

Hal's look spoke volumes. "God alone knows what Libby will say," he said at length. "She hated the woman on sight."

"Not to mention dear Robin, who is—how did you phrase it—not quite honest?" Justin grinned. "I see I shall have to watch the fellow!"

Hal groaned. "I have a feeling of impending disaster!" he said. "Within days we shall have Mary and Guy Armstrong, not to mention Cecily, Jane and that awful husband of hers, my father and Jacqueline, all arriving."

"Jacqueline?" Justin queried in dismay.

"She can hardly be excluded. She's my father's wife," replied Hal irritably.

"She's trouble, especially for Libby," said Justin with conviction.

"Well, she's going to have help, in the form of your father's wife, may God help her!" said Hal, "Come on, we'd best get back and break the news to Libby."

❧

Chapter Five

Libby heard the sounds betokening arrival with an inner groan. Hal's diffident confession had filled her with dismay. She'd disliked Johanna almost immediately, and had hoped never to have to be long in her company again. The thought of her making a prolonged stay at Westwood was enough to drive her to distraction.

Reluctantly, she laid aside her melancholy thoughts and bent for a few minutes over little Harry, who was sleeping soundly, a wooden horse clasped uncomfortably in his arms. She glanced up and smiled at the nurse.

"He seems quite well now, doesn't he, Alys?"

"Yes, Mistress," she replied calmly. "It was no more that the sniffles. I said so at the time."

"Yes," agreed Libby humbly, "I know I do fret. Now, do you think this new nursery maid will do?"

"'Tis Jack Tomson's lass, Mistress, she's as sound as a bell. This is her dream, you know, and she's that placid. I always did think Nan Wooley was too flighty for a wet-nurse. Always looking in the mirror and tying up her hair with ribbons! If you ask me, she had designs on Master Hal."

"Yes, I rather gathered that," sighed Libby. "Well, I'd best go and greet my guests. Heaven knows the next time I'll get to be with my little darling."

"I shall be here, Mistress, so don't you fret," soothed the girl. "And you just make ten minutes everyday, to come and sit with him. Remember, it's not six weeks yet since your own lying-in."

Libby agreed and hastened away, wishing she didn't still feel so very tired. She paused at the head of the stairs to smooth her silken skirts and settle the lace of her sleeves, and then proceeded to the hall below, only to stop short at the sight of the visitor talking to a harassed Bess.

"Jacqueline!" Libby cried, in anything but delighted accents.

"Oh, hello Libby, 'tis you!" Hal's stepmother turned to reveal her elegant figure clothed in a travelling cloak. Her sharp eyes ran in an assessing manner over the younger woman. "Zounds! Libby, you have aged this past year! How old are you? You look thirty, if not a day! Where did you get that gown? It does nothing for you!"

Libby blinked in the face of so comprehensive an attack. "Welcome, ma'am," she said politely. "I was not expecting you quite so soon."

"Non, I didn't want to bury myself in the country either," she snapped, "but my husband, he is being tiresome!" She shrugged her shoulders in the manner of her French countrymen. "I think all husbands are tiresome. Is Hal tiresome Libby? And your clerk, Bess, is he tiresome?"

"Justin, who is a lawyer, stepmother, not a clerk," cried Bess, her cheeks flushing and her eyes flashing, "is quite perfect!"

Jacqueline opened her eyes wide. "So, in spite of the fact he has got you so you look like the side of a house, you still defend him? You little fool. Ah, but your Papa is displeased with you, Bess, and won't be happy to see you breeding, either!"

"Why should I care for that?" Bess retorted. "He's never shown the slightest interest in my happiness, so why should I care for his?"

"Quite the tigress, I see, now you have something to defend!" Jacqueline sneered, "And you Libby, are you still so besotted with your handsome husband?"

"I still love Hal dearly, yes, stepmother," she replied with quiet dignity. "May I take your cloak for you?"

"Non, Marie shall do that. Marie, haven't you got my jewels from the coach yet? Take them to my chamber, and make haste."

Hal, entering in the wake of the servant woman, quickly summoned a smile. "Jacqueline, how are you? Good heavens, did we expect you today? Come, let me help you out of that dusty cloak. You must be tired to death travelling in this heat."

"A glass of wine would help slake my thirst, yes, Hal," she said. "As 'tis plain neither your sister nor your wife can think of such a thing."

"Oh, I am sorry," said Libby shaking herself. "I didn't think of it. I was just so surprised. I'll call Thomas."

"I think we are all taken at a disadvantage," smiled Hal. "Are my father's plans changed then? I thought we waited on his coming for the ceremony, but Mary hasn't arrived yet, nor Jane."

"His plans are changed," Jacqueline announced flatly. "He says he cannot be sure he'll get here this week at all. He says we are to arrange everything for Friday, and he'll see what he can do."

"Oh," said Hal, who'd been expecting something of this sort. "Does Richard Shearsby know this?"

"Your father, he says, you'll do the pretty, and make everything right," she replied serenely, taking a seat at the table. "He says he'll leave everything to you."

"And the dowry?" asked Hal. He came to sit opposite, as the servant returned in Libby's wake, bearing spiced wine and a dish of comfits and little cakes.

Jacqueline shrugged. "I know nothing of dowries," she said without concern, taking a cake and biting into it.

Hal met Libby's eyes, resignation in them. They were both well aware of how easily Sir Francis was able to pass on any duty he deemed disagreeable to Hal, and especially how he was inclined to do so if money was involved.

"How can Hetta be married without a dowry?" Bess asked in dismay, coming to sit next to Hal. "Mr Shearsby won't allow it to go ahead!"

"Perhaps she'll have to elope like you, Bess," said Jacqueline her eyes flashing. "Where is Hetta? I expected Hetta to be here, to greet one who has been like a mother to her these past five years."

"We had no knowledge of your arrival, Jacqueline," said Hal. "Father promised to send word, but plainly didn't. Hetta will be out walking in the garden with Will Shearsby."

"With her bridegroom? Without a chaperone?" cried Jacqueline in horror. "Zounds! Hal you are wanting her to be ruined, like this one?" She indicated Bess with a wave of her hand. "To be with child before the wedding?"

"I went a virgin to my wedding bed, Jacqueline," cried Bess, her face red. "I doubt that you can say the same!"

"If it was a wedding!" Jacqueline sneered as she sipped her wine.

"As one of the best lawyers in the country, Justin made sure his union was legal, Jacqueline, as well you know," said Hal, beginning to get angry as well. "I do hope you've not come to create discord among us all at this time, for if you do, I shall have to ask you to leave."

Jacqueline nearly choked on her wine. "This from you, Hal?" she cried reproachfully. "I did not expect such discourtesy from you, but then, five years with nothing but rustics and trades people about you—"

"Jacqueline!" Hal got to his feet. "Either guard that

tongue, or quit this house. You may be my father's wife and entitled to respect, but if you cannot treat others equally, you are no longer welcome."

Libby and Bess stared, for neither had expected this. Jacqueline's eyes narrowed to mere slits of fury. "Guard my tongue, Hal, yes I must do that! And so must you, but first we must reach an understanding! Send these fools away, I will speak to you on a private matter."

"Neither my wife nor my sister are fools!" he said shortly. "Nor have I anything to say to you that cannot be said before them."

"No?" she cried, her eyes glittering wrathfully, "On your head be it then."

"Hal, it is of little matter," said Libby getting to her feet. She could see how Jacqueline was lashing herself into a fury, and knew the only way was to let her think she'd achieved a victory. She smiled at him tenderly and briefly covered his clenched fist, "Bess and I have a hundred and one things to do. Pray excuse us!"

"Ah, Libby, she has the great sense," said Jacqueline, bitterly. "Go, Bess, run along after her. Find Hetta for me."

"Well, Jacqueline?" asked Hal curtly as the door closed. "What is it you want to discuss so urgently?"

"I came ahead of your father, Hal, because I must speak with you," she said quietly, some of her fury fading now she had his full attention. "But come, sit down, do not loom over me with the black face!" She made a fluttering movement with her hands. "Happen I am a little short tempered. I will try not to let the fools irk me, but it is not without reason, Hal."

Hal sat down, refilling his glass, and looked at her enquiringly.

"I am with child, Hal," she announced.

Hal looked surprised, for she and his father had been married five years with no hint of a child. "Indeed ma'am," he said politely, "you and my father must be pleased."

"Ah, do you play the fool now, Hal, to try my patience?" she cried in exasperation. "I have not told your father!"

Hal had a dreadful premonition. "Why not, ma'am?" he said, his mouth suddenly dry.

"Because the child—he is yours," she said.

Libby, who had not gone outside with Bess, but into the kitchen to tell the cook of the latest visitor, came back into the screens passage at this point, and stood rooted to the spot.

"Don't be ridiculous," said Hal sharply. "How can your child possibly be mine?"

"Ah, Hal, don't be like this," cried Jacqueline. "Did you not call at my house in London three months ago, because the old man, Libby's father, had died?"

"I was looking for my father, yes," he agreed, his breath coming fast.

"Sir Francis was away," she reminded him. "And did we not dine together, you remember, yes?"

"Yes, I remember it perfectly," he said quickly. "We dined together, you offered me the freedom of your bed, I declined, and we parted!"

"Not all night through, Hal," she purred. "Surely you recollect the next morning?"

Libby heard the scrape of his chair as he got hastily to his feet. "I remember awakening next morning to find you in my bed, yes," he said quietly.

"And did I not say how I fully understood your scruples, at you not wanting to take me in your father's bed."

"Jacqueline, you talked a whole lot of nonsense then, as you do now," he replied, but Libby could tell from his voice he was desperately afraid.

"Nonsense is it, Hal?" Her laugh was mocking. "Tell me, how drunk were you?"

"Damned drunk," he admitted. "Sickened by your willingness to betray my father, almost dead drunk, but not so drunk as not to be able to—"

"Are you sure, are you certain, Hal?" she asked, and Libby could hear the triumph in her voice. "For I swear to you, that when I came to your bed at dawn that morning, you had no scruples. None at all!"

"No!" said Hal violently.

Justin opened the door and entered the screens passage from the courtyard, starring in puzzlement at Libby, white-faced and frozen.

Hal's voice came again, "No, Jacqueline, you lie!"

Libby met her brother's amazed look, and with a sob of anguished dismay, pushed past him into the courtyard.

"No, Hal, 'tis so," Jacqueline was saying calmly the other side of the screen. "You are the father of my child."

Justin stared after Libby. He half-turned in astonishment, wondering if he could believe his ears.

"So you say, but I don't agree," Hal continued doggedly.

For a second Justin hesitated, wondering if he should run after his sister, then Hal's heated words decided him. He walked purposefully into the hall.

"Your pardon, for this interruption," he said looking at Hal. "But you've chosen a curiously public place for what is, I am sure, a very private discussion."

"Ah, 'tis your lawyer friend, Hal," said Jacqueline. "No doubt he will give you the advice, as he always does."

"He is your stepson, too, Jacqueline!" Hal retorted in a harsh voice.

She dismissed them both with a gesture. "I go and leave you to talk! Non, I say no more now. Later we talk again!"

"Thomas!" Hal went to the screens door to call the servant. "Pray show my stepmother to the guest chamber," he said curtly.

They stood in silence as the man, laden with baggage, followed Jacqueline up the stairs. Justin took Hal's empty glass, re-filled it and led him into the small parlour.

"Is it true?" he asked.

Hal stood, as if turned to stone, turning glittering eyes upon him, "Do you believe her?"

"I am asking you," Justin replied, meeting his eyes.

Hal looked down to the wine in his glass, and then tossed it off. "I would that I knew," he replied bitterly.

Justin looked appalled. "You don't know?"

"How much did you hear?" asked Hal, sounding exhausted.

"Just her—her accusation," Justin replied blankly, "and your denial." Then, as Hal said nothing, he cried. "For God's sake, Hal, tell me what the devil's been going on! Could it be true?"

Hal laughed bitterly. "Last February, when your father died and precipitated us into this bloody mess, I went to London looking for you. It had been an absolutely terrible day. It was pouring with rain and I got caught behind two heralds, four mace-bearers, a host of trumpeters, and two troop of horse. It was the declaration of war against the Dutch. There was a great multitude of people rejoicing and shouting from Westminster to Temple Bar and back. I knew there would not be an inn that was not full to overflowing, so I turned about and went back to my father's house in Whitehall. Only, he wasn't there."

He sighed. "I should have left, gone to an inn, but it was a foul night. I was soaked to the skin and Jacqueline offered me a bath and supper. I succumbed to creature comforts. She also offered herself as a bedfellow. That particular comfort I refused, pretty forcefully!

You'd think, being a fellow of some sense, I'd have taken better care of myself, but no. I told myself I'd put Jacqueline in her place, and yes, depressed at the contents of your father's will, at my failure to even think of where to find you, and at the frailty of my stepmother's conduct, I foolishly allowed myself to drink too much."

Justin grimaced. "Just when you needed all your wits, too," he said sympathetically.

"Indeed," agreed Hal. "I recollect making a somewhat unsteady way to bed, and sleeping like the dead, until late next morning, when I awoke to find my stepmother abed with me."

Justin groaned. "Your recollections are hazy."

"Non-existent," he replied bluntly. "Truth compels me to admit we were both naked, a matter I remedied quickly enough to make her laugh. She swore I was, in the English phrase—'Shutting the stable door after the horse has bolted'—God, how I hated her at that moment!"

"Yes," said Justin with feeling. "It can't be a position one can escape from with any degree of credit."

"Exactly," agreed Hal bitterly. "I left at once and conducted my enquiries from the Golden Lion thereafter."

"Did you think to, well—to tell Libby?" Justin asked.

"Good God, no!" cried Hal, "Are you mad? What am I to confess to a good wife—that I was, at best, a damned fool, who was seduced like a green wench? Or at worst a lecher who'd lie with his father's wife! No, I thank you; I kept mum about it then, and shall now! Whatever she wants, Jacqueline shall have! Libby must never know. It would destroy forever any credit I had with her."

"Hal," Justin came to grip his shoulder. "Hal, old fellow, when I came into the hall, Libby was rooted to a spot in the screens passage. From the look on her face, she heard everything."

Hal's face drained of colour. "Then I am finished," he said with the calm of defeat. "Oh, God, what shall I do? She'll never forgive me!"

"Be calm, Hal," soothed Justin. "Libby is a reasonable woman, you have but to explain."

"Explain!" he cried. "Are you mad? Explain to a wife, only recently delivered of a dead baby, that you've got another one on your father's wife!"

"Libby knows Jacqueline, she knows her devious nature, Hal," he said earnestly. "Tell her the truth, explain how it happened!"

"How can I explain what I don't know?" he shook his

head, as if to clear it of confusion. "She'll never believe me if I can't tell the truth—and how can I tell the truth if I don't know it?"

"What shall you do?" Justin asked, worried by his apparent apathy. "You must do something, or this will become a dreadful misunderstanding."

"I don't know. I must think," Hal replied dully. "I've got to find out what Jacqueline wants, yet before I can do anything, I must know what is in her mind."

"Would you like me to try to explain to Libby?" Justin asked doubtfully.

"Yes! No! Oh—I don't know what to do for the best," he cried. "Yes, perhaps, if she saw you, you could explain to her, speak to her, but she won't understand, how could she? And I must speak to her, try to tell her —but not now. I've got to think first."

"I'll go and see if I can find her," said Justin, casting him a worried look. "Hal, you'll be sensible won't you? You'll not do anything foolish?"

"Don't you mean anything *more* foolish?" he replied bitterly. "Yes, I'll try to keep from further folly for the next hour or so."

❖

Chapter Six

Justin spent some time searching for his sister in growing anxiety, and finally found his own wife, in company with Hetta and her betrothed, in the formal garden.

"Ah, Bess have you seen Libby?" he asked urgently.

"Libby, yes, she was in her herb garden, I think," said Bess. "Is something amiss?"

"No, no," he said in an unconvincing tone. "No, I just want to talk to her. Excuse me, Hetta, Will." He hastened away, in the direction of the herb garden, leaving them all rather puzzled.

"Libby!" he called as he looked around the door. "Libby, are you there?"

"Yes," she replied in muffled tones. "Over here, by the digitalis!"

"Digi—what?" he asked.

"Tall purple spikes," she replied looking up to see his

face as he appeared. "Is something amiss?"

"Yes, very much so," he replied joining her. "I've been talking to Hal."

"Oh," she replied carefully picking the seedpods. "Have you?"

"What do you mean, 'oh'?" he asked in amazement. "You heard the same as I did, didn't you?"

She cast him a fleeting glance. "Yes, well I don't know, did—did they say much more?"

"No, very little," he said, perplexed by her attitude. "Libby, why aren't you furiously angry?"

She sighed and turned towards him more fully, so that he could see she'd been weeping. "What is the point in being angry?" she asked, "Jacqueline is so beautiful and she's always loved Hal. And he—he—I think would like to love her, but for his father."

"Are you mad?" Justin was amazed. "Are you just going to give in, not put up a fight?"

"No, no I don't think so." She smiled a wobbly smile. "Anyway, I deserved it, didn't I, for listening at doors."

"Listening at doors? What? Did you deliberately listen?" he demanded, beginning to get angry with her.

"No, no, I just overheard by accident." Her smile disappeared, and tears slid down her cheeks. "No, that's not true, I went to the kitchen as an excuse. I should have gone with Bess, but I wanted to know, and now I do."

"Listen!" He took her arm and led her to the stone seat set against a wall. "I've talked to Hal, and he's as wretched as you are. It was all a mistake! Hal went to London to look for Bess and me, didn't he?"

She nodded, wiping her cheeks on a very damp handkerchief.

"He went to his father's house in Whitehall, and there found Jacqueline alone. He says he knew it was a mistake, but he was cold, wet and weary, so he accepted her invitation to supper."

"Poor Hal," she sighed. "Yes, he would have been cold and wet. The weather was dreadful."

"He was also, he says, offered Jacqueline herself, which he was prompt in refusing. Unfortunately, he was foolish, in his manner, so that he annoyed her, and then drank rather heavily."

"Yes, he was in low spirits at the time. We'd been expecting to inherit father's money, which Hal planned to give to you and Bess so that you could return. It seemed to be the answer we were looking for. Then, at the reading of the will, all the money went to Johanna! It left us feeling as if nothing was ever going to straighten out."

"Never mind all that. Don't you see? This was Jacqueline's method of revenge, to trick Hal like that."

"Yes," she said doubtfully. "Oh yes, I can see that."

"And further revenge now, to come here causing even more trouble." He glanced sharply to her. "That's her idea, of course, it always has been—to cause trouble between you and Hal."

"Yes," she agreed to his words mechanically.

"You do understand, don't you, how it happened?" Justin asked, not convinced she'd truly listened to a thing he said.

"Oh, yes," she said her voice breaking a little. "I understand perfectly. Shall we go back to the house now?"

"Yes." He glanced at her tightly clasped hands. "Have you all you need, then?"

"All I need?" She stared up at him, her eyes reddened with weeping and blank with misery.

"Herbs?" he glanced about him. "I thought you came here to pick more herbs."

"No, I came here to think," she replied quietly. "And to collect some seeds. One gathers herbs in the morning after the dew, and before full sun. Seeds, in the heat of the afternoon, when they are fully dried out." She opened the palm of her tightly clenched hand, and glanced at the small dark seeds sticking to it, then she leaned over the bed, and brushed them off. "I don't think I shall need these after all," she murmured.

With Justin still trying gently to put across Hal's defence, they walked back through the formal gardens. As they came to the house, the sounds of horses and a coach came to their ears.

"Oh, no!" cried Libby, despair warring with weariness in her voice. "Is that Mary and Guy arrived already?"

"No, not Mary," said Justin with a groan. "Our dear stepmother, and if I am not mistaken, there is another coach coming across the park, too!"

"Oh, yes," said Libby faintly. "That will be Jane. Hal's sister Jane, from Wychbold and her husband, Philip Eustace."

She joined him at the door, in time to see another coach join the first on the gravel. Thomas was already there, in attendance on the carriage, which Justin recognised as on hire from the Green Man at Adamsholme. As he watched, its overdressed occupant was handed down, and looked about her with a satisfied air. She was, he noticed with an inward shudder, be-ribbon, be-laced, perfumed and curled to within an inch of her life.

"Stepmother," he said stepping forward, as Libby hesitated over whom to greet first. "How delightful to see you."

"Justin!" Her over-bright smile faded at his irony, but reappeared as she caught sight of her quarry. "Libby! My dear, dear Libby! See, I am come, just as I promised that delightful husband of yours, to lend you my aid! As soon as dear Hal told me of your difficulties, I knew I owed it to your poor, dear father, to throw all other considerations of mine aside, and fly at once to your rescue!"

Libby, looking stunned, briefly emerged from Johanna's overpowering embrace, to meet the frank, twinkling eyes of a young woman her own age.

"Libby, how are you?" Jane contented herself with clasping her hand. "I'm so pleased to see you again. You do, of course, remember my husband, even though I believe he was from home the last few times you and Hal have called."

Libby, smiling and entering mechanically upon her duties as hostess, managed to conceal her dismay as she looked at Philip Eustace. Four years ago, when Jane had married him, he'd been a pretty, petulant boy with engaging manners, when he'd chosen to use them. She was now confronted with a man, thin to emaciation, whose skin stretched taut over the bony structure of his bloodless face. He smiled a ghastly grimace, although his eyes were hard and angry.

"Madam," he said, bowing over her hand. "Are you prepared for a guest little better than a wraith?"

"All my guests are welcome, sir," she replied, her ready compassion stirred.

"I do hope I'll not give you much trouble," he said, his tone curt, almost offensive. "For I bring with me my own keeper! This is my second cousin, Ambrose Carver, who fulfils the twin duties of companion and nurse."

"Mr Carver," thankfully Libby turned to him in greeting. She saw a handsome young man, a little older than Hal, as fair as Hal was dark, with a merry smile and a calm air of tolerance she found refreshing.

"Mistress Westwood, I do trust my arrival won't inconvenience you," he said politely.

"How can it possibly be of enough significance to incommode her," snapped Philip Eustace. "Jane will have written half a dozen letters warning of your coming, and singing endlessly your praises. Mistress Westwood has a house half the size of the county, and servants enough to fill it, I dare say!"

Ambrose agreed with his cousin pleasantly, and smiled in a droll way to Libby, saying, as Hal arrived and greeted Philip, "I beg pardon for my cousin, madam, the journey has fatigued him, rather. I knew it would, but he insisted on coming. I only hope it doesn't make him worse."

"Can it do so?" asked Libby.

"Oh, indeed," said Jane, who had overheard the question. "Philip's physician said he should not attempt the journey in this heat, but he feels that, as the end is the same, what does it matter what time he spends on the road."

Libby pressed her hand. "I am sorry," she said. "It must be hard for you."

Jane smiled enigmatically. "Hard, yes, but not so very hard as it would be for many another wife."

Libby, who knew from Hal just what she had suffered at the hands of her husband, smiled a little, her attention taken by the effusive welcome Johanna was giving Hal. She met his eyes fleetingly, recognizing the horror and embarrassment there.

"Yes, well," she said, raising her voice, "please, won't you all step inside the hall, where there is some refreshment laid out, before Thomas shows you to your chambers."

⚜

The next time Libby had a moment to herself was shortly before supper. The arrival of Mary and Guy Armstrong, with his sister Cecily and the new baby, had come hard upon the heels of the other guests, and all at once her house was full to overflowing.

She stood hesitating at her toilet table, dabbing a little rosewater on her brow to cool it, wondering what, if anything, could possibly be done to improve her own appearance. She'd tried pinching her thin cheeks, but that had only brought a few seconds of colour, which soon died away, leaving her almost as pale and drained as Philip Eustace. She was constantly wondering what to do.

Jealousy was a fearful thing, she knew that, and she'd always been jealous of Jacqueline's power over Hal. She could understand it. Jacqueline was a beautiful woman, and she, Libby, was nothing if not ordinary. So in her way, she'd made a virtue of her very ordinariness. She couldn't hope to compete in beauty, but she could and had been a good wife these past years, except in the one thing. Yes, she kept house for Hal, attending to his wants, listening to his hopes and fears, reading his law books, to be able to keep pace with his conversation; and she had produced the heir he wanted. But since that time she felt she had been failing, failing three times now, to provide another son. And now Jacqueline, who already had beauty and a fascination that Libby couldn't explain, was carrying Hal's child. Libby's own sweet babies lay dead in the churchyard—the latest one with the earth still fresh on top of its tiny coffin —as Jacqueline swelled with another.

Tears filled her eyes, and trickled slowly down her cheeks, dropping faster and faster on to her lawn collar. Going through the discomfort of a pregnancy and the nightmare of childbirth were nothing compared to the anguish of having empty arms at the end of it all. Yet, that was not the worst she had to endure, or was she hovering on the edge of madness?

She recollected Aunt Kate telling her how, after her fifth baby had died, she had been a little mad with grief for a time, and that after that occasion she'd never allowed herself to think of the child before being brought to bed, or she surely would have gone mad.

Was Libby in that position now? Was she not truly responsible for her actions? Would she have put those digitalis seeds in Jacqueline's tisane? It had been her intention, as she'd sat there, gathering them from the pod. Yes, her mind had run over that, and the juniper berries—darting from killing Jacqueline, to just inducing a miscarriage—but had stopped there. The thought had come to her, that it wasn't only Jacqueline's child, but Hal's, too. That had been all that stopped her. Not care for Jacqueline's life, not fear of the consequences, but the thought in her mind, that in spite of everything, Hal might want the baby.

The door opened abruptly, and Hal entered, his face strained and pale. "Oh, Libby, I—I was hoping to—to catch you." He saw her tears, and hastened to her side.

"My dear," he crouched beside her, looking wretched. "I don't know what to say. I would never willingly cause you grief, and yet I have done so to such a degree that I don't know what to say or how to—"

"Hal," she turned to him, interrupting and embracing him fiercely. "Oh, Hal, I do so love you!"

"Libby!" Shame flooded his face. "I don't know what to do, or how to explain. Justin says I should have told you at once, but I felt such a fool, and I knew how the thought of Jacqueline always disturbs your peace. Then, when our dear little son was born dead, I wondered if that wasn't a punishment, and feared to tell you, lest you turned from me. So I held my tongue, and now I look ten times worse."

She held him close, smoothing back his hair. "Do,

do you think she tells the truth?" she asked, hoping she sounded disinterested.

"I would give anything to be able to say I think she lies," he replied frankly, his voice muffled in her hair. "But I can't swear to anything, my dear, I—I cannot swear! I am almost sure, but I was—" he paused and then said quietly, "very, very drunk."

"What shall we do?" she asked. She wondered if she could confess to him her earlier plans and her feelings of guilt, yet she held back, for fear of shocking him.

He raised his head and looked into her face. "What, no recriminations, no angry words?"

"Did you mean it to happen?" she whispered.

"As God is my witness, I meant it not to!" he said fervently.

"Then there is no more to be said. What must we do?"

He hugged her convulsively. "I don't deserve a wife like you. You are too good to me," he muttered.

Her heart warmed at the fierceness of his embrace, and she clung to him for a few seconds before saying: "No, you are too good to me, Hal. Too kind, too understanding of my whims and crochets, but never mind that now. I love you, that is all that is important."

"And I love you," he replied kissing her.

She smiled faintly, willing herself to believe him. "What shall we do about Jacqueline?" she asked. "She seems intent on making trouble."

"As is her way," he agreed. "As for what to do, I have no notion, but that I must hear what she wants first." He looked keenly into her eyes, "That means I shall have to meet with her. You understand that? You won't be fretting yourself, thinking I am going to her because I want to?"

She smiled under his scrutiny and agreed, "Most probably."

"Then you shall accompany me," he replied.

"For all the world as if I were your keeper! I think not, indeed," she laughed unhappily.

He looked rueful. "Yes, she would say something unpleasant like that, wouldn't she? Ah, I have it—if summoned to her presence, I'll take Justin with me."

She smiled at the thought and then sighed. "Oh, Hal, I do hope she doesn't spoil the wedding."

"Come now, don't fret, we'll find a way round this. Nothing shall spoil Hetta's wedding, not when we've all worked so hard for it," he replied, giving her another hug. "Now we must attend our guests, I'm afraid."

❧

Chapter Seven

Justin sat on the window seat in the hall, a heap of papers was laid out before him, but his brain refused to concentrate on the matter in hand. He was only too well aware of his stepmother, parading the length of the hall in her cheap, new finery.

He shut his eyes in an effort to blot out the picture, which made him so very angry. He couldn't recollect being this angry in many a long year. No, not even at the turn of the year when he'd quarrelled so bitterly with his father. He'd been angry, yes, but not furious, as he was at this moment when Johanna Danvers walked back and forth within his sight.

It was his money. Every penny of it! He'd worked many long hours, since he was first able to read and reckon, helping his father. It had been his more agile brain, which had turned their business from a mediocre country town man of law, to lawyers who were sought out by many of the gentry in the surrounding area, lawyers who had links with the capital. It was he, and he alone, who'd altered the tone of their office, making it tidier and more welcoming. He had used his education as a stepping stone to wealthier clients. Now he'd lost it all, and to a slut of a woman who'd waste it all on useless finery in less than two years.

Bitterness welled up inside him, blurring the papers. At Christmas, he'd been so confident. He'd finally got his beloved Bess, an alliance that, whilst it was most certainly a love match, couldn't but help his position locally. He fully expected in the fullness of time to become a wealthy man. Now, because of this jade, who strode up and down, so anxious to show off her shoddy taste, the very best he could hope for was to become his sister's pensioner. How could his father have been such a fool?

"Well, stepson, you have little enough to say for yourself." Johanna came to take a stance before him. Anxious not to be late for supper, she'd made herself ready far too early, and now couldn't sit in her nervousness. She needed reassurance that she fitted into this gathering.

"What would you have me say?" he demanded, his eyes hostile.

"You might at least make an effort to talk to me, to put me at ease in a strange house, you who know it so well!" she hissed.

"Put you at your ease?" he replied, in mocking tones. "Oh I see, yes, well, let me show you about this place you've so schemed to visit, come!" He stood up and cast his arm about him, "This is the Hall, and there on that wall is the tapestry which was swathed about the body of Mr Westwood's uncle, the previous owner of Westwood, when he was murdered by his illegitimate son. If you look closely, you can still see the blood stain! Is this the sort of information you want?"

"No, no indeed!" she cried, shrinking back. "I merely thought you might tell me which chamber is which, and where to go, Libby is so taken up with her guests."

"I see," he marched across the hall and threw open a door. "This is the dining parlour, I rather think the table gives a clue to its use, but let us be sure if nothing else. This, to one side of the door, is the great parlour, where Libby commonly sits of an evening. Here is the door to the ruined wing. Down that corridor, beyond the screens, are the kitchens, buttery and still room."

"Yes, yes, I see," she said recoiling from him, for he had never made his dislike and distain so very plain before.

"Is that enough?" he sneered. "Are you at your ease yet, or do you want more of me?"

"You—you might admire my gown—I suppose," she stammered, trying for a lighter note.

Once again, his glance flickered over her contemptuously. "I've seen cattle trapped out for market before," he replied. "Neither am I an old fool, to be taken in by silk and lace."

The colour flared to her cheeks, further enhancing the paint. She gasped, and then made a good recover. "So, we see your true colours now your precious Hal isn't by to be impressed. No, you may not be an old fool, but tell me, dear stepson, who has the money?"

"You do," he replied curtly, as pale as she was red-faced. "But don't wager a penny on keeping it long enough to enjoy it."

"Justin, pray, do not—" Libby entered, her tired face creased by a worried frown. "I beg you will not get into a dispute. Madam, please do not bait my brother. He is far from well."

"I am well enough, Libby," said Justin curtly.

"I am not the one bent on trouble," cried Johanna incensed. "Don't bait your brother? Did you not hear how he insults me?"

"Pray madam, hush," Libby cast a look over her shoulder. "We don't want everyone to know we are at odds. Please, we must try for a little civility, even if we can't always agree."

"I am not the one who is uncivil," Johanna cried. "Direct your words to that brother of yours. I don't know what poor, dear, Philip would have made of his children treating me so."

Libby directed an anguished look at Justin, who shrugged. "Our stepmother feels she should be put at her ease by a tour of the house, Libby," he replied.

"Oh, I beg pardon," Libby replied. "I have been so busy with my guests that I never gave it a thought. You know where your chamber is, I take it?"

"Yes, though I didn't think to be tucked away at the back of the house. However, I understand you are full of family and so must not stand on ceremony," replied Johanna with an injured air. "Indeed, as your father's wife I did think you might take a little time to show me about this great house. Oh, your father was so proud of you living here. I told Mistress Capel, the baker's wife, that I was coming to Westwood Palace, as we call it in Adamsholme. Not but that I am sure poor, dear Philip would be glad to see all his money being spent to fix up the old place, with fancy fa-las and the like. I told her how your father never could bear to deny you anything. He'd happily go without to make sure you had what you needed to support your position here at Westwood."

Libby, who had been forewarned by Hal and Justin, took this with but a blink of her eyes. "Indeed, madam," she replied. "I think he looked on my marriage as the crowning glory of his achievements. I have some time before my guests come down for supper, and I am happy to show you whatever you want to see. Would you care to see the new building works?"

"Building? Oh, fusty work!" she exclaimed. "I shall get my linen soiled. No, I am more interested in the house itself. Is it very old?"

"No, madam," replied Libby. "The main part was constructed in 1620, by Hal's grandfather, on the site of the original Tudor house built by Hal's ancestor at the dissolution of the monasteries. He had been award-ed the land by King Henry VIII for his assistance in negotiating the divorce of Anne of Cleeves."

"Good heavens! How you do know the history so well," marvelled Johanna. "Oh, aren't those the tapestries your father had made as a gift to you to replace the one ruined by that dreadful man who murdered Hal's uncle?"

"Yes," said Libby, pausing at the small chamber at the foot of the stairs. "The tapestries father gave us are so fine. He sent all the way to Arras in France for them. As you can see, they depict Joshua at the battle of Jericho. They were so lovely that we put them in here, where we can protect them from the sunlight. Hal now calls this the Jericho Parlour."

"Yes, I know, he was so disappointed. He quite thought they would go in the Hall," replied Johanna, walking into the room to examine the tapestries.

"I know he did, and Hal and his aunts appreciated the gesture. Indeed, we did try hanging them in the Hall, but there were so many because Father was always so generous. It was Aunt Margery's suggestion that we use them in the small parlour. It had always been such a cold chamber, we never sat there, and now we can use it all winter if we want. Besides that, Sir Francis had sent a full-length portrait of himself done by Mr Kneller, to commemorate his knighthood, for the other end of the Hall."

"Oh, I can see it is easy to offend a country lawyer of little account, rather than Sir Francis, who is in the King's pocket," sniffed Johanna.

"I'm sure no offence was intended," said Libby

pacifically. "But, Aunt Margery said the original tapestry was too valuable as it was given by Good Queen
Bess to Hal's ancestor. It wasn't ruined, so they sent it
to the weaver's at Mortlake, and they managed to repair
it and remove most of the stains. I don't know that Hal
wanted to re-hang it, but Aunt Margery insisted. So, it
is back in its original place, only slightly the worse for
wear."

"Yes, poor, dear Philip said how his gift was slighted
by Mistress Kingscott."

"Indeed, you are wrong, madam," said Libby indignantly. "Aunt Margery much admires these hangings.
I am certain she wrote something of that effect to my
father last year."

Mistress Johanna shrugged this aside, going to raise
the heavy hangings. "Poor, dear Philip certainly laid
out his money to good effect," she remarked, following
Libby up the stairs. "But then, he thought nothing was
too good for his daughter."

"I loved my father dearly, too, madam," said Libby,
trying not to snap. "Here we have the gallery. Not a
long gallery, alas, though it does stretch the length of
the house, and could, if we ever had time, provide a
winter walk. The paintings are of Hal's ancestors. That

is Henry, Hal's uncle. That is Francis, his father, who had the house built. And that little one over there is Edward, son of Edmund Westwood. Oh, and those cannonballs piled in the hearth there, and at the other fireplace, are from the west wing. Hal had them brought in here from the ruins when they began work. They are from the cannon fired by the Roundheads when they attacked the house. Henry, Hal's uncle, held out against the Parliamentarians for four days, you know, after the Battle of Stow. Hal said they shall remain there by the fire to remind us all of the folly of a war between brothers and uncles, fathers and sons. Hal says it must never happen again." Libby turned and retraced her steps to the Hall.

"Well, I should think not," Johanna agreed, "but the war is all in the past now, it all happened long before you were old enough to understand. Why, Philip wasn't even in the country."

"It still affects us all today, madam, and it is vital that we don't forget," said Libby firmly. "Never again must England be divided against herself."

"Yes, I can see how it must affect you, my dear," said Johanna benevolently, "I know Philip was for Parliament, and it must be difficult for you, living as you do at bed and board with these Royalists."

"No, indeed, it is not," she replied lightly, "for I am a Royalist, too. I've met the King and would not hear a word spoken against him."

"They say he has a way with women," Johanna remarked, sniffing.

"Justin, I've been thinking—oh, I beg pardon madam," Hal came down the stairs quickly.

"How very nice it is that you and my stepson are such good friends," said Johanna, abandoning Libby and Justin, and turning her attention on Hal. "Poor dear Philip was always so proud of how well Justin fixed his interest with the Westwoods."

"I don't think it was anything quite so cold-blooded as fixing an interest, madam," said Hal, surprised by the venom in her voice. "Justin and I met first at my wedding to Libby, and then he came to help us a few weeks later. The sterling work he did then made us all so grateful to him, there could never be any future talk, but of affection."

"Actually Hal, on our first meeting, after your wedding, if you remember," said Justin from his seat at the window, "I'd come to see if my sister was married to a murderer, as reports said."

"So you did!" Hal laughed. "God, I'd forgotten that

at first I was generally thought to be my uncle's murderer! What had you in mind, Justin, if I had been?"

"I'd have defended you to the best of my ability," he replied. "Whilst getting Libby away from you as quickly as possible."

"Aye, the answer of a true lawyer." Hal replied, smiling at him affectionately.

"Aye," Johanna agreed, "truly cold-blooded."

"I prefer to think of him as cautious," said Hal, his face troubled. "For I know well, once Justin loves, as he does my sister, there are no bounds to his affection."

"I see you have a good opinion of him, at all events," Johanna said quickly. "Are your opinions of all females quite so flattering?"

Hal looked puzzled. "You look quite charming, Mistress Danvers," he replied, wondering what was required of him. His eye was suddenly taken by his sister Jane coming down the stairs, slightly in advance of her husband and Ambrose Carver. His mouth dropped open slightly, and he quickly closed it with a snap, glancing hurriedly to Justin. If they weren't careful, disaster loomed ahead.

⚜

At supper, Justin kept his attention manfully upon his

dish of venison, never daring to meet the eye of his wife, his sister, or Hal. The overwhelming desire to laugh was present, he guessed in almost all seated about the table that evening. A difficult meal, Libby had said, and she'd not known the half of it. Hal, at the head of the table, urbanely kept up a light flow of conversation, in a mechanical manner, which suggested his thoughts were elsewhere. In this, he was aided, as ever, by Libby. Guy Armstrong occasionally responded, taking great care whilst doing so never to meet the glance of another. A certain twitching about his mouth and the fact that twice Mary had reproved his words with a mere look, told Justin that he too trembled on the edge of laughter.

Justin was sure that Guy had in him an equally wild desire to provoke the temper of—if not the stranger at the table—then Jacqueline for whom he had a cordial dislike. Both Jacqueline and Johanna Danvers were in the foulest of moods it was plain for them all to see, as was indeed the cause of the problem. Justin could fully comprehend the tragedy, and even, to a certain extent, sympathise. He might only be a husband of six month's standing, but he already understood the feminine mind quite well. Bess was essentially very feminine, and so he could well imagine how she would have felt, had she came down to supper to find not one, but two other women in almost identical gowns.

Jacqueline's was obviously the most costly. Of the finest claret-coloured silk, it was so superbly fitted and low cut as to leave very little to the imagination. The lustrous material was divided and caught back by jewelled clasps, to show a petticoat of azure blue damask, whilst sleeves, hem and neckline were lavishly trimmed with a delicate cobweb-like lace. Without a doubt, it was the creation of a master, plainly the latest in high fashion at Court, and rather ridiculously elaborate for a simple supper in a country house.

By contrast, the gown worn by Jane was, he supposed, a simplified version of Jacqueline's. In a similar shade of silk, but cut more moderately, with a decorous fichu of fine lawn about her shoulders, it might well have passed by unremarked by any, but for Johanna's gown.

Schooling his features, he glanced her way again, as if to confirm his impressions of his father's wife. He acknowledged how a woman with little intelligence, no taste and a willingness to waste good money could make herself look a fool.

Once again, the gown was of wine-red silk, but not

of such good quality, he noted, as either of the others, although, on it's own, perhaps, he wouldn't have noticed that. Shoddy and shiny it, too, fitted her more ample form like a glove designed, he supposed, to maximize her charms. Once again, it was heavily trimmed with lace, which was neither good quality, delicate, nor he noticed distastefully, particularly clean. The divided skirt was held back not by expensive jewelled clasps, but by large bows of blue ribbon, and a third adorned her frizzled hair.

In all honesty, Justin could see why Jacqueline was so furious, for Johanna was a parody of herself. Indeed, as he looked, it became clear to Justin, that in the way the three women wore their gowns, one beheld their character. Jacqueline, polished, elegant, overdressed, making it plain by her manner how she despised everyone else at the table. Jane, modest, simple, elegant, and rather shocked to find herself in such company. His stepmother, vulgar, bold, determined to use his money to further her pretensions.

"Yes," Libby was saying to Mary, "a baby boy, born last Monday, so he'll be of an age with your little one, but not so strong, I fear. Or, so Aunt Margery writes. They've named him Henry."

"Not very original," said Mary tartly, "but then the Kingscotts use a very limited number of names."

"It's not as if they have been particularly lucky either," remarked Hal. "But, I suppose every man wants a son to follow him. I must plead guilty, and you must too, Guy!"

"At least I only named him Guy," he agreed, "I could have named him for my grandfather, Sampson!"

"He'll thank you for that," said Justin with a grin. "As a bearer of an unusual name, I swear our child will be called John or Jack or William, anything but Justice, Liberty, Democracy, Faith, Hope or Charity!"

Everyone laughed at this, apart from Johanna, who drew herself up. "I'm sure your father named you for the best of reasons, Justin. And surely, 'tis a name to assist you in your profession, or at least it would have been if you'd kept to it!"

"You are mistaken, madam," said Justin, unable to keep the dislike from his voice. "My father didn't name us. Not me even, with an eye to our future professions. It was my maternal grandfather, John Hailsham, who named us. All his children, poor souls, were named for abstract virtues. Our dear mother, I do believe, was called Verity."

"So from truth came Liberty and Justice—is that not

fitting?" asked Guy with a smile.

"Fitting enough, although I find it disturbing that Verity died giving birth to Democracy, who soon followed," said Justin with a sad smile. "It bodes ill for our future, I feel."

"Truth, like love, never dies," said Ned who'd been but giving half an ear to the discussion, being more content to gaze upon Cecily's sweet face. "It can be obscured for a while, be masked by evil, but love must eventually come shining through, like the sun after a storm."

Hal looked amazed at this, and made the mistake of meeting Justin's eyes. Justin's saw his lips quiver as he swiftly glanced away, and was conscious of an unholy desire to chuckle. He reflected, that the oddest occurrences were plainly predestined. What else but a calamity of this potential magnitude could have driven the stricken look from Hal's eyes.

"Me, I do not follow you, Monsieur Clerk," said Jacqueline rudely. "Who is this truth? What is democracy? You talk in riddles, to confuse us all and make us think you are so clever."

"Madam, Democracy was my baby sister, who died many years ago," Justin replied politely, but with an edge to his voice. "I beg pardon that you cannot comprehend my words, perhaps they are rather too plain and English for you."

"Plain and English," she echoed. "Yes, indeed, those two words go together. Plain and English—the language, the country, the people—especially the females!"

"Because English is a remarkable language, stepmother," said Hal, his eyes flashing, "its words have many meanings, totally incomprehensible to a foreigner. Plain in English means unadorned, simple, like the truth. I don't think many of us would deny the truth to be one of the most beautiful things we know. Therefore, call us plain and English if you will, we know it for what it means."

"Oh, well said, Hal!" Mary applauded.

Philip Eustace, who'd been looking unalterably weary, laughed ironically. "Will your beautiful truth set me free, Westwood?"

"The truth must always set you free," said Hal seriously, "if you have the courage to face it." He met Jacqueline's eyes as he spoke, and hers narrowed like a cat's.

"The truth being, that if you repent and put your trust in the Lord, He'll carry you through the ordeal you dread," said Libby gently. "In Him, we can find courage, when all else fails."

"Speaking of courage—Guy, do you hunt with us tomorrow?" asked Ned, who was still plainly wrapped up in his own thoughts. "It's not the capital country you are used to, but if you are truly thinking of taking Elmley Park, perhaps you should see some of its disadvantages."

Guy grinned at his single-minded brother-in-law, "Thank you for the invitation, but my purchase of Elmley Park is dependent on several other, more pressing factors."

"Are you going ahead with it, Guy?" asked Hal.

"I am seriously considering it. Now, thanks to the late Mr Danvers, I am something of a wealthy man! A damned shame, Justin, he didn't live to see the ship come in."

As the talk about the table became more general and a little more relaxed, Jacqueline, patently ignored by her stepchildren, grew angrier and angrier. Her dark eyes flashed as the laughter grew, and the wine in the cups emptied. How dare they dismiss her so? Mary sitting there with Guy, looking as if butter wouldn't melt in her mouth—she'd poisoned her husband to get a younger, more handsome lover. Hal, pretending she didn't exist—he'd seduced his father's wife, and now was trying to escape the consequences. Bess, who'd defied her father and married a tradesman—flaunting her expectant child, as if it wasn't the next thing to misbegotten. Jane, sitting so silently beside her death's-head husband—had he, too, been helped on his way by something in his food? Ned, so single-minded, he never even gave her a second glance, yet plainly worshipped that silly child Cecily. Even Hetta, the youngest, the child she'd lavished all her attention on in the past, seldom had time for her, but dogged Libby's footsteps, as if Libby knew anything!

Meanwhile, Johanna Danvers sat trembling in a like fury, for all that she had a smile fastened to her lips. She had schemed and planned to get here, where she felt she had a right to be, and it was such a hollow victory. She had been expecting—she didn't quite know what, but it wasn't this, that was for sure. She'd gone out of her way on her arrival, to tell Libby that she'd come expressly to help her through this difficult time, setting aside her own personal sorrow. And all she got in return for her kindness had been a blank look followed by such insipid politeness, which was worse than an insult. But that was the Westwoods entirely. Polite, but so distant, making sure by the formality of their manners that she understood she could never be one of them. Of course, they'd never say anything so obvious out loud, but their feelings echoed about her just the same, making her feel desolate and so utterly alone.

Her eyes narrowed as Guy Armstrong leaned over, whispering into his wife's ear. Then, Mary's eyes slid to Johanna's gown as she smiled and smoothed her own silken sleeve unconsciously.

Yes, Johanna could so easily guess at what he'd said, and she didn't care. Defiantly, she lifted her chin. She'd given six shillings the ell for this silk—both the pedlar and Mistress Harrington, the seamstress, had agreed that it was the finest. It was plain that the cut of her gown was superior, for the sister, Jane, looked a positive dowd in hers.

As for the Frenchie, who seemed to think she was so important—well, if one wanted to look like a courtesan, rather than a respectable widow, that was her business. Anyway, it was plain that the Frenchwoman had endless money to spend on gowns. She didn't know what it was to scrape and save just to look decent, to bargain just so much on getting a husband before one's looks went, and even then, to end up with an old man.

None of them, not one of these Westwoods, knew what her life had been like, what sort of privations she endured growing up with her mother and step-father both such penny pinchers. These Westwoods, petted and pampered as they were, in truth none of them cared.

But she'd show them! They'd be sorry they'd slighted her. Justin clinging to the edge of the family, think-ing by his hasty marriage that he'd finally become one of them. And Libby—Libby with her demure smile, and self-satisfied domesticity. They both thought they'd finally been accepted, but she'd show them that these Westwoods never accepted anyone who wasn't one of them.

Thankfully, the meal came to a close, and the servants removed the food whilst the females settled themselves about the hearth, Jacqueline taking the chair closest to it and hunching her back to the remainder of the com-pany. Bess, Mary, Hetta and Jane going into a huddle over old memories, so that Johanna once again felt an outsider, and knew not what to do, as Libby was called away by a domestic crisis.

"Won't you sit by me, Mistress Danvers, there is a cooling breeze here by the window," said Cecily, glancing doubtfully to Johanna's face, which aptly mirrored her emotions. "In such a family party as this, it can be a little awkward for outsiders, but I know the sisters see each other so seldom—" she hesitated as the man servant came in and hovered at Hal's elbow.

Hal paused in the telling of an instance at the Assizes, and turned from Guy and Justin to listen to the servant, whilst Philip Eustace berated his poor cousin at the foul taste of the draught he'd just procured him.

Chapter Eight

"Master Hal," Thomas the manservant met his master's eyes doubtfully.

"What is it?" he asked patiently as Justin and Guy chuckled.

"'Tis Goody Stokes, sir."

"Goody Stokes?" he repeated in surprise.

"Yes, Master Hal, she says she's come to tell Mistress Hetta's fortune. She says she's done it for most of you before your weddings."

Hal frowned. "Has she?" he asked. He thought for a moment, then dimly recollected being accosted by the woman within weeks of his first arrival at Westwood. He glanced about him. He was desperate to avert the quarrel that Jacqueline was sure to cause before the night was out. He nodded, "Oh yes, yes, well, ask her to step in please, Thomas."

He turned back to his sister adding, "There Hetta, yet another attention from our neighbours, though not so tasty as Squire Franklin's game. Goody Stokes is come to tell your fortune."

"My fortune?" asked Hetta in lively astonishment.

"Yes, it seems she does so for all the family before their marriages," Hal replied, smiling a little at the puzzled faces of his sisters.

"She never did so for me," said Mary.

"Her mother certainly did so for your uncle and Aunt Margery," said Libby. "Or, so I recollect your Aunt Margery saying."

"She did tell your fortune, Mary," said Jane. "Mine too, she told me to tell you of it, but I didn't care to, for yours was as ill as mine."

"Mine didn't make sense," said Bess. "at least, not until my wedding."

"What was it?" asked Justin. "You never said anything about it at the time."

"Well, I forgot, to tell the truth. She told mine and Ned's together. It was last summer, wasn't it, Ned? You were furious with her."

"It was stuff and nonsense!" he replied sharply.

"No, it was so!" said Bess. "She told me:
*Wed by daylight—wed in sorrow; Wed by candlelight—
alive tomorrow.*"

"Good Lord!" said Justin blankly.

"At the time I dismissed it, like Ned, for who is wed by
candlelight? It wasn't until I was, that I understood."

"What was yours, Ned, to make you so angry?" asked
Hal, laughing a little at this ingenious history.

"I can't remember," Ned said, looking uncomfortable.

"I must confess," admitted Hal, "I can't recollect mine
well either at this distance. It was something about God
giving health, Harry (Uncle Henry you know) giving
wealth, and freedom for fine sons or something." He
chuckled. "I do remember fastening on the second as
the most important at the time to an impoverished
youngster."

"I remember Ned's," said Bess. "It was:
*Under a blanket of snow, in a world turned upside down
by the Lord of Misrule, many a fine fellow loses his heart,
to become an everyday fool.*"

"But that was true, too!" cried Mary staring. "Ned
did lose his heart to little Cecily last Christmas, in the
midst of a snowstorm! By heavens, Jane, I would I'd
heard mine before I married Sir Edward."

"Take first fire of pain and fear, then one Lemmas kiss, and within the year, you shall have five and thirty of bliss," said Goody Stokes, as she entered quietly.

"Good God," said Guy Armstrong. "How did you know of the kiss?"

"Goody has an eye for these things," she replied blandly.

"What did you tell my wife?" asked Philip Eustace, into the small silence that followed this.

Goody Stokes, a plump old woman, shuffled wearily to the table and set her basket on the floor with a ghost of a sigh. Her white hair was drawn back from her rosy lined face, and two bright eyes looked out from under craggy brows. She looked across the table at the wraith before her, her face impassive.

"No life, nor joy, from man, nor boy," she said clearly. *"For your life will only begin, if you invite the lady in."*

Again, there was silence as this was digested, then Philip Eustace fell to laughing weakly. "How very fitting!" he gasped. "Oh Janey, how very fitting!"

Hal cast him a look of dismay and hastily intervened, "What can you tell young Hetta, if you please, Goody? She, as much as any of us, needs your advice."

Goody Stokes turned to Hetta, who was regarding

her warily, and smiled.

"*Colour me blue, colour me green, the fairest Westwood I've ever seen. Will she be wise, will she be witty? Never no matter, as long as she's pretty!*"

"Oh, that's a nice fortune," cried Cecily, who had taken a seat next to Hetta. "Do you do them only for the Westwood family, Goody?"

"It has been my custom, Mistress, but I can make an exception with you, as you'll become a Westwood."

"Will you then, please?"

"Nay!" cried Ned quickly. "Don't you hear, Cecily? They are seldom favourable."

"There was naught amiss with yours, young sir, was there?" Goody Stokes chuckled.

"No," he agreed reluctantly. "You were right, I was a fool to fear love so, but I don't want Cecily—"

"To be touched by an ill wind?" the old woman asked. "*Tempered is the wind to the shorn lamb, bound up in wool is no love, facing the storm side by side is the finest love any can prove.*"

"So it is, Goody," said Hal, with a nod of approval. "We thank you for your trouble, now will you join us in a cup of wine, and rest yourself a little?"

"Thank you, Master Westwood, I will," she replied,

coming to take the chair he indicated opposite Jacqueline and thankfully receiving the cup of wine he bought to her with his own hand.

"Your excellent manners stand you in good stead, Master Westwood, coming as they do from a good heart. Ah, but its warm out there, still. 'Twill be a restless night for one and all."

"Will the weather hold until my wedding day, Goody?" asked Hetta politely.

"If it's not delayed beyond the end of the week," said Goody, sipping her wine.

"You gave me no rhyme, Dame, before my marriage," said Jacqueline suddenly, her dark eyes flashing.

"You weren't married in England, Mistress," replied Goody. "I cast your fortune all the same and did the rhyme, waiting on your arrival, but so long passed, I guessed you'd not care to hear it."

"Was it so very bad, then?" demanded Jacqueline quickly.

"Bad, no, it held a warning, but it is too late now, for the first part, at least," replied the old woman calmly.

"I dare swear it is all nonsense anyway!" said Johanna, disliking this conversation where she held no part.

"Is it, Mistress?" The old woman turned her head and

glanced Johanna's way. Suddenly, her eyes narrowed and she became perfectly still, blinking rapidly, then she added after a pause, "You have no plans to travel I hope, Mistress—out of this land—out of England?"

"None whatsoever," replied Johanna blankly.

"No, indeed." Goody nodded her head in a satisfied manner and sipped her wine, saying, half to herself, *"It would be as well not to take a trip to Jericho."*

"You can go to Jericho, if you don't tell me immediately what my rhyme was," interrupted Jacqueline. "You were talking to me, not a provincial, vulgar trollop!"

Johanna's eyes flashed. "I thought most trollops were at Court these days," she said with gritted teeth.

Goody Stokes hastily finished her wine and rose to her feet. "Very well then, Mistress," she said before Jacqueline could reply. "If you wish to hear my warning, be it on your own head:

Married to one, but loving another, without care you'll destroy the son, and not the brother. God's gift is yet within your grasp, snatch at it and you'll breathe your last."

A deep silence fell at this and seemed to echo about the hall, attracting Philip Eustace's attention once again. "Well, Dame," he said, his eyes were glittering with fever and a hectic flush coloured his thin cheek. "Can you not tell my future?"

"All can tell your future, good sir, 'tis written in your face," she replied compassionately. "Your fortune, however, that might yet be attained."

"My fortune," he sneered. "I thought they were one and the same."

"Never make that mistake," she replied. "They have little to do with each other. *Turn aside, young sir, renounce your evil ways, the Lord will reward you with peace at the end of your days.*"

"Pshaw!" he cried. "You talk like a praying priest."

"The Lord sends the truth in many differing guises, good sir," she replied tranquilly. "It is for you to recognise it."

Philip Eustace waved this aside. "I've heard all this before. What have you to say to my cousin Ambrose? You've told everyone's fortune but his. Come now, tell him the worst, too."

Goody glanced to the young man thoughtfully. "I have already told it in part," she said softly, "but if you want it clearer: *Give up the pretence, and put aside your mask, happiness will shortly await you, if you dare but ask.*"

"That's you damned to misery then, Ambrose," sneered Philip. "You never dare anything."

"Life has not taught me to be sanguine," he replied gently.

"Is that what someone who dares is?" asked Ned. "Sanguine?"

Hal laughed as Goody picked up her basket and prepared to depart. "I suppose he must be, Ned, or he'd never dream of trying. Goody, let me escort you out." He walked with her to the door of the hall calling, "Thomas, tell Dicken to saddle a horse and take up Goody Stokes, 'tis too warm a night for so long a walk."

"Thank you, Master Westwood," she said, looking up into his shadowed face. "And be at peace, meet your fears head-on. The woman is evil and her tale is a tissue of lies."

He looked into her eyes. "Do you truly tell me so, Goody?" he asked diffidently.

"I do. Now, go back to your guests whilst I stop into the kitchen for a word with Clarice. She promised me some raspberries to make my cordial."

⚜

The evening didn't last much longer. Jacqueline, in a

fury, soon took herself to bed, and the rest of the women were not long in following. The men sat later over a cup of wine, but Ned was anxious to be gone because of his early start for hunting. Finally, Hal made his way to his chamber to find Marie waiting for him with a message, which did little to improve his temper. He dispatched her with a curt reply and went about his usual preparations for bed. Hal waited until Libby—so worn down with weariness these days—fell asleep, before seeking out his stepmother.

"So, Hal, finally you find time to attend me!" cried Jacqueline, as he entered her chamber in response to her bidding. "I sent for you over two hours ago."

"I had to wait for Libby to fall asleep," he replied in hurried, anxious tones. "She is worn out. This wedding is going to be too much for her. She's not yet strong enough."

"Not strong enough!" she repeated contemptuously. "Yet neither she, nor you, have apologised for the insults I had to endure in your house this very evening."

"Apologise?" he repeated blankly. "What insult, Jacqueline? What are you talking about?"

"That woman, that trollop, who sat opposite me at dinner, mocking me in that terrible gown!" she cried.

She strode up and down, swishing the short train of her gown as if it were a tail.

"Oh, that," he said, his tone indicating how unimportant he thought it. "Just exactly what did you think we could have done, Jacqueline?"

"Done? Done!" she cried, only further incensed by his attitude. "I don't know what you could have done, but I know a man would have done something!"

"Plainly, I am not a man then," he replied dryly. "For my instincts told me to ignore what was, after all, a very unimportant matter."

"Unimportant!" she gasped, fury making her shake.

He smiled faintly, puzzled. "Why are you in such a rage, Jacqueline? It's not as if you lost out by the comparison. You must be aware that you are infinitely more beautiful than that sorry creature!"

"She made me look ridiculous," she cried somewhat mollified. "Aping her betters!"

"I think she made herself look ridiculous," he replied calmly.

She was silent a space, walking back and forth in an agitated manner. Then she asked sharply, "So, Hal, what have you to say?"

"To say? Nothing!" he replied. "You said we'd talk further

later. Then you sent for me like a servant, and as I didn't want Libby distressed by all this fuss, I came now."

"Ah, and Libby will be distressed, I think, when she hears of this," replied Jacqueline with satisfaction in her smile.

"Libby already knows, Jacqueline," he replied. "I have no secrets from my wife."

"She knows?" cried Jacqueline, the smile wiped abruptly from her face.

"Yes," he replied calmly. "She knows all about your tricks and what a fool I was, and like me, she thinks you are bluffing! I've no doubt you are pregnant, and that you've often betrayed my father, but not with me."

"Oh, and you are so sure are you?" she retorted, her eyes glittering once again. "Have you forgotten how we laid together last February?"

"I've forgotten nothing," he replied rather less calmly. "I recollect only too well awakening with a thick head, a foul taste in my mouth and an ugly sight in my bed."

"An ugly sight?" she cried angrily.

"What else could you be, my father's wife naked beside me? You'll remember, I made haste to depart from your side."

"Oh, yes, I remember that, and what a handsome

body you have Hal," she jibed. "I also remember you were much more welcoming on my arrival."

"I doubt that very much, Jacqueline," he replied quickly, reddening. "I am not often drunk, for I know the effect it has on me. I sleep like the dead. It would have been impossible to arouse me."

"Oh, I aroused you, Hal!" she replied with a laugh. "I can always arouse you!"

Once again, he reddened. "This is beside the point," he snapped. "You sent for me. What do you want?"

"What do I want?" she repeated coldly, for his tone was abrupt. "It should be obvious what I want. I need—I demand your support!"

"My support?" he replied frowning. "In what manner?"

"Your papa, Hal, he doesn't yet know of this!" She laid her hand upon her flat stomach. "He will be angry, oh, so very angry, for you understand, he no longer shares my bed."

Hal looked surprised. "Oh, I see, so he'll know at once it cannot be his child," he said in dismay.

"Non, it could not possibly be his. He has not shared my bed, not this last year or more since he was angry with me over a silly, trifling affair!" She shook out her long, black, silky hair. "Everyone at Court has a lover," she declared sullenly. "He himself has the mistress, as is right and proper, but he said I was a whore, and a trollop, and now no more he comes to my bed."

Hal looked even more dismayed, but said firmly, "Your only option, Jacqueline, is to tell him the truth. He'll be angry, yes, but I doubt it'll be unexpected news if what you say is true."

"Non! Non, you don't understand! You don't listen!" she cried angrily. "He threatened to send me back to France."

"Well," he said wearily. "Isn't that what you want? You hate England."

"To France, alone and in disgrace, with no money!" she exclaimed. "I'd be worse off than before! No, I tell you, Hal, this way is best! After all, 'tis likely you are the father of my child, which makes him so precious! So, I'll tell Francis, and he'll soon forgive you, for you are the son he loves best of all."

"No man loves a son who has betrayed him, even in error!" said Hal coldly. "I can't stop you telling my father lies, but I shall deny what you say, and tell him the truth from my point of view."

"Then I shall tell everyone you forced me," she snarled. "That in a drunken rage, because I rejected your advances, you forced yourself upon me! Oui!" she cried in triumph, as he stared at her in disbelief. "I don't think your precious Libby would like to hear that! I don't think she'd be so forgiving, do you?"

"You wouldn't dare," he said indignantly. "No one would believe you!"

"Non?" she taunted. "No one? Yet you were drunk Hal. Marie helped you to bed, didn't she? And it is well known you have the grand passion for me, Hal! Oh yes, they'll believe it. They'll say—as you English do—no smoke without the flames!"

"Fire," he corrected mechanically, unable to quite believe the depths to which she'd sink.

"Fire then," she shrugged her shoulders, "but 'tis true, non?"

"Non—no!" he returned, shaking himself from the grip of disbelief. "No—yes—I don't care, I'll not do it, Jacqueline! You can threaten me as you will, but I'll not bow to your threats! I've been a fool, yes, but I'll not compound my folly!" He walked to the door.

"Wait, Hal!" she cried angrily. "I warn you, I will do this thing! I make not the idle threat!"

"And I warn you, Jacqueline, if you do, you'll be sorry," he countered, and closed the door on her. ❧

Chapter Nine

Ned, whistling cheerfully under his breath, paused at the head of the flight of stairs, to buckle his belt securely. He glanced up, as the beautiful morning shone through the high window, a feeling of joy in his heart. He had a day of hunting ahead of him, with his beloved Cecily to come back to in the evening.

For a few moments, the promise of the chase paled beside the thought of an afternoon in a perfumed bower with his love, but then he remembered he'd arranged to meet up with Guy and Ambrose Carver in the stables. He consoled himself with the recollection that his sisters would never allow him and Cecily to lose themselves in a shady nook as he started on down the stairs. His whistle died as he rounded the turn of the stairs. He stopped dead in dismay at the sight of a prostrate figure.

For quite half a minute he stood there, frozen to immobility. That the woman was dead, he instinctively knew. The angle of her head against the doorjamb of the chamber told him her neck was broken, even though her face was hidden from view by her long, dark hair.

"Jacqueline!" he gasped in horror. And at that thought, he spun about and raced back up the stairs. He hammered on the door panels of Hal's bedchamber, before bursting unceremoniously in.

"Hal! Hal!" he cried. "Jacqueline is dead! She's fallen down the stairs and broken her neck!"

Hal sat up, his hair all on end, sleep and bewilderment written all over his face.

"Jacqueline!" he repeated as Libby struggled up, too. "Jacqueline, dead?"

"She's fallen on the stairs and broken her neck against the door of the Jericho chamber!" repeated Ned, and as he spoke he turned very pale.

"Are you sure?" asked Libby, as Hal, with an oath, tumbled from the bed. "Can you be certain she is dead?"

"I can see her neck's broken as plain as day," Ned said as Hal thrust his legs into his breeches. "Her head's sort of rammed against the door. Shall I fetch Justin from next door?"

"Justin? Yes, yes do," said Hal, tucking his nightshirt in untidily.

"Hal!" cried Libby as Ned bounded away. "Hal, look at me. You—you didn't—didn't do anything—anything foolish, did you?"

He stopped and stared in astonishment. "Anything foolish?" he repeated, disbelief in his tone.

"Yes," she could see anger leap into his eyes, yet fear drove her forward. "I mean, I thought you might have—have thought of—of pushing her, not—not to kill her of course, but to—to—"

"Let me understand you," he said, rage leaping into his voice, and incredulity into his bright eyes. "You fear I may have pushed my stepmother down the stairs, not to kill her, so to speak, merely to rid her of any child of mine she might carry. Is that it?"

Tears filled her eyes. "No, no!" she cried. "I am merely being foolish, I just thought that—that it—it might have seemed—"

"Hal, do you come?" cried Ned from the doorway, where Justin was joining him, clad only in a nightshirt.

"Yes, yes." Abruptly he turned from her, and joined Ned and a sleepy Justin in the corridor.

"You say she's dead, Ned," said Justin, shaking his head as if to clear it. "But how? I mean, did you touch her? Is she warm?"

"No need to. You'll see for yourself. 'Tis like when a stag—look there!" he halted dramatically at the bend of the stairs. "See for yourselves!" he repeated.

Both men looked down the flight of stairs to the turn where the woman had fallen so awkwardly. Her arms were flung out, as if she'd tried to save herself, her head caught at an awkward angle, almost bent under her neck. Even as they stood there, shocked, Justin couldn't but notice odd things. Her shoes were still on her feet. Her petticoats, with their layers of grimy lace, were all akimbo, showing her stockings loosely gartered about the knee. Then, as he went to say, "She didn't fall from up here then—"

Hal interrupted by saying, "That's not Jacqueline!"

"What?" cried Ned. "Yes, it is! Don't you remember the gown?" His voice trailed off as he recollected the previous evening. Hal suddenly stumbled forward down the stairs.

"Don't touch her!" cried Justin as Hal knelt beside the corpse, pulling her shoulders into his arms. Her head fell back against him, proving Ned's theory correct. He smoothed away the dark hair to reveal the deathly face, with a wound on the temple and blood down one side of her cheek.

"Oh thank God!" he cried devoutly. "Thank God, I thought 'twas Jane."

"You shouldn't have moved her, Hal," cried Justin. He had followed down and now looked at the ghastly countence of his stepmother.

"I thought it Jane," Hal repeated. "I knew by the ankles it wasn't Jacqueline, but I thought it was Jane!"

Libby, who arrived in time to hear this, drew back a little into the shadows. He knew Jacqueline's ankles so well, as to be able to distinguish her body!

"But you might have disturbed any clues," Justin was saying.

"Clues?" repeated Hal. "The woman tripped and fell and broke her neck. It was an accident." He glanced up into Justin's face and saw Libby above. "Or did you, like my wife, assume that if it was Jacqueline, I had murdered her," he laughed bitterly. "I see by your face it is so!"

"Not murder, no," said Justin, glancing back up to Libby, who stood looking as pale as her nightgown. "No, at least, I don't know, it's just—" he hesitated, looking into Hal's angry eyes. "There was something—something about the way she's fallen—something odd!"

Hal frowned, some of his fury dying. "Odd?" he repeated. "Odd, in the way she's fallen? If you ask me, the whole thing is damned odd!"

Guy Armstrong's voice proceeded him. "I say, Ned, do you—Oh, beg pardon, Libby. I quite thought—" Guy hesitated at the head of the stairs, his mouth dropping open, his initial embarrassment at the sight of his sister-in-law in her nightgown fading. "Good God, is she hurt? Who is it Hal?"

"Mistress Johanna Danvers, and yes, she's dead." Hal replied, laying her back down and closing the sightless eyes.

"Dead!" he echoed in consternation. "By God, how did she come to trip?"

A gleam entered into Hal's eyes. "My own question, Guy," he replied.

"In the dark, mayhap," suggested Guy. "For she is still dressed, and yet why should she be fully-dressed?" He paused a few steps down, and stared intently. "I say, Hal, there is a thread attached to this banister here!"

"A thread?" cried Justin, starting back up the stairs. "Where?"

"Well, a cord more like, here on the second stair down," said Guy, bending to pick up the loose end. "And yes, here is a like piece the other side!" He stretched them out to join in the middle.

"The constable must be fetched," said Hal with decision.

"You are the justice," said Justin. He slowly turned to Hal as the implications of this occurred to him, as he too understood what Hal was saying.

"I know, but in my own house, I can do nothing. Ned, hasten to the stables, dispatch a rider for the sheriff in Maucester, and send Dicken for Wat Higgins."

"Can—can you not move her?" asked Libby from dry lips. "You do realise, don't you, that she did do it? She did take a trip to Jericho."

Hal frowned at the hysterical note in her voice. "Jericho? Oh, the chamber! Well, yes, but—"

Justin glanced up at her face. "Libby is right," he said firmly. "She needs to be laid in a more fitting place."

"She is past earthly dignity now," said Hal coldly.

"As we have already disturbed her anyway, and enough of us have seen her to vouch for her position on the stairs, I can see little point in leaving her," said Justin.

"And she is going to rather incommode traffic," said

Guy, coming to take the corpse's feet as Justin lifted her shoulders. "Where shall she be put?"

"On trestles in the chapel, I suppose," said Hal as he seemed to pull himself together. He waited until his brothers-in-law had lifted their burden, then descended the last few steps, gathering up a key and calling for the servants.

Chapter Ten

"So, let me understand you, Mr Edward Westwood," said the sheriff, his cold eyes running over Ned's innocent face. "You saw a body of a woman on the stairs, and assumed it to be your stepmother, Jacqueline Westwood, wife to your father, Sir Francis, yes?"

"Yes, it was the gown, you see," said Ned, as if that explained everything.

"Yet you, Mr Westwood," he turned to Hal, "you feared it was your sister Jane—a Mistress Philip Eustace?"

"Yes, I knew it wasn't Jacqueline. It wasn't her ankles," Hal replied in dull tones.

They'd all had time to dress fully now, and tried to eat a little breakfast. Hal's head ached relentlessly and each of them sat uncomfortably recollecting a similar circumstance not six months ago.

The sheriff raised his brows at this. "You recognised

the ankles of your father's wife, but not your sister?" he asked, in a manner Hal didn't like.

"I have seen rather more of my stepmother than my sister of late years," Hal replied in a stately tone, and then, seeing the amused glint in the sheriff's eye, wished he'd kept silent.

"And you, sirs, did you have no guess as to the lady's identity?" continued the sheriff, glancing first to Justin, then Guy.

"I recognised her petticoats, but only after Hal had revealed her face," said Justin. "I, too, imagined it to be Lady Jacqueline Westwood."

"Wife of Sir Francis Westwood," noted the sheriff.

"I just thought it was a dead body," said Guy bluntly.

"You assumed her dead then, Mr Armstrong?" asked the sheriff.

"Yes," said Guy. "The way her head was hanging over Hal's arm, there was no other thought. Though I did ask if she was hurt, like a fool! I wonder why one does?"

"The mind often refuses to accept the reality of that which the eye sees," muttered Justin.

"And you gentlemen had nothing to do with it?" asked the sheriff of Philip Eustace and Ambrose Carver.

"I arrived on the scene just as she was being carried to

the chapel," said Ambrose quietly.

"Ah yes, you were due to hunt with Mr Edward West-wood?" the sheriff referred to his notes.

"And I was in my bed until half an hour ago, and would infinitely prefer to return there," snapped Philip Eustace. "If your eyes are used to accepting reality, you must see I have no part in this."

"I can see you are a very sick man, sir," replied Sheriff Hughes, with the nearest approach to compassion Hal had ever seen, "but I cannot, alas, acquit you on that score."

"Dying man, Sheriff," he corrected, "and as such, I have little interest in the fate, or otherwise of fellow mortals."

"Exactly," agreed the sheriff pleasantly. "Now, let me understand. The confusion arises, does it not, as a result of three of your guests, Mr Westwood, sitting down to supper in the same gown last night?"

"Not the same gown, but mighty similar gowns," said Hal. "The same colour, certainly;"

"It was one of the funniest things I'd seen in years," said Guy. "But I tell you something—I'm damned glad my wife had on a blue gown."

"Funniest thing?" queried the sheriff, frowning.

"Good God, man, are you a bachelor?" grinned Guy.

"As it happens sir, yes," the sheriff replied stiffly.

"Ah, that explains it," said Guy. "You'd not understand the fury, especially of Madame Jacqueline. By heaven, if she'd had a tail, she'd have lashed it!" he chuckled openly. "Aye, and your stepmother wasn't much better, Danvers. For all her sweet smiles, underneath, her eyes were darting daggers! 'Twas only your wife, Eustace, who held herself with any dignity."

"My wife is so used to public humiliation, I dare swear the wearing of a gown of similar hue as two other women was but a minor irritation," he replied dispassionately.

An uncomfortable silence fell at this, and the sheriff looked intrigued, but fastened on an earlier point.

"Mistress Johanna Danvers—your stepmother, Mr Danvers?" he asked mildly.

"Yes," agreed Justin.

"A recent acquisition, I do believe," the sheriff continued politely.

"My father married the lady last February," he replied.

"And died within a fortnight, if my information is correct," he said. Justin nodded shortly as the man looked up. "Leaving, as I understand it, his fortune to her?"

"No, the bulk of Mr Danvers's estate—the late Mr Danvers's estate—went to my wife, Liberty," said Hal sharply. "That is to say, the business, the house and the lawyer's office. Mistress Johanna Danvers inherited only the money."

"A business you had been largely instrumental in making successful, Mr Danvers, or so informed sources tell me," remarked the sheriff blandly.

"I had some hand in doing so of late years," agreed Justin evenly. "But that was before I left my father's affairs, to pursue my own career in London."

"On your marriage to Mistress Elizabeth Westwood, last Christmastide?" Sheriff Hughes asked softly.

"Yes," agreed Justin and he could feel everyone holding their collective breath.

"Misfortune appears to dog you, Mr Westwood," the sheriff remarked into the silence, which followed.

"Misfortune?" said Hal curtly, disliking his tone again.

"On the first occasion of our meeting, some years ago now, your uncle had met an unpleasant end," the sheriff said softly. "Then last Christmastide, a brother-in-law was poisoned, in your presence. Now, your wife's stepmother has met with an untimely accident."

"My misfortune, if it can be called that, is to have a

large family," said Hal coldly, not liking the direction of his questions. "My uncle, God rest his soul, was foully murdered by his bastard son."

"Who conveniently broke his neck," said the sheriff, "before he could be brought to trial."

"My brother-in-law was poisoned by his mad cousin," continued Hal, anger tightening his voice. "A lady we all made strenuous efforts to prevent from doing herself an injury."

"Yes, it was the same four of you again, was it not?" asked the sheriff. "You, Mr Armstrong, who wanted to rescue your sister—yet have since married the widow of the deceased, I do believe! And you, Mr Edward West-wood, you are engaged to Mr Armstrong's sister. Now, why were you there Mr Danvers? Oh yes, you had just married Mr Westwood's sister Elizabeth. What a tightly-knit family you are!"

"No different, I dare say, to any dozen others in the county," said Hal, through gritted teeth.

"And all this investigated behind closed doors, by you, Mr Westwood, as justice of the peace," added the sheriff.

"That was necessitated by six foot snow drifts," said Hal sharply. "And no, I didn't investigate the murder of either Sir Edward Jolyon, or his unfortunate drab. Mr Danvers did that for us."

"Oh yes, Mr Danvers, who was so diligent in proving Mr Francis Westwood innocent of murder originally, that he won his daughter's hand in marriage," the sheriff said with a sneer. "Was it to pursue an illustrious career as an investigator general, that you went to London?"

"No," said Justin baldly.

"No?" he repeated. "What, then, was your employment in the capital, sir?"

"I was a clerk, sir, to an attorney at law," said Justin sharply.

"A clerk, when you'd been a partner to your father?" the sheriff asked with a considering look.

"A clerk," replied Justin. "My father and I quarrelled on the occasion of my marriage. Which, as you well know from gossip, was a clandestine affair, with neither the consent nor favour of my wife's family. In these circumstances, my wife and I decided to remove to London, away from all connections."

"Yet not entirely severing them, sir, for here you are but five, six months later, back in the heart of your family."

"My wife's health, and my sister's wishes meant a return became a necessity. As my sister had been left my father's business, she needed someone to run it. I was her obvious choice, and my wife, being well gone with our child, also wished to return to the peace of the country and the heart of her family."

The sheriff nodded with apparent amiability and a silence fell for a few minutes, so that a fly could be heard buzzing against the windowpane.

"Do you recall the terms of your father's will, Mr Danvers?" asked Sheriff Hughes, as the knots began to slowly untie in Hal's stomach.

"Only broadly, without consulting the document," replied Justin, his face pale.

"What, for example, happens in the unlikely event of your stepmother's demise?" the man asked, looking again at the sheaf of papers he held.

Justin shrugged his narrow shoulders. "As I've already said, without consulting the document I cannot say, but I imagine the usual provisions are in place."

"These are?"

"That Mistress Johanna had to survive her husband by a fixed term, usually thirty, sometimes sixty days, otherwise the residue would return to the bulk of the estate."

"Would you be surprised to learn the term was ninety days, Mr Danvers, and that it falls due today?"

Justin stopped, his mouth dropping open. "Ninety days is unusual," he agreed. "But surely—" he paused, plainly calculating the time span, "yes, it falls due to-day, Midsummer."

"Yes," the sheriff spun around to Hal, "but you, Mr Westwood, you knew that!"

"I?" Hal looked astonished, "No, I never knew that."

"Yet you read the document, did you not?"

"I read the will, yes," agreed Hal blankly, "but I'm damned if I took all the details in."

"Yet you are known to be a remarkably able man," replied the sheriff softly.

"I may well be so," he retorted, "but I am not a man of law. If I have a legal document, I consult one."

"And your man of law is?"

"My brother-in-law, Mr Danvers," said Hal nodding in his direction.

"But of course, Mr Danvers."

"It is plain you suspect both Westwood and Danvers in having a hand in this," said Philip Eustace impatiently. "Must the rest of us be so incommoded, then?"

"Suspect Mr Westwood and Mr Danvers?" repeated the sheriff. "I was under the impression you all assumed it an accident."

"Only a fool would do so, after seeing a length of thread stretched across the stairs!" snapped the dying man.

"Yes," agreed the man thoughtfully, "only a fool." He seemed to shake himself and come to a decision. "None of us here are fools. So, gentlemen, these are the facts. Mistress Johanna Danvers was either pushed or called down the stairs. She tripped on a length of string secured across the second stair down, thus clearly making it an intent to injure, if not kill, the lady. I must therefore look upon the accident as murder."

He glanced about at the tense faces. "The added complication appears to be in the gown the lady was wearing. So I ask myself, if indeed she was the intended victim—or the unfortunate victim of a case of mistaken identity. Bearing this in mind, I am forced to enquire into the affairs of three ladies, not one."

Guy sighed heavily. "You are making this damned complicated, Hughes!" he said. "I can't see why it couldn't all be a tragic accident."

"Accident?" asked the sheriff. "As you are plainly not a fool, sir, perhaps you'd be prepared to explain?"

"Well, young Ned here, was bound to be first up for the hunting. Perhaps someone decided to—to play the fool with him, and trip him up in his enthusiasm, and Mistress Danvers unsuspectingly came down earlier."

"Very early indeed, as she hadn't been to bed," said the sheriff dryly. "As for playing the fool with young Mr Westwood, I don't think I'd feel very reassured, if I thought someone would try to trip me down such steep stairs. Did you think to do so, sir?"

"Me?" said Guy aghast. "Good Lord, no! I can't imagine, no. I was thinking more of a young person, Mr Carver perhaps, or—"

"Or your sister, Cecily?" the sheriff supplied.

"No, no!" cried Guy angrily. "Cecily wouldn't want to harm a hair on his head, but Mr Carver seemed much taken with my sister yesterday evening, and I wondered if he might have thought to make Ned look a fool. To even injure him a little, and keep him out of circulation."

"I can assure you, my dear Armstrong, you misread the situation entirely," sneered Philip Eustace. "Any enmity my dear cousin might feel would be directed toward the young lady, not the young man."

"I feel no enmity, nor unnatural interest in any," protested Ambrose Carver vehemently, his colour rising.

"Might we get back to the point at issue?" asked Hal.

"It's a good try, Guy, but hardly tenable. That piece of thread means it's murder, and of necessity, Justin and I are suspects."

"Not only you and Mr Danvers, Mr Westwood, but any who would like to be rid of one of the three ladies dressed in red last night. That must include you, Mr Eustace, with regard to your wife, and you on two counts, Mr Westwood, for I gather you have some dispute with your father's wife, too. And that is not to mention your wife, who benefits from Mistress Johanna Danver's death."

"My wife!" cried Hal angrily.

"Indeed, does she not inherit it all now, under her father's will?" the sheriff asked.

"But she'll give it all to Justin anyway!" cried Hal in exasperation. "How could you truly think Libby would kill for gain?"

"I am looking for motive, Mr Westwood, and if what you say is true, then Mr Danvers certainly has much to gain by his stepmother's death—and his wife as well, of course."

"Oh, throw the fellow out, Hal!" cried Guy angrily. "Next he'll be accusing Mary."

"As I understand the matter, sir, 'twas only the untimely death of Mistress Avis Soames that scotched the rumour that your wife—the then Lady Jolyon—had poisoned her husband," said the sheriff.

"Why, you upstart, Roundhead cur!" cried Guy, leaping to his feet. "I'll have your heart for that!"

Chapter Eleven

"So, the sheriff now views us all with deepest suspicion," explained Hal to his visitors later that day. "And I do feel that if you and your father would prefer it, Will, we should put off the wedding."

"Well, Hal, I'll not deny the rumours are flying about," said Richard Shearsby. "And that my wife is most distracted by them, but it's all stuff and nonsense, as I told her." He scratched his ear thoughtfully. "To my mind, Hal, the wedding had better go ahead on Friday, as planned."

"Oh please, sir," said Will, earnestly.

Hal smiled grimly. "I thank you for your vote of confidence, Richard. It means a lot, I can tell you." He sighed heavily. "I must also tell you that my father is unlikely to be here for the event, and that I am delegated to deal with the dowry, and give away the bride."

"I'd not have it any other way," said the older man. "Truth to tell, I don't deal that well with your father, Hal."

"Yes," said Hal vaguely. "Well, if I am still a free man come Friday, and not under arrest for the murder of my wife's stepmother. And you are both sure you are perfectly happy to go ahead with the wedding—we'll do that, shall we?"

"Surely Sheriff Hughes can't be such a fool as to suspect you, Hal?" cried Will indignantly.

"By the time Guy Armstrong had broken Sheriff Hughes's nose, and we'd dragged him from his throat, I was surprised we weren't all arrested. It certainly took all of Justin's best efforts to keep Guy from jail for assault, and how it will all end I dread to think," sighed Hal. "Now we have that dreadful man of his, Sergeant Hoskins, poking his nose into our private affairs and the promise of another meeting with Sheriff Hughes, this evening, when he should be patched up and recovered from this morning's affair."

"What do you think of moving the wedding, Hal?" suggested Richard Shearsby diffidently. "If you'd feel happier, if it would help at all, I'd be willing to hold it at my place."

"Thank you, Richard, for the offer," said Hal warmly. "And if all else fails, I shall be tempted to agree. But, if we might leave it for a few days to see how we go, I mean, the preparations are well under way, they have been for weeks, of course. Libby would be bitterly disappointed if it wasn't held here, but in the circumstances—"

"Yes, yes, exactly," said Richard hastily. "Yes, we'll see what the next few days bring. I'll come over on Tuesday or Wednesday, and consult with you again, Hal, but in the meantime, shall I not take Hetta and this young fellow back with me?"

"That, indeed, would be a splendid idea," said Hal grimly. "Yes, if Sheriff Hughes will allow it. I'd be obliged if Hetta could get away from all this. Perhaps you might take young Cecily Armstrong, too, if Guy will consent. She can keep Hetta company, and would, I think, be better out of all this."

"So," said Guy later that day as he stood in the doorway with Hal to see his sister off. "Hughes wasn't totally unreasonable, then."

"No, surprisingly, in view of your behaviour, he was

agreeable to letting the girls go. And Mistress Shearsby has got her wish of getting her son out of this place," snapped Ned, who was dismayed by the developments that took his beloved away.

Guy nodded gloomily. "What a transparent ploy!" he remarked.

"One can't but feel compassion for the woman," sighed Hal. "After all, would you want your nearest and dearest in such a place as this? I'm only surprised Richard Shearsby wasn't sent to cancel such an unfortunate connection."

"I don't think Will would stand for that," remarked Guy.

"Aye, but with my father up to his usual tricks over the dowry, they'd be within their rights," said Hal bitterly.

"Your father really is something of a rascal, Hal," remarked Guy. "Has he yet paid a dowry on any of his daughters?"

"Mary's was paid to Jolyon," Hal replied coldly, who didn't like to hear his father criticised. "I don't recall that you asked for one, and although Jane's was paid to Philip Eustace, I doubt whether we'll see one penny of it back in jointure."

"Ambrose says he is all to pieces," agreed Ned. "He

says Philip Eustace has been living on credit for the past six months, but now he's not likely to outlive his father, he can't get any more. Which is why he chose to come to the wedding. I think Ambrose fears he'll not leave after the wedding, but batten on to you, Hal."

"Who exactly is this Ambrose fellow?" asked Hal sharply.

"He's a distant cousin, a poor relation. It would seem that Philip Eustace's father pays Ambrose to keep Philip under control. He's his keeper, not his lover."

"Yes, that wasn't exactly evident," said Guy, as if glad to have this matter cleared up.

"There's naught amiss with Ambrose, beyond having a handsome face. He's a fine fellow, he rides, hunts and shoots with the best of them," snapped Ned.

"Not all Philip Eustace's companions have had a taste for petit point, Ned," said Hal with a grin.

"The ones I met did," said Ned bluntly. "I tell you, Ambrose isn't like that. He hates the thought of Eustace and his friends."

"One can understand his point of view," said Guy. "The Eustace fellow's a snake if ever I saw one. He repels, even as one feels sorry for him."

"Mmmn," agreed Hal gloomily. "And here's another

such." He indicated Sheriff Hughes coming through the gatehouse. "Remember now, Guy, an apology is essential, and if you could thereafter hold your tongue unless directly spoken to, it would be better for us all."

❧

Even with the required apology extracted from a patently unwilling Guy, it was still a very tense gathering which met in the parlour about an hour later to listen to what Sheriff Hughes had to say. He spoke with some difficulty, for his top lip was still cracked, and his nose much reddened. His eyes had that strange look, which indicated they could be black by the next day.

"Very well," he said bitterly. "As we are now all gathered here, perhaps I might be allowed to begin my enquiries into this matter."

"Who is this horrid little man, Hal?" demanded Jacqueline. "And why must he ask questions of us? Are you not the justice?"

"Yes, I am, Jacqueline," he agreed with a sigh, realizing that his troubles were only just beginning, "but as I am a suspect, I can hardly hold an investigation."

"You, a suspect?" she cried. "Why, why should you

want that woman dead, unless it was to rid the world of her horrible bad taste?"

"Jacqueline!" began Hal, but the sheriff looked up.

"Bad taste, Lady Westwood? Yet, I understand you and she had tastes in common. Did you both not wear the same gown last evening?"

"Non!" said Jacqueline, her eyes flashing.

"No?" he repeated blankly, taken off guard. "But my information was—"

"Her gown was nothing like mine!" she snapped interrupting him. "Save that the hue was perhaps similar! It had no style, was cheap and tawdry, and ill-made! In fact, it resembled my gown as much as you resemble Hal, who is the gentleman!"

"I really do feel, Lady Westwood, we will gain very little if this matter is conducted in this present climate of rancour," remarked Justin calmly, as the sheriff clenched his jaw in annoyance. "Sheriff Hughes is obliged by law to ask his questions, and you are likewise obliged by law to answer him fully."

"English law!" she spat contemptuously.

"This is England, m'lady," he replied equally calmly. "One feels for you in your desire to return to France, but unfortunately for us all, you must—and shall

—remain in England for the time being."

Jacqueline's eyes narrowed at his sarcasm. "Don't take that tone with me, Monsieur Clerk," she snapped. "You think to ally yourself to the Westwood family, and so go free of murder! Has this fool asked himself who benefits most from this murder?"

"Yes, he has," said Sheriff Hughes tartly. "And the answer is: Mistress Liberty Westwood, or by extension, her husband."

"Hal!" cried Jacqueline taken aback. "Hal? Don't be a fool! Hal couldn't kill that woman. He is the gentleman!"

"Gentlemen have been know to kill before," Hughes snapped. "Before you leap so hurriedly to your stepson's defence, you might like to stop and think that it may have been a case of mistaken identity. You may have been the intended victim."

"Me?"gasped Jacqueline, blankly incredulous."Me? Who would want to kill me?"

"Half the family, I should think," Guy muttered under his breath.

"Ask yourself, Lady Westwood, who had you quarrelled with so bitterly, not a few hours earlier?"

"Quarrelled?"she cried, her hand stealing to her

throat, shock in her face. "You mean Hal?"

"Did you and your stepson not quarrel yesterday afternoon upon your arrival here?" he demanded.

Fear stole into her eyes, and she glanced uncertainly to Hal, who sat woodenly as he suddenly recollected his words. Would Hal perhaps try to kill her? No, it was unimaginable! "I—he—yes—yes we did disagree," she stammered, disconcerted for the first time. "But Hal," imperiously she turned to Hal, demanding his attention. "Hal, explain to this fool!"

"Explain, Jacqueline?" he replied, his mouth suddenly dry. "What would you have me explain?" He, too, recollected their quarrel and realised how dreadful many of the things said would sound in retrospect.

She glared at him, opening and shutting her mouth a few times, as she, too, understood. Then she snapped, "Oh, you are a fool, Hal! Attend me, Monsieur Sheriff, this is my stepson. I have known him since he was a green boy. We quarrelled, yes, but we often quarrel! It is our way. We have both the quick temper, the loud words, angry shouts! Then it is gone—pouf—forgotten!"

"Is that so, m'lady?" the sheriff asked urbanely. "So, you'd have no cause to think Hal Westwood might want to push you down the stairs?"

"Surely," said Justin, into the silence which followed, whilst Jacqueline looked distinctly frightened and did not answer. "If one were to push, so to speak, there was a chance of the victim missing the cord and falling?"

"Lady Westwood, I am awaiting your reply," said Sheriff Hughes, ignoring this attempt to divert his attention.

"I do not reply," said Jacqueline making a recover, "because I do not reply to so foolish a question!"

"And you are still not replying, m'lady. I require an answer."

Jacqueline rose to her feet. "I do not have to listen to this fool!" she cried. "Non, Hal didn't try to kill me!"

"I rather think," said Guy, as she swept from the room, "that is what is called a splendid exit!"

"Will I go after her, sir?" asked Sergeant Hoskins from the doorway, giving them all an unpleasant jolt, for they had not realised he was there.

"No, leave her be," the sheriff replied sharply. "I'll talk with her again later. But I'll take this chance to remind you all—" he turned back to the party gathered there— "we meet like this because it is less inconvenient. I could summon you all to give accounts of yourself on oath."

"I'm sure we all appreciate your forbearance, Sheriff Hughes," said Justin hastily. "We, as God-fearing English folk, comprehend the law. Unfortunately, my wife's stepmother is of foreign extraction. In France, I do believe, the only law is the whim of the King."

"Much as it was here, but a few years back," Sheriff Hughes agreed. "But, in this country we fought to make us all free and equal. The law applies to us all, rich man, poor man, we must all give account of ourselves where there is a murder."

"And so we are ready to do," agreed Hal, disliking this attempt to remind them how they'd been on opposing sides in the war. "If you will but proceed?"

The sheriff met his eyes, "Very well. At what time did you retire last evening, Mr Westwood?"

"I?" he replied. "Justin, Guy and I were the last to go to bed. It was past midnight, because you left at midnight, Ned, saying you were hunting. And you kept saying, Guy, you were thinking on joining him."

"It was five and twenty minutes to one o'clock when we went up the stairs," said Justin. "I looked at that clock there, Hal."

"And Mistress Danvers, she had retired when?" asked the sheriff, making a note of the time.

"Oh, early on, she is to have a—oh, you mean my father's wife. Yes, I'm not sure," said Justin.

"It was when Libby retired," said Hal. "Mary and Jane went up shortly after Bess to see the baby. Didn't they, Guy? Jacqueline had gone by then, in a temper. Libby and Cecily were unpicking some embroidery of hers which had gone awry. And all three, Libby, Cecily and Hetta went up, and Mistress Johanna followed quickly. I thought she wanted to talk to you, Libby. Did she?"

"Yes," said Libby quietly. "She came to my chamber and begged to be allowed to see little Harry sleeping. Then, she sat and talked of her child and how he'd be a companion to Harry."

"She was generally happy with her future, she had no qualms at bearing a child as a widow?" the sheriff asked.

"She made it plain she wouldn't remain a widow long," said Libby, a spark of anger entering her eyes. "It would seem once her child is born, she was to marry her cousin, Robin Dwyer."

"Does that anger you, Mistress Westwood?" he asked, observing this.

"Yes, it does!" she replied tartly. "Especially as it was obvious that her cousin is—and probably always was

—her lover, and therefore most likely the father of her child!"

"Libby!" cried Hal in warning.

"I am not going to lie to Sheriff Hughes, Hal, that is the truth. Yes, I was angry with her, I believe she cheated my father. She ousted my brother and she was trying to convince me that she was a good woman. To make a fool of me, in effect! I didn't like her, and I'm not sorry she's dead, but I didn't kill her."

"Thank you, Madam, you've made your feelings very clear," replied the sheriff, as Justin groaned and covered his eyes with his hands. "Unfortunately, the law requires, if possible, proof that you didn't kill your father's wife."

"Proof must be in the fact that there was no body on the stairs when we went up to bed, and that my wife was, by that time, already asleep," said Hal sharply.

"And what is more to the point, the cord couldn't have been stretched across the stairs, otherwise we'd have tripped up it," said Justin.

"I agree with that point, Mr Danvers, but it would appear that there was nothing to stop any of you from leaving your beds to stretch the cord across the stairs after retiring. Indeed, one of you must have done so."

"Libby was already asleep, as I told you," said Hal sharply.

"Indeed you did, Mr Westwood, but you seem to assume that she remained so throughout the night."

"Yes, or I would have woken," he retorted quickly.

"Madam," the sheriff turned to Libby. "Did you sleep soundly the whole night through, as your husband suggests?"

"No," replied Libby. "My son was wakeful, I heard him cry and went to speak to his nurse." She smiled faintly at Hal's amazed expression. "I get up most nights, Hal. It is you who sleeps so very soundly, not I."

"It is a habit of mothers, I do believe, Libby," remarked Guy, smiling. "Mary seems to spend half the night wandering about the house in her nightgown."

"Indeed, and did you last night, Mistress Armstrong?" asked the sheriff swifty.

"Now, wait one moment!" cried Guy, his hackles rising again at this question. "I wasn't speaking to you but to—"

"Guy!" cried Hal sharply then, as Guy glared at him, he added, "Let Mary speak. What can she have to fear? She has no possible desire to be rid of Mistress Danvers."

"I don't trust this fellow, Hal," hissed Guy, in an undertone. "He's as like to try to suggest something completely mad, like Mary being touched in the head. He's already accused her of murdering her husband, next he'll be saying childbirth has addled her brain!"

"Not if you don't suggest it!" murmured Justin dryly.

"Well, do you trust him?" whispered Guy sharply.

"Gentlemen, if Mistress Armstrong could be allowed to speak?" interrupted the sheriff.

"Yes, I was wakeful last night," replied Mary looking troubled. "Baby slept until a little before two o'clock, then he stirred. His nurse was with him, but I slipped into her chamber, to make sure he was taking his feed."

"This was at two o'clock, Madam?" he asked, making a note of it.

"A little after, perhaps a quarter or twenty past the hour," she agreed doubtfully.

"And you saw nothing at this time?" continued the sheriff.

"No," she said, but there was the merest hint of hesitation in her voice.

"Madam?" he asked quickly.

"I saw nothing," she repeated, "but heard breathing."

"Breathing?" the sheriff repeated blankly.

"Breathing, laboured breathing, as if someone had been running and, I caught, just a glimpse."

"Of what?" he demanded.

She shook her head, looking perplexed. "I don't know, something white, a handkerchief, the edge of a nightgown. I only saw it with the corner of my eye, and it—it rather frightened me. It was very dark and eerie, so I ran quickly back to my chamber." She glanced up to look at her family, her expression half mischievous, half embarrassed. "I thought it perhaps a ghost!"

"We have no ghosts here, Mary," said Hal firmly.

"Yet you say you saw nothing, Mistress Westwood." The sheriff glanced in exasperation to Libby. "Neither did you hear anything! A woman falls to her death down the staircase, yet none of you hear anything! Do you not find it strange, when so many of you say you were wakeful?"

Justin glanced unsurely to Bess. "We did think we heard a noise like—well like a cry, but thought it an owl." He admitted ruefully. "It was late, and I was dozing, I think. Bess roused me asking what it was."

Bess sighed and looked distressed. "Yes, I thought perhaps I had dreamed it. I often do dream things now I don't sleep well."

"You often dream things," repeated the sheriff grimly. "At what time was this?"

"I could not say for sure," said Justin. "It must have been after Libby went back to bed."

"Why do you say so?" demanded the sheriff.

"Because I recognised Libby's steps. I heard Harry cry and Libby pass our door, and then later come back. This was when I was still wakeful."

"It was close to half past one when I was awake," said Libby. "Little Harry was sound asleep again by ten minutes to two o'clock."

"Were there any other nocturnal guests abroad last night?" asked the sheriff with resignation.

"I was up at half past three," said Ambrose Carver. "Cousin Philip was in some pain. Mistress Eustace came to tell me he needed some drops in wine to help him sleep."

"You keep such drugs in your possession, Mr Carver?" asked the sheriff sharply. "Mistress Eustace doesn't hold them?"

"No, she does not," he replied shortly.

"Why is that?" asked the sheriff, scenting a mystery.

"My father, in his wisdom, deems it so," said Philip Eustace, his emaciated face bitter. "It seems I've been known to get my wants from my wife by force in the past. So, the only things which give me relief from pain are kept in the hands of one stronger that they might torment me. Yes—" he said glancing about the shocked company, his eyes glittering, "it is a sorry tale, isn't it? A dissolute husband, who inflicts any amount of cruelty on his wife, needing to be saved even from himself!"

"It is certainly a most unedifying story," agreed Hal curtly. "One which must make my sister long for the promised release."

"Oh, your sainted sister isn't such an angel!" cried the sick man viciously. "What do you say, Master Sheriff, to a charge of poisoning? Maybe that's why my father insists one of my family holds my medicines."

"It's a lie," said Ambrose Carver quietly. "Mistress Eustace is held in affection and esteem by her husband's family. I was introduced into the household at Mr Thomas Eustace's behest to use what means I could to protect Mistress Eustace from any further abuse, any physical abuse. I fear she is still obliged to listen to the sad fantasies of a sick young man."

"Oh, hold your prosy tongue, Ambrose," Philip Eustace snapped, "and fetch me a cup of wine."

"By your leave, Sheriff, I do believe we would all

benefit from a cup of wine," said Hal. Then, as the sheriff sighed and nodded curtly, Hal got up and went to call a servant, adding as he turned back, "Perhaps a little wine will ease us along. This looks like it will be a matter not soon settled."

Chapter Twelve

"Was there anyone else from their beds last night?" asked the sheriff, some time later, when they'd all been served with wine. "You, sir," he turned to Justin. "You and your lady, you weren't tempted to get from your bed and see what the noise had been?"

"No," said Justin. "My wife finds it difficult to sleep at the best of times, and it was a hot night. If I had left my bed each time she heard a noise these past few months, I'd never have got any sleep. As it was, neither of us left our chamber, from when I entered it at half past twelve until Ned woke us shortly after dawn this morning."

"Dawn was, if I'm not misinformed, at about four o'clock this morning," said the sheriff.

"Yes, it was already rumoured in the sky at half past three," agreed Ambrose Carver.

"So, it would seem if you were awake then, Mr Carver, and both Mistress Westwood and Armstrong awake at two thirty or thereabouts, the deed must have been done between half past two and three thirty. Were you awake at that time, Mistress Eustace?"

"Yes, perhaps a little earlier," she replied softly. "I awoke from a deep sleep, to hear Philip tossing restlessly and groaning in pain."

"You'll note, she heard me," Philip Eustace said nastily. "She doesn't defile herself by sharing my couch of pain! No, she keeps herself as far away from me as possible! When I die, it'll not be in those slender arms. Will it, my dear? I'll not pillow my head on your soft breast as I breathe my last!"

"By heaven!" cried Ambrose Carver. "Why should she support you when her arms—all her body for ought I know—is but one mass of bruises from your punches and pinching! I wonder you even dare to think of breathing your last in the arms of one you've treated so ill!"

"I pray you, Ambrose, don't rise to his bait," whispered Jane tearfully.

"Oh, so meek and demure! 'I pray you, Ambrose!' I'll warrant you don't pray him when you are abed together, whore!"

"Eustace, if you don't stop that vicious mouth of yours, I'll see you don't suffer a moment's more pain, by stopping it for good!" snarled Hal. "What my sister has had to endure at your hands beggars belief, but she has done it without a word of complaint and with a quiet dignity you cannot comprehend."

"I think I now have a fuller picture of last night's movements," said the sheriff, choosing to disregard this fracas.

"You don't seem to have achieved much for all that," remarked Guy sharply.

"No, Mr Armstrong, I don't," the sheriff replied with equal tartness. "And that's because none of you have told the truth, save Mistress Libby Westwood."

"Not told the truth? Damn you, man! How dare you call us liars!" cried Guy angrily. "Hal, will you sit by and tolerate such insults?"

"You must understand, it is difficult for Mr Westwood," said the sheriff silkily. "He, being a justice of the peace, fully comprehends his own failing."

"The information I am withholding is strictly my own affair," said Hal, his face rather white.

"In murder, Mr Westwood, as you well know, there can be no privacy. But no matter, as justice, you know you are obliged to tell the truth on oath in court."

Hal, if anything, looked even paler at this.

"Of course," continued the sheriff, "if there are matters of privacy, then 'tis surely better to deal with them here and now within this small circle. Anything not relevant to the murder shall not be brought forward." He paused, looking from one to the other. "If you've understood me, I'll repeat myself. Is there any matter you'd like to discuss, Mr Westwood?"

Hal swallowed. "You refer, I gather, to the matter of the quarrel between my father's wife and myself?" he asked from a dry mouth.

"I do, indeed. Come, you are no fool, Mr Westwood, you must see how it looks."

"Yes," Hal agreed. He gritted his teeth, closed his eyes momentarily, and then said quietly, "My father's wife arrived here yesterday to tell me she is with child." He paused, as everyone looked surprised. "And, that she believes me to be the father of that child."

There was a dead silence at this, then Mary cried: "Oh, Hal, how could you?" in appalled accents. "Oh Libby, how terrible!"

"Hold your tongue!" cried Guy, in the sharpest tone any had ever heard him use, his eyes on Hal's face.

"Is this claim true, Mr Westwood?" asked the sheriff, his eyes flickering to where Libby sat, scarlet-faced, with downcast eyes.

"Well, of course it's not!" cried Ned angrily, before Hal could reply. "By God, you saw what a woman she is for yourself! She'd accuse a saint, that one! If you're looking for someone likely to do murder, look no further than Jacqueline! She's as likely to push the other trollop down the stairs for spite because she wore the same gown."

"I do not know," Hal spoke with some difficulty.

"It is a possibility, though," the sheriff concluded.

Hal nodded, his shoulders bowed.

"Well, I can't believe it!" cried Mary, indignation in her lovely eyes. "When I think of the tone you took with me, Hal, over my love for Guy! At least I was betraying a devil of a man who cared nothing for me, whereas you—"

"Will you hold your tongue, Mary!" cried Guy, rounding on her fiercely. "Or must I take a stick to you?"

Mary closed her mouth in amazement, her eyes mirroring her thoughts.

"Unfortunately, Mr Westwood, this information doesn't clear you," the sheriff began, a shade uncomfortably, seeing the effect of Hal's words.

"It, in fact, puts him in a worse position," snapped Justin, "and, has lost him all credit with his peers!"

"Oh, I don't know about that," said Philip Eustace. "I'm rather impressed! I used to think you such a dull dog, Westwood, but I suppose still waters run deep, eh?"

"In view of your words, Sheriff Hughes," said Jane suddenly, "I feel I must show you this note." She darted an apologetic glance to Ambrose Carver. "I'd sooner not conceal anything."

The sheriff looked surprised, taking the folded paper she handed him, and straightening it out. He read out loud: *"Meet me in the walled garden at dawn. Do not fail."* He glanced up, "It is not signed."

"No," she replied quietly.

"Whom do you think sent it? Where was it found?" he asked, quickly.

"It was amongst my jewels—in the case," she stammered. "I—I thought it had come from Ambrose— Mr Carver." One look to his face told her it hadn't, and she felt her skin burn hot as her soul shrank within her.

"Mr Carver?" said the sheriff, his eyes going to Ambrose's amazed face.

"No, I did not send it," he said. Then, seeing Jane's scarlet cheeks, he added, "I had wanted to, many times this last month. I'll not deny, I adore Mistress Eustace, but as I believe her to be a woman of impeccable virtue, I'd never send such a note."

Jane closed her eyes, her colour fading a little, her heart, in spite of its constriction, singing out at this confirmation of her wildest dream.

"Mistress Eustace, you didn't take up the assignation?" asked the sheriff.

"No," she replied. "No, I would not do so. My duty is to my husband." Then, she smiled a joyful smile, "But I wanted to, quite desperately."

"Oh, such virtue!" sneered Philip Eustace. "I see I am indeed fortunate to be alive, and it was not my death which was plotted."

"But was the trap for you then, Jane?" asked Bess, looking bewildered by all the revelations.

"I hardly know," Jane replied, looking in a frightened manner to her brothers.

"It is a matter of who sent this—and whether they also set the cord across the stairs," said the sheriff, looking puzzled. "I vow, there was never such a murder with so many motives." He broke off as voices were heard from outside, and suddenly the door was flung open, to herald the entrance of a man.

"Well met, Hal, Ned!" cried Sir Francis Westwood. "You were, of course, expecting me? Where is the bride? Bring on the groom! I am arrived. Everything can now go forward!"

Chapter Thirteen

It took Justin a long time to find Hal that evening after supper. He finally did so in the untidy room which formed part of the stable yard, where Hal met his steward and dealt with his tenants.

"Your father is asking for you, Hal," Justin said, noting that, although he was surrounded by ledgers and accounts books, the ink had dried on his quill and his eyes had an unfocused look.

"I cannot see him," Hal replied mechanically. Then, seeming to come to himself, he dipped his pen in the inkwell, and casting Justin an unfriendly look, bent over his books. "Pray tell him I am detained, and will consult with him on the morrow."

Justin, realising from the look, how Hal hadn't forgotten his moment of doubt on the stairs, carried a stool to sit down opposite him. If he was going to quarrel with

Hal, he might as well be comfortable. "I don't think hiding here will improve matters," he said bluntly.

Hal met his gaze, his own eyes glassy with arrogance. "I am not hiding, but dealing with matters which require my immediate attention," he replied coldly.

"You've thought of a way of preventing the sheriff from arresting you tomorrow?" Justin asked provocatively.

Hal's eyes narrowed slightly and then dropped again to his papers. "No," he admitted.

"That, surely, must be the most pressing matter requiring your attention," Justin replied, his tone tart. "But no, you are engaged in deciding on a twenty year lease on Two Oak Farm. Vital matters indeed;"

"Vital for Jack Tade, especially if I am arrested tomorrow. He'll get no decision for months, if ever," retorted Hal, stung by his sarcasm.

"You have so little faith in justice then?" asked Justin, with equal tartness.

"I thought I did. But, if justice decides I must lose my good name in its interest, I begin to wonder," replied Hal quietly.

"Did justice decide that? I thought you did."

"Either way, the end result is the same," he snapped. "I am branded libertine, fool, betrayer of my own father, murderer. What matters it now?"

"It matters greatly!" cried Justin angrily. "If you weren't so full of self pity, you might give a thought to my sister, made to look a fool, too."

"Libby isn't made to look a fool, she's pitied for having so wicked a husband!" he snarled. "Not that it will matter to her, she believes me a murderer anyway."

"Don't be a bigger fool than God made you!" cried Justin impatiently. "Libby believes no such thing!"

"Oh, not a murderer of malice—I'm not even man enough for that!" he retorted, his tone anguished. "No, she thinks I meant to push Jacqueline, in order she might miscarry of my baby, and that I pushed Johanna in error in her place. A bungler and a murderer!"

"It doesn't seem to occur to any of you—not even the sheriff—but if a cord was stretched across the stairs, there is no need to push! In fact, a push might actively prevent a death, by promoting a stumble! Don't you understand? They are two totally different sorts of murder!" cried Justin emphatically.

"Do you think the type of murder truly matters to Libby?" Hal cried. "Do you think she cares if her stepmother was pushed or stumbled? The woman is dead, and she believes I did it!"

"No, she doesn't!" cried Justin, shaking Hal's arm in exasperation. "Oh, for a moment, it might have passed through her mind, as it did mine. By God, the case was desperate enough, but even as the thought occurred, it was dismissed! I know you to be many things, Hal—an arrogant fool, a stiff-necked pedantic stickler for the truth, but a murderer? The sort of fellow who'd push a woman down stairs, never! Hell would freeze over, and you'd see Libby and Harry sold into slavery before you'd rise your hand to harm a woman."

Hal blinked rapidly, dropping his gaze quickly to his books to hide sudden tears. "I do trust I can still engage you as my advocate," he said in a choked voice.

"Oh, you damned fool!" cried Justin, grasping Hal's shoulder in quick comfort. "I would that you'd held your tongue, though! You've given Hughes a brilliant case!"

"You think I don't know it," he said, his tone muffled. "Oh, Justin, what am I to do?"

Justin squeezed his shoulder again. "I would to God I knew," he muttered. There was a short silence, then Justin said in tones of greatest resolve: "Well, we'll just have to find out who did it ourselves."

"Hughes doesn't seem to be overly preoccupied by any of that," sighed Hal. "I think he was confused, and then when I spoke, it gave him the ideal opportunity."

"We must think this through," said Justin. "If we—" He broke off as the door opened and Ned entered.

"Hal, father was asking where you were," Ned said, glancing to his brother uncomfortably.

"We are discussing how we are to prevent Hughes from arresting Hal tomorrow," said Justin. "We need more time to work out who did kill Johanna!"

"Right," said Ned, nodding a quick agreement. "Yes, how can we do that? I suppose Father didn't help, in ordering Hughes from the house in that manner. Nor, so openly applauding Guy's assault! But what can we do? I mean Hughes is the sheriff of the county. We can hardly hold him imprisoned or any such thing, can we?"

"No, I don't think that would improve my already rock-bottom reputation," said Hal bitterly.

"Hal, none believe it," said Ned awkwardly. "I mean, Libby was telling Mary and Jane what did happen."

"Oh God!" cried Hal. "Now they know I am a drunken fool, too!"

"Better that, than a libertine, surely," said Ned bluntly. "Or do you truly prefer the credence of Philip Eustace?"

"I would prefer to emerge from this with my skin and some degree of credit," snapped Hal.

"Yes, but—" began Justin, only to stop again as the door was once more pushed open.

"Hal, your father wishes for your attendance." Libby entered, her wan face and red eyes telling their own story.

Hal looked up, meeting her eyes. "Can you ever forgive me?" he asked humbly.

"Can you ever forgive my moment of doubt?" she returned, in a whisper.

"Gladly!" he replied, holding out both hands.

"Joyfully!" she said, coming to take them and raising her face mutely to his. As they kissed across his books, Mary entered, saying, "You don't deserve her, Hal."

"Hal, your father is raising all hell looking for you," said Guy, who followed. "He seems to think that the only way for you to prove your innocence is to get roaring drunk." He grinned, in a puzzled manner. "I must say it has its attractions!" Then, as he met Mary's eyes, he added hastily, "Merely a jest, my love."

"There is very little humour in this whole situation, Guy," she remarked waspishly. "Hal, Libby has explained everything, and if she is satisfied then I suppose we must be. Although, I'd be failing in my duty as your elder sister if I didn't—"

"Sit down and hold your peace, woman," said Guy,

grabbing her about her waist and pulling her onto his lap. "Is this the conclave to decide what to do?"

"Justin and I were discussing my defence,"agreed Hal.

"You don't think Hughes will be fool enough to try to arrest you, do you Hal?" cried Mary shocked.

"What would you, Mary?" he replied wearily. "I have the reason for wanting both women dead, I have the means, and Libby cannot guarantee I didn't leave my bed."

"This piece of cord, has anybody seen it before?" asked Justin, who'd been sitting quietly. "I mean, is it something which is part of the house, Hal? Or has it come with one of your visitors?"

"I've never seen it before," said Hal blankly. "It is but a piece of twine, such as might be used anywhere."

"And indeed is was," agreed Justin. "You have some like it in the stables—or on the farm?"

"Not that I recall," said Hal. "'Tis not something one often needs, but no, I've not—"

"Hal!" Bess, her face full of anxiety, appeared in the doorway, Jane close behind her. "Hal, Father says you are to come immediately! He is growing most annoyed, and he says he'll not have his son hiding away in corners, like a rogue!"

"Dear God!" cried Hal in exasperation. "Is this not

my own house, that I must be sent for like a servant! Tell my father, no, stay—I'll tell him myself!"

"Hal," Justin caught his arm. "No more confessions, I beg you."

Hal brushed him aside and strode angrily from the room. He went past the kitchens and entered the main part of the house, his family coming more slowly behind. He turned into the Hall and would have entered the parlour, but that his father's voice reached him from beside the great fireplace, where he sat with Jacqueline.

"At last, young Hal!" cried Sir Francis, rising to his feet to display himself, dressed in the height of fashion. "I've been sending for you all evening! Come and join us in a cup of wine to chase away the glooms."

"You'll excuse me, sir, I have business to attend to," Hal replied shortly, crossing to the stairs.

"Business, pooh! You've a man for that! Come lad, this glum look won't do. Put on a brave face, and we'll meet that fool of a sheriff tomorrow, together!" he boomed with a hearty laugh.

"Forgive me, sir, but I am a landed gentleman, I cannot so easily shuffle off my responsibilities to a servant. The people at Westwood are used to my hand at the bridle."

"Then they take advantage of your good nature, lad,"

said Sir Francis urbanely. "Come, ease back, take a cup with me, all can be attended to on another occasion."

"That may well be so, sir, but I do not wish it. It is my will that I attend to the matter now, and not waste my time in idle drunkenness. Here at Westwood, my decision is final. As my guest you are welcome to drink as you see fit, but I will not join you. Goodnight."

"Wait, Hal. Damn you, sir, wait I say! I am your father. I demand your obedience!" cried Sir Francis, anger leaping to his voice.

"Sir, ever since I came to manhood, I have obeyed you in everything—done your duty when you were too idle, run your errands which you found distasteful, and shouldered many burdens rightly yours, that the world might view you in a better light. Tonight I say enough is enough! I am weary, sick at heart, and I will not perform at your will, like a dancing bear! My obedience in matters filial you must always have, but my presence is my own to decide! I'll bid you goodnight."

The rest of the family, who had arrived during the latter part of this speech, stood frozen in the hall, not knowing what to do in the face so comprehensive a snub.

Sir Francis Westwood, however, was well used to such

things. "You know, my dear, that boy gets more like Henry every day," he said to Jacqueline with a shrug. "No sense of humour at all these days! Guy, Mary, come and join us in a cup of wine. Jane, where is that husband of yours? Is it true, as Jacqueline says, he'll not last the summer?"

❧

Chapter Fourteen

"Oh, 'tis you," Sir Francis Westwood sourly eyed Justin with disfavour, as he entered the small parlour the next morning.

Justin gathered together the papers he'd been reading, the result of a wakeful night thinking with Hal. "I was about to leave, sir," he said, his tone icy.

"No, stay. Where is Hal?" Sir Francis asked, raising a hand.

"Hal has been attending to his people since first light," said Justin, with whom Hal had shared his darkest fears. "He has gone to set his house in order before church, believing as he does, the future is rather uncertain."

"This is nonsense," said the elder man testily, more in irritation than conviction. "Look, I've heard it said you bid fair to become one of the best lawyers in England. Is it so?"

Justin shuffled his papers again. "It has been suggested I have abilities," he agreed with legal understatement.

Sir Francis glared at his down-bent head. He disliked the man, and hated the fact he'd married his daughter out of hand. "I suppose this marriage of yours is legal," he snapped. "It had better be, with my Bess swollen like a ripe fruit."

"I took great care that it was," Justin replied curtly.

"Then I suppose I'd better give it my blessing," Sir Francis replied with a grand air of magnanimity.

"Bess will be pleased, sir," remarked Justin.

"But you don't give a fig!" Sir Francis snapped in quick understanding. "I could break you, boy, if I wished!"

"You could try," corrected Justin, losing some of his calm.

"Oh, so there is a spark of spirit in that scrawny frame," Sir Francis sneered. "Look, I need you to save Hal from this charge, the same way you did for me."

"Hal has already engaged my offices," replied Justin curtly. "But, alas, I doubt I shall be equally successful."

"Why, in God's name? You cannot believe Hal guilty!" cried Sir Francis.

"I know Hal to be innocent," he replied. "Unfortunately, the situation he is in is difficult in the extreme."

"How so?" demanded Sir Francis.

"One of the first questions asked in a case of murder is who benefits. In this case, Libby does and there, by extension, Hal."

"From what I understood of Mary's foolish chatter, Libby intends to give it all to you," Sir Francis snapped irritably.

"She may only do so by law with Hal's consent—she being a female and having no property of her own," replied Justin. "The law couldn't even consider such an event. As far as the law is concerned, Hal gains if his father-in-law's wife falls down the stairs. If, however, she fell in error, and the trap was set for another of the ladies, then Hal, having quarrelled with your wife, is also a suspect."

"This seems the most flimsy of cases, you should be able to knock it asunder at once!" cried Sir Francis. "Is a man to be hauled off to court each time he falls out with a female? The prisons would be awash with people!"

"I imagine your wife has not informed you of the cause of the quarrel between herself and Hal?"

"My wife? No!" he said curtly.

"I believe Hal wishes to keep a similar silence," agreed Justin.

"What the devil is going on here?" snapped Sir Francis Westwood. "Mary clammed up last night, and so did that husband of hers, who is usually so full of himself. What did Hal and Jacqueline quarrel about?"

"That is a question you must put to your wife, sir," said Justin.

"I'm putting it to you!" Sir Francis replied sharply. "I get nothing but tears from Jacqueline and the usual desire to leave England immediately."

"Hal doesn't want you told, sir," said Justin in a manner to indicate he didn't agree.

"Well, I want to be told. I'll not be kept in the dark!" he roared. "I'm not a fool, nor a child!"

"It would appear, sir," said Justin, with a slightly malicious air, "that your wife is with child." He paused, as Sir Francis looked surprised. "And that she insists the father is Hal."

"Hal!" Shock and such outrage appeared on the old man's face, that all at once Justin felt ashamed of his desire to hurt him.

"So she claims, sir," he muttered, glancing away.

"I—I cannot believe Hal would—would do such a thing!" Sir Francis stammered, for once in his life taken aback.

"Not of malice, sir," said Justin, quickly eager in his desire to exonerate Hal. "He had reason to take shelter in your London house last spring late one night, in his search for Bess and I."

"Aye, I recollect him telling me of it," agreed Sir Francis curtly, still much bewildered.

"It would seem, or so Hal says, that Jacqueline—" Justin hesitated. Last night, listening to Hal, he'd told himself he'd enjoy pricking the bubble of Sir Francis Westwood's esteem—after all, his father-in-law never missed an opportunity to plant a thorn in his side. But now, confronted with his stricken old eyes and white face, he felt mean-spirited. "Your wife took the occasion to offer Hal the freedom of her bed. An offer Hal was prompt in refusing. Alas, he wasn't so strong-minded when it came to a bottle of wine, and freely he admits he crawled to bed as drunk as he'd ever been."

"The damned young fool, tell me no more," cried Sir Francis, his face grey. "The treacherous scheming hussy! To try that trick again, I vow I'll take a stick to her, I will! But Hal—by God, how could the lad fall for such a trick?"

"Hal is honest, and naïve, in that he expects others to act honestly, too." Justin sighed, as if this were a failing that he didn't share.

"The stupid fool!" cried Sir Francis. "The child won't even be his, but one of those young blades she goes about court with! Yet the fool would go to the scaffold, rather than betray her honour?"

"No sir, you've not understood. Under duress, Hal told Sheriff Hughes. Thus convincing him that if he hadn't killed Johanna Danvers for gain, he'd done it thinking she was your wife. To Hughes's mind, the scandal brewing would call for a desperate remedy."

"Not so desperate as to require Hal's life," said Sir Francis bleakly.

"Hal feels rather than hurt you, or cause such scandal, he'll keep silent as long as possible," said Justin, with a sigh.

"Well, Jacqueline won't, even if I have to beat it out of her," said Sir Francis vindictively.

"Even supposing you to be successful, sir, there is still the scandal of it all. None knows better than you how a rumour of this sort will fly about. You are still said to have killed your brother—even with a free pardon and another found guilty."

"People will always believe what they choose," replied Sir Francis sharply. "Malicious tongues ever seek to believe the worst of a man." He paused, thinking deeply.

"So, what are your solutions, Mr Lawyer?"

Justin sighed. "We must find out who did kill Johanna," he said practically. "It wasn't me, and it seems the sheriff has no thoughts in that direction, as Bess and I were wakeful until dawn. Plainly, it wasn't Bess or Libby."

"But Libby had equal opportunity with Hal, didn't she?" demanded Sir Francis, frowning.

"She did, but the sheriff appears convinced of her testimony. Mostly, I think, because he dislikes Hal so from the last occasion they met."

Sir Francis nodded. "So, if it isn't you—and it isn't Bess, Libby or Hal—who is it then? Not Ned, surely? Nor Mary, or Guy?"

"I'm not sure who he thinks of," sighed Justin. "He dragged up the affair at Sidworth Castle last Christmas."

"Aye, Guy said he hit him," chuckled Sir Francis. "I wish I'd seen it."

"It never does one's cause any good to alienate the officers of the law," remarked Justin coldly. "Hughes has some suspicions of us all, I do believe. Indeed, none of us can prove we didn't set the trap."

"Well, in that case, what do you intend to do?" demanded Sir Francis.

"There are two matters I need to follow up, and Ned is assisting me. Firstly, there is the matter of the letter Mistress Eustace received, and then there is the cord itself. It seems none of the household recognise it. Therefore, it must have come with one of the guests. I've sent Ned across to talk to Cecily and Hetta, to see if they know anything of the matter."

"And me, I am yours to command," Sir Francis said. "What would you have me do?"

Justin eyed him thoughtfully. "I have three tasks for you," he said bluntly. "Firstly, get the confession from your wife, by what means you must! Neither Hal nor my sister needs additional problems to irk them at this time. Secondly, don't abuse the sheriff or his man, verbally or physically, when they next make an appearance here. A lot more is achieved with a soft word than a hasty blow. Thirdly, if your daughter finally has your blessing on her marriage, you might be so good as to inform her yourself. It would make all the difference to her."

"It must have relieved your spleen to get rid of that," Sir Francis remarked, getting to his feet. "I don't know that your acidity isn't every bit as brutal as my shouts. I'm away to escort my family to church, but I'll see what I can do after that."

✤

In spite of his promise, Sir Francis returned from church, his mood one of gloom. The lengthy sermon, which had given him too much time to ponder Justin's words, only enhanced this.

He had been the butt of a similar trick many years ago. He could well believe Jacqueline would use the same method to incriminate Hal, in an effort not only to save herself from his anger, but to cause maximum distress to Hal and Libby, too. Yet, whilst he acknowledged the truth of this, he rather shrank from all the furore of it all. Did it truly matter who the father of her child was? In his heart, he no longer cared. He would deal with it as he saw fit, he decided, and after dining with his entire family, he sought solace in the gardens. He still needed time to think.

A long walk only served to depress him further, for he could see plainly Hal had everything in good order. The fields were full of crops, the woods well-tended, the beasts fat and disease-free. Even all the repairs were up to date. The ruined west wing, which still showed blackened spars to the sky—a potent reminder of how short a while ago this land had been riven with war—

was about to be repaired. Yet, it seemed to Francis there were still countless wounds which hadn't been healed and more which grew worse as time went by.

At last, he turned his steps back to the house, joining the yew walk and entering the formal garden. There he found Libby, Bess and Jane sitting working on a garland of dried flowers and herbs.

"I assume this to be for Hetta's nuptials, should they still take place," he remarked with would-be geniality, taking a seat amongst them.

"Yes," said Libby, "Aunt Margery showed me the instructions in one of her books. Do you not think it will look pretty?"

"Very," he replied in a bored tone. "Hmmm. Margery, when will she return?"

"We look to see her and Aunt Kate any day now, sir," said Bess. "We had a letter only yesterday, saying that they would return for the wedding."

"I feel her presence is needed here," he replied. "Perhaps she can make some order out of this chaos. Tell me," he turned to address Libby, "did you construct a like garland for Bess's marriage bed? If so, it was truly effective, for I see her lawyer has wasted no time in getting a child on her."

"None at all, sir," replied Bess calmly. "Although it being midwinter when I was wed, I had to be content with a posy of herbs, rather than a garland."

There was a short silence as Jane and Libby exchanged a meaningful look. Then, Sir Francis said in a testy manner, "Your husband informs me your marriage is legal, Bess."

"He is one of the most brilliant lawyers in the land. How could you doubt it, sir?" she returned. She realised suddenly, with a lifting of her spirits, that she was no longer afraid of him. "You surely, Father, with your history, would know Justin makes no error in such matters."

"He would appear to have made a colossal one with regard to his father's estate," replied Sir Francis maliciously. "Whereas you, my dear," he added, turning to Libby, "you appear to have played almost as clever a game as that slut who was killed."

"Do I, sir?" replied Libby, not liking his inference. "I'm afraid I am not good at any games. If I should inherit anything, I shall give it all to my brother anyway. I believe it to be his by right."

"Indeed?" he snapped. "As a lawyer's daughter, I must defer to your knowledge, but I'd have thought anything you inherit became your husband's, and would therefore be at his disposal!"

Libby glared at him, knowing this to be the truth. "Hal and I have discussed this matter, and are agreed on it," she said, trying hard not to sound defiant.

"I would certainly advise him to take that view whilst this murder is being looked into," said Sir Francis, nodding in an annoyingly smug manner.

Libby glared at him. "I do not think Hal requires advice," she said pointedly.

"Certainly not from a female," he agreed urbanely. "One who must naturally have little or no idea of the importance of such matters. No, my dear, you stay with your pretty fripperies. They are much more suited to your situation."

Again a silence fell on the party as Jane began to fix the little bunches of dried flowers into the garland.

"So, Bess," continued Sir Francis, trying to inject more cordiality into his tone. "You are married and will shortly produce a fine son for this husband of your own choosing."

"The Lord will decided on whether it's a boy or girl," replied Bess. "It matters not for Justin and me, we shall love the child anyway and keep it safe, as good parents do."

"Your husband tells me you'd like my blessing to your union," Sir Francis continued, as if she'd not spoken. "Although, I can't see much evidence of you caring one way or the other myself. Perhaps it is he who'd like the approval of your family."

"We do have the approval of most of our family, sir," Bess replied, unruffled by his manner. "If you care to add yours, I shall be glad, but it matters little to Justin, I do believe."

"When I was a lad, none would have dared to marry without the express consent of their elders and betters, let me tell you, young lady!" Sir Francis snapped, irritated by her air of calm. "You may think yourself very fortunate you've been received back here. Twenty years ago, you'd have had your name removed from the family for what you've done! Now it would seem, daughters may choose to ally themselves with any jack-come-lately, and expect to be welcomed back into the fold without so much as a word!"

"I think attitudes have moved forward in a more liberal manner since the war," agreed Libby sweetly. "Each generation makes a little progress. After all, you cannot fault the choices of your daughters. Guy Armstrong has much improved his fortunes since his marriage, and

Justin shortly will."

"And now Jacqueline tells me this Carver fellow is hanging about you, Jane, even before your husband is dead!" he cried tartly, ignoring this also.

"Ambrose Carver has been sent by old Mr Eustace to care for Philip," said Jane. "I think, sir, if you'd had more care of the sort of men you married your daughters to, they may not have been so arbitrary in their next selection."

"It is as well a man has sons," he grumbled, getting to his feet finding he was achieving nothing. "They say daughters are a solace for one's old age, but it seems to me they become sharp-tongued scolds!"

They watched him stalk off in silence. "If that was a blessing," sighed Bess, "it was hardly graciously given."

"I think the pill might have been swallowed more gladly," remarked Libby, "but that my father left his money away from Justin. Now, inevitably, it is seen as already family money and Sir Francis will decry its loss forever and a day, when I give it to Justin."

"Justin won't take it, Libby, you know he won't," sighed Bess as she watched her father stalk away.

"Then, I shall give it to my godson," she said. "For I claim the right to be godmother to your baby."

"Oh, I do hope so, Libby, if God is willing," Bess replied, smiling as her eyes welled with tears.

"Come, we should shed no tears over Hetta's garland if we want it to bring her good luck and a house full of stout children," said Jane.

⚜

Chapter Fifteen

Sir Francis Westwood glanced at his wife as she sat brushing her long, black hair late that night. It had been a lengthy, tedious day. He had not needed Justin's words to tell him something was wrong. It had been so for some time now.

The truth was that he was too old for her, in fact, this last year he'd begun very much to feel his age. It wasn't just that he'd finally been sickened by her treachery, more that he realised what a disservice he'd done Jacqueline in marrying her.

"So, my love, you've had an exciting time here," he said, as she showed no sign of joining him in the poster bed.

"Exciting, non!" she replied. "Tiresome, oui!"

"But I understand this fool of a man, Hughes, believes you to be the intended victim," he continued.

"He is, as you say, the fool!" she replied with a shrug.

"And, that young Hal is the murderer," he continued urbanely.

She shrugged her shoulders again. "He thinks we all are the murderer in turn. First Hal, then Libby and her brother, then Mary, then Hal again!" she said.

"I can see his reasoning in thinking Libby or her brother the murderer," Sir Francis continued thoughtfully. "She stands to gain a considerable sum from her stepmother's death, and Hal told me some foolish tale about it being tied up so tight he couldn't touch it. And, that even if he could, he'd agreed with Libby to give it to her brother. But as for this nonsense of a quarrel between you and Hal, well what is that all about?"

"Must we discuss this, Francis?" she cried. "My nerves are so upset by everything, that I can't think anymore!"

"You aren't required to think, my dear, but merely remember. Or shall I ask Hal for his version?" he asked, a hard note entering his voice.

She hesitated, once she could have been sure that Hal would have defended her come hell or high water, but no more. He might, of course, just remain silent, but she had doubts about that. Anyway, even if he did, she knew Justin or Libby wouldn't show a similar reticence.

"I haven't liked to say anything, Francis," she said slowly, moving to the bed. "I know how much Hal means to you, how you hate to be told bad things about him! It is true, too, it is my fault," she added cunningly. "Only, I never gave it thought, he and I are of an age. I thought of him like a younger brother."

"Indeed!" said Sir Francis, unable to keep a faint note of irony from his voice.

"It was back in the winter, Francis, remember, you were in France trying to find out what the Dutch planned," she said, as she slipped into bed beside him.

"I remember it well, yes," he agreed.

She wriggled into his arms. "Hal came to the house. He was in London looking for Justin and Bess, just after Libby's father had died. Naturellement, as your son, I bade him stay for supper and overnight. He was cold and wet and weary after his journey. I know you'd not have me do different."

"Indeed no, who is welcome at my house if not my son?" Sir Francis said, moving slightly so that he could still see her face in the candlelight.

"We had supper together, Hal and I. I was a little unhappy and lonely, Francis, being alone for so long. And Hal was dispirited also, so we drank a bottle of your wine, Francis. And Hal perhaps drank another bottle, I cannot recollect, but Marie had to help me get him to his chamber."

"Not a pretty tale," agreed Sir Francis. "I'd have thought my son could have held his wine better than that."

"Between us, we helped him undress," she continued quickly. "Then, Marie said she'd get a pan in case he spewed and went away, leaving me alone with him. It was then he turned on me like the mad man." Cleverly, she hid her face in the sleeve of his nightshirt. "He had said things in the past, Francis, which I had ignored, for I know he isn't happy in his marriage to that mouse Libby. And, I cannot deny, that evening he had laughingly suggested he shared my bed, but even so his attack took me by surprise! Oh Francis, I didn't want to have to tell you this—but he forced me! He was like the mad man, his strength was that of three men, he held me down and he forced me, Francis—me, your wife—in his drunken lust!"

"Indeed," said Sir Francis calmly. "And where was the faithful Marie when this was going on?"

"I told you, she'd gone for the pan," she sat up abruptly. "What is this Francis, are you not angry?"

"Oh yes, I am very angry!" he replied coldly. "But,

tell me, you did not scream, or call out for assistance? Don't we keep a house full of servants to come to your aid?"

"Call out?" she repeated, feeling as if the ground were slipping from beneath her. "Call out and have all the servants come running to see your son raping your wife? I thought anything than that! I fought him like the tigress. I scratched and beat at him with my fists until they bled, but he was stronger. I could do nothing until Marie came to my aid. She hit him with the pan and so helped me get away."

"I see," he said thoughtfully. "Leaving Hal for dead, presumably?"

"Non, he was knocked out," she replied, feeling bewildered at his reaction. "Marie and I locked ourselves away from him until the morning."

"You didn't summon the constable?" he suggested.

"Francis, this is Hal we talk about, your best-loved son. I could do none of this without the shame and scandal! I thought only of you—of your grief to know your son was such a monster!"

"And it was for this laudable reason that you showed an equal reluctance to tell me?" he asked, brows furrowed.

"How could I destroy your illusions?" she agreed,

sinking back against him. "My pain, my outrage, was nothing beside your grief."

"Thank you my dear," he said cynically. "So, what did you quarrel with Hal about on your arrival? Did the sight of you again inflame his desires? Did he so far forget himself as to attack you again?"

She frowned. He wasn't behaving as he should. True, the words were correct, but the mildly scornful way in which they were uttered was disconcerting.

"Non," she said dully. "As I say, I tried to put it from my mind. I told myself, I was part to blame and resolved to have more care in future. But then, something I could not have dreamed of happened. Oh Francis, I don't know how to tell you! He—Hal has got a child on me!"

"You are with child?" he said quickly, for this part he'd found hardest to believe.

"Oui, three months gone!" she replied. "And it is Hal's! I told him as soon as I arrived, I was so worried and frightened. I begged him to help me tell you how it happened, but he abused and reviled me. He said I was the slut and the strumpet and that he'd deny everything. Then when I told him I must confess to you, he threatened me, Francis. He said if I dared, I'd be very sorry, and then the next day Johanna Danvers is found dead at the bottom of the stairs, after wearing the same gown as me! I tell you Francis, Hal did it. He is frightened of the scandal and so tried to kill me!"

For a few seconds, Francis's allegiance wavered. Could it have happened so? But then, common sense took hold. "I'll speak to Hal of this!" he said, getting from the bed.

"Non, Francis! Where do you go at this hour?" she cried.

"To see Hal," he returned. "I should have spoken to him last night, or today. I could see he was troubled, but thought it better to let it lie if he didn't want to talk."

With this, he caught up his bed gown and went out, leaving her prey to fury. He walked along the corridor and into the gallery, going to tap lightly on the door of Hal's chamber. When there came no answer, he slowly opened the door and peeped in. Libby slept soundly in the bed, but there was no sight of Hal, so just as softly, he shut the door and went quietly down the stairs.

A light shone under the door to the Jericho parlour and he wasn't really surprised to find Hal and Justin in conclave together. Nor, to see the defensive look in Hal's eyes as he looked up to see who had entered.

"Sir?" he said at once, a question in his voice as he

got to his feet.

"No, no, sit I'll join you," said Sir Francis, coming to the pretty gate-leg table and taking a seat opposite his son. "Is that a flagon of wine you have there, Justin? If so, I'll gladly take a glass."

Justin obediently poured the wine, passing it to him and saying, "I have to thank you, sir, for taking the trouble to talk to Bess. It would seem your words have relieved her mind of great care, and any who can do that for my wife earn my gratitude."

"Yes, I profited by one piece of your advice, young man," he replied taking the wine and sipping it. "But I wasn't man enough to face the other." He grimaced. "I'm getting old, you know—and what is much worse—I'm beginning to feel it. I never did before." He was silent for a space, looking into the depths of his wine. Then he glanced up to meet Hal's eyes. "Justin told me this morning of your dilemma. I wish you could have found it in your heart to tell me yourself."

Hal went white. "Justin should learn to keep his tongue," he said sharply. "As I would have done, sooner than injure you, sir."

"Nay, you can't injure me," said Sir Francis softly. "I've injured myself! I knew what she was when I married her. I thought I could control her, but it would seem I was mistaken!" He seemed to shake himself, finished off his wine and passed the glass back to Justin for a refill. "So, to business! It was as Justin told me, I take it, you were drunk and she tricked you."

"You have the first part correct, sir, I was drunk," Hal replied, colour flooding into his face. "The rest, as the poet says, is a blank."

"Damn!" said Sir Francis. "That drunk?"

"And therefore, surely incapable," said Justin swiftly. He was aware that it was important to both men that somehow they could each leave the interview with a modicum of respect.

"Most likely," agreed Hal evenly.

"More than likely, surely," persisted Justin.

"I could not swear to it," replied Hal. "Indeed, I could swear to nothing but waking the next morning with a head cracking asunder, a mouth like a sewer, and Jacqueline naked in my arms."

"By heaven, boy!" cried Sir Francis, anger sparking at the vision this conjured. "How came you to fall for such a harlot's trick? You're not a green-sick moonling, but a man full-grown. Haven't you met up with the wiles of a drab before?"

"Yes," he agreed, "but I did not expect to do so in my father's house. I felt there I could be safe. I didn't lock my door as I might have done at an inn, for fear of a thief stealing in to take my purse, so why should I imagine my father's wife would steal into my bed?"

"Because you knew Jacqueline of old!" Sir Francis cried, even angrier at the truth of this. "You've had trouble with her before, and should have expected it again!"

"I did, and I thought I'd made my position clear when she offered herself to me!" Hal snapped in return. "I did not mince my words, nor trouble too much about courtesy, but spoke plain and to the point of my contempt of her betrayal of you!"

"By God!" he cried. "I listen to you, and hear a maid undone! Have you no blood in your veins? Or has marriage to that mouse of a wife sapped it all!" roared Sir Francis.

"Stop me if I'm wrong," cried Hal, "but am I now to be taken to task for not bedding your wife?"

"Well, at least we'd know where we stood if you had!" he snarled.

"Gentlemen," said Justin, judging it time to intervene. "This is nothing to the point! May I suggest, sir, that as you've already indicated, Sheriff Hughes be told on the morrow that Lady Westwood carries the child of her lover—a courtier, I believe you said, sir?"

"It could be any one of half a dozen, for all I know!" said Sir Francis huffily. "But I'll not disclose the secrets of my marriage bed to that fellow Hughes. I shall inform him the child is mine, and force Jacqueline to tell him that you didn't quarrel!"

"But we did," said Hal, "and that woman of hers, Marie, heard us—and probably Thomas, too."

"What does that matter? They'll keep a still tongue in their heads if you pay them handsomely enough," returned Sir Francis.

There was a small silence. Then, Hal said evenly, "I don't think you fully comprehend my situation, sir. I am justice of the peace. I represent the law to the people who live here."

"Exactly, and as a justice, you must know the best way to manipulate the law," said his father.

Again, there was a silence. Then, Hal said quietly, "I would sooner be disgraced before all, than do that! Indeed, should I even contemplate such a thing, I would be disgraced forever!"

"Good God, what a nonsense you make of everything! You are but a justice—why, such men take bribes every day! Aye, and worse too, I dare say!"

"Bad luck to them, then!" said Hal, who was now very pale. "I do not. And I do not forget that my forefathers spent their lives, that I might be able to bring the law to every Englishman, whosoever he be, wheresoever he lives. I count myself fortunate that such a trust is given to me, and I will never, ever abuse it."

"None are asking you to abuse it!" cried Sir Francis, exasperated. "Merely, not to disclose the intimate secrets of our family to a tribe of rustics when it can be prevented!"

"Not legally, it can't," said Hal sharply.

"Oh dear God!" cried Sir Francis. "That I should live to see my son turn into Henry before my eyes, forever pratting about right and wrong!"

"It's as well I learned right from wrong with Uncle Henry, for I never learned it from you!" cried Hal furiously.

Sir Francis looked amazed by this, and by the anger in Hal's tone. "So you won't do as I ask?" he cried blankly.

"I shall tell the truth when asked," returned Hal.

"But you'll not volunteer it?" said Sir Francis, quickly.

"No more shall I evade it," replied Hal contemptuously. "Can you not understand, the principles are far too important."

Sir Francis sighed. "You'd make a bad spy," he said dryly.

"I would not want to make a good one," said Hal loftily.

"No!" said Sir Francis. "But you'll not refuse to accept my title when I die, and I got that by spying."

"We must pray, sir, I am not put to the test. Perhaps I'll pre-decease you," snapped Hal coldly.

Sir Francis sighed and glanced to Justin. "I shall be guided by you," he said. "What must I do?"

"Get your wife to confess to her lies," said Justin firmly. "If she'll admit Hal is not the father of her child—and that Hal knew this—then there can be no reason for him killing Johanna in error."

"And the case against him for killing her on purpose?" asked Sir Francis.

"Virtually non-existent," said Justin. "He has as good a one against me—or Bess or Libby—it could be any one of us."

"Then, how do we resolve the matter?" cried Sir Francis, exasperated.

"By finding the real murderer," Justin replied wearily.

"That's what you said last time, and the time before," said Hal bitterly.

"And we have found the murderer, each time!" cried Justin indignantly.

"But not been able to prove it, or bring them to trial," said Hal.

"No," agreed Justin. "That's why this time there must not be any errors. This time, we must—and shall—find the murderer and see him brought to justice."

⚜

Chapter Sixteen

Ned smiled and waved as he caught sight of Cecily at the end of the long walk at Shearling Court. She waved in response and walked slowly to meet him. All at once, Ned's happiness dissipated. Usually, Cecily ran into his arms on their meeting. Had she grown tired of him? Was this a result of the likelihood of Hal being arraigned as a murderer?

"Cecily?" he said, a quiver in his voice, holding out his hands in appeal.

She darted a quick look over her shoulder, and ran the last few yards into his arms. "Oh Ned, Ned, how I've missed you!" she cried, hugging him close. "I shall get such a lecture from Mistress Shearsby, but I don't care. I need to feel your arms about me." She raised her face mutely to him, and he responded by kissing her lips with enthusiasm.

"Mistress Armstrong!" came a stentorian cry. "Do my eyes deceive me? By heaven, Miss, if you were a daughter of mine, I'd beat the flesh from your back!"

"Who is this dragon?" hissed Ned, as Cecily guiltily fell away from her lover.

"'Tis Mistress Shearsby, Will's mother, poor lad. She has harried both me and Hetta ever since we arrived Saturday! Good heavens, it's not quite forty-eight hours since we arrived, yet it seems like a month!" said Cecily, shrinking away from him as a figure turned into the long walk from the side and stood, arms akimbo surveying them.

Ned firmly took up Cecily's hand and walked forward to greet the woman.

"Mistress Shearsby, your servant, ma'am." Ned stopped a few paces from the grim-faced figure, and swept a bow worthy of Hal, using as he did, his feathered hat to emphasise the movement. "I am Ned Westwood. I beg pardon of this intrusion, but I met your husband in the stableyard, and he bid me find my love and my sister in the garden."

"I see you favour your brother, Mr Westwood!" she snapped, her eyes cold. "Fine words and empty gestures!"

"I am honoured to do so," said Ned, with a patent honesty. "For there can be no finer model to my mind."

"Oh, indeed, and will you follow him to the gallows too?" she retorted.

"To the mouth of hell, if need be, ma'am," he replied tartly, not liking her tone. "For where Hal goes, I go, knowing he has a purpose in all things that can disgrace none."

"Well, I tell you to your head, my fine fellow, he's a disgrace to his name, and brings shame on all those forced to consort with the likes of him!" she cried, her eyes flashing, for she'd not expected so doughty a response.

"And I tell you, Madam, you are mistaken!" he replied firmly, but politely, feeling Cecily quail at his side. "My brother could never bring shame upon any but those poor fools who allow themselves to be dictated to by the vagaries of scandal and rumour! If it so happens you are one of these pitiful creatures, then say no more. I will remove from your circle all such who offend you immediately. Cecily, run and fetch Hetta. We Westwood's don't stay where we are on tolerance!"

This was uttered very much in the grand manner of

his father, and made Cecily open her eyes wide in dismay, for Mistress Shearsby was near gobbling with fury at such a response for so young an adversary. Luckily for Hetta's wedding plans, Mr Shearsby came into view, with Hetta on one arm and Will on the other.

"Ha! Well met, young Ned!" he cried. "I see you've found your Cecily, and thereafter weren't so keen to find your sister, I'll warrant!"

"On the contrary, sir, I had but this moment dispatched my betrothed to seek out Hetta," Ned replied stiffly. "Hetta, go to the house with Cecily and gather together your things. Mistress Shearsby would rather not be incommoded by us a moment longer."

"Now, hold!" cried Mr Shearsby, as Will gave a wail of dismay. For, by now they'd drawn level and could see from Mistress Shearsby's face, a quarrel of magnificent proportions was in full swing. "I'm sure my wife said no such thing. We are more than happy to have such sweet young ladies here!" he smiled encouragingly at Hetta.

"Indeed," said Ned politely. "But sweet or no, they are both kin of my brother, and I feel certain neither will stand by, and allow his name to be traduced."

"Not if we have a choice, Ned," cried Hetta, who had plainly tolerated enough of her future mother-in-law.

"If you have come to take us home, by all means let us be gone this moment! I am tired of hearing Hal's name blackened by those who know nothing of the matter."

"Hetta!" cried Will in anguish, turning in appeal to his father.

"Let her go, you young fool!" cried his mother. "She's naught but a pretty face, and there are those to be had by the dozen without dark stains on their names!"

"Madam, oblige me by holding your tongue," said Mr Shearsby sharply, as Will began to dispute with her hotly. "Will, silence. Now come, shall we not all repair to the house to settle this over a cup of wine? Ned, my boy, you are not an unreasonable fellow, I know. You'll understand how it is. My wife is fretted by those dreadful rumours, and so spoke out of turn!"

Coaxingly, he took Ned's arm, keeping a hold on Hetta and nodding to Will and Cecily to follow, he led the way back to the house. "I must admit, my boy, the tales are getting pretty lurid now," he continued with a grimace. "One cannot completely blame my wife for her doubts, you know, for according to the latest reports, Westwood is a hot bed of licentiousness and debauchery!"

"Reports, as ever, sir, are merely that," said Ned stiffly.

"Indeed, indeed," soothed the older man. "But you know what folk are like—and they say there is no smoke without fire!" He cocked his head to one side, to invite a confidence. "Now, this tale of your brother being the lover of his father's wife, is that not very shocking?"

"Indeed it is, sir," said Ned warily. "But as you know Hal, you'll know how to treat it."

"Oh yes, yes indeed," the older man agreed hastily. "But how do such tales get about, I wonder?"

"Imperfect knowledge added to gossip, I should think," said Ned. "My father's wife is an excitable woman —French, you know," he added, as if that explained everything.

"Yes, yes, I have met the lady—a great beauty of course," he added, casting Ned a sidelong look.

"Yes," agreed Ned. "A beautiful woman, in a foreign sort of way, but excitable—unstable almost—and incredibly jealous."

"Ah yes, they can be, especially as they get older and their looks begin to fade!" he glanced to Hetta, at his side. "But you don't dislike her, my dear, she's been your mother for some years now, that I do know."

"Since I was a child," agreed Hetta. "No, I am fond enough of her, I know my duty, I hope. But Jacqueline has not the ability to inspire affection, there is little warmth of heart in her."

He nodded again as they all entered the house, calling to a servant to bring refreshments. "Now Ned, my boy, let's clear up this little matter, shall we?" he said with would-be heartiness.

"Nothing could be simpler, sir," said Ned. "An apology from Mistress Shearsby, and the promise to hold Hal's name as dear as I do, and it shall all be forgot."

Mr Shearsby gaped at Ned. "An apol—well yes, yes that is indeed—well, you must understand how it is, Ned," he faltered, lowering his voice. "It is as we were just saying, when a woman reaches a certain age, don't you know, the beauty is well—fading and some of them—well they become, as with your father's wife, a little jealous, prone to—to odd humours. My wife now, she has a great affection for Will, don't you know. He is her special pet, and it's hard for her to see him with nothing but eyes for this young puss!" he pinched Hetta's chin affectionately. "Not but that's not exactly how it should be, but the jealousy, you see, is still there."

"I see perfectly," said Ned. "And I'm afraid it is something which will have to resolve itself one way or the other. I'm sure you, too, will understand, Mr Shearsby, that I cannot leave Hetta here in this climate of censure." He glanced to his sister, not entirely sure about her feelings, but determined to deal with the matter as he saw fit. "In fact, taking everything into account, I am wondering, Hetta, if we'd better not delay the wedding, until everything is clearer in our minds."

"If you and Hal think that best, Ned," said Hetta promptly, with her usual docility. "Then, I shall be guided by you."

"Father, no!" cried Will, who came in, arm in arm with his mother and Cecily, in time to hear this. "Sir, I beg you will not agree to this! The wedding has been set for Midsummer's Day since Candlemas!"

Hetta smiled, "There is yet Lammas and Michaelmas, Will," she replied. "And I for one would sooner not be beholden in such a manner, but enter matrimony with my name unsullied."

Ned, who knew from Justin how unlikely they were to be successful in this, began to feel he'd over played his hand, but had reckoned without Will Shearsby's love.

"Hetta, no! My love, I beg you!" Before them all, he went on his knees to her. "My darling, there is no need for delay! Hetta, don't refuse me now, I beg you, but let the marriage go forward on Friday at Midsummer, as planned."

"But your mother is expressing doubts, Will," said Ned. "She feels it would be foolhardy to ally yourself with a family set to become a byword for scandal, and we can't but acknowledge her point. We Westwoods are a proud family. If you doubt one, you doubt all, and if you doubt all, then better to have nothing to do with any!"

"No," said Will stubbornly. "I don't agree. I know I owe you a duty, Madam, but I know the Westwoods. Sir, I beg you will speak to my mother, and bid her mind her tongue."

Mr Shearsby looked appalled. "I fear it's rather more than keeping silent, my dear," he said uncertainly, glancing to his wife's ravaged face as she viewed her son on his knees before another woman. "Ned here demands an apology, too."

Mistress Shearsby returned his look with one of disbelief. "An apology for speaking the truth?" she cried. "Hal Westwood murdered his uncle for his inheritance, his sister's first husband to free her from the scandal of bearing another man's child, and has now murdered his wife's stepmother to free her inheritance, if it wasn't to stop his stepmother bearing his child! The man's a monster and the whole family so steeped in infamy, that I wonder at your readiness to leap into such a marriage! She has bewitched you, my son, with her eyes and her pretty face, don't you see that! She's as evil as they all are! Don't you understand the danger you'll be bringing here, if you wed the vixen? Poisoned he was, her sister's husband! Poisoned, and who do you think she'll start upon here?"

Resisting the impulse to state the obvious, Ned shrugged. "I rather think you have your answer, Will! Hetta, Cecily, pray run and gather your belongings. I'll escort you both back to Westwood now."

Within half an hour they were hacking slowly along the country lanes in the direction of Westwood, and Ned was apologising.

"I'm sorry Hetta. I think Hal would say I overplayed my hand," he admitted ruefully.

"No matter, Ned," she replied cheerfully. "I was tired of apologising for my existence to that woman anyway."

"Yes," said Cecily, "and it wasn't going to get any better, was it? You could tell she'd be forever reminding you throughout your married life how lucky you were to have married into their family!"

"Quite," said Hetta, tossing her curls.

"But, aren't you upset?" asked Ned, glancing to Cecily. "I mean, don't you love Will? Won't you be unhappy without him? I'd be in despair of Cecily rode out of my life, as you've done his."

"I think he was pretty despairing, too," said Cecily with a sigh. "Poor Will."

"Silly!" laughed Hetta. "I've not lost Will—at least I don't think I have. I'd best not speak too soon, I suppose, but he's so—so dependant upon his parents. He makes excuses for his mother, saying how she loves him, which isn't true. She wants to make him mind her—as she does her poor husband—by her terrible tantrums. So, now he has a choice—either he can follow me, or stay with her."

"But what if he doesn't follow you?" asked Ned, as Cecily nodded her agreement at this strong-minded course.

"Then I shall be utterly miserable," said Hetta with a wobbly smile, "but, at least I shall be miserable on my own account."

"And it will help to know, that if he hasn't the strength to come after you, he's not truly worth it," said Cecily.

"It won't you know," said Ned. "It will hurt just as much if you are right or wrong," he sighed. "However, in the general misery ahead, I doubt one more thing will matter."

"Is it truly so bad, Ned?" asked Cecily incredulously. "The rumour was not wrong, then?"

"Not in essence," he agreed gloomily. "Justin is despairing. He told me I've to find out about this piece of cord, but I can't see it helping much." He produced it from his doublet. "I was supposed to ask Mr Shearsby and Will if they recognised it, but I forgot in all the furore!"

"But it's mine!" said Cecily in astonishment. "Surely you knew that?"

"Yours!" cried Ned, in blank amazement. "Are you sure?"

"Yes, yes. Don't you recollect me telling you how my trunk lock broke, just as we were leaving? The baby was screaming, Mary was in one of her fusses, and Guy in a temper, which exploded when all my shifts tumbled into the dust! He stuffed them all as they were, dusty and soiled, willy-nilly back into the trunk and tied it about with a piece of cord poor Joe had to fetch from the stables! That's why I had to run to the laundry yesterday before we could leave. All my linen had to be washed afresh!"

"But, yes, of course!" he said. "I had forgotten, at least I didn't even connect it, but how is it Guy didn't recognise the cord?"

"I don't know," she replied, shaking her head. "Unless it was because he was in such a temper, because he was! After all, Joe tied all the knots. Do you think it's important?"

"I don't know," he replied with a frown. "Justin seemed to think it might be! What happened to the cord? Once you arrived, I mean, what happened to it?"

"Well, I can't think," said Cecily blankly. "We arrived, our baggage was taken up to the chamber, I was sharing with Hetta again, as I often do. Do you recollect, Hetta?"

"I remember you telling Libby all about it, and Mary coming in to laugh at Guy's fury, and Libby saying how she'd get Delia to wash your shifts fresh for you," said Hetta thoughtfully. "And Delia coming to unknot the cord. Yes, I can see her doing it, and her putting it on the chest beside the trunk, then little Guy woke up and we all went to see him."

"So we did," agreed Cecily. "And by the time we'd admired him and Harry, Delia had disappeared with my linen and the cord was gone with the trunk."

"Yes," agreed Hetta. "The cord had disappeared, too."

"So we must talk to Delia," said Ned. "Perhaps she'll —hello, who's this riding so hard?" he ushered his charges to the grass verge at the side of the lane and brought his horse to stand before them, alert, his sword at the ready. But in the event he relaxed, grinning.

"No need for alarm!" he said, amusement in his voice. " 'Tis your lover, Hetta, come to claim you!"

Hetta allowed herself a small smile, and then schooled her countenance to express mild dismay.

"Ned!" Will Shearsby pulled his horse to a slithering halt alongside them, "I didn't think to overtake you so quickly!"

"We're in no great hurry, Will," he replied. "What's amiss? Did we forget something?"

"Yes, no. That is—I've—I've come to say our wedding shall go ahead, Hetta, as planned," he announced addressing his betrothed. "I've spoken to my father, and he agrees. I'm coming to Westwood with you now, and shall remain there until we are married. If he can persuade her, my mother will join us on Friday, if not, just my father will come."

"I don't know that I agree anymore, Will," she replied pertly, somehow rather irked by his air of complacency.

Of course, this was what she wanted, but she was rather piqued with him, and didn't see why she shouldn't tell him so. "I—all we Westwoods—have been insulted by your mother. I don't know that I care to wed into a family which thinks so little of mine!"

A look of blank astonishment crossed Will's pleasant face at this display of petulance. He opened and shut his mouth a few times, glancing to Ned, as if for guidance. Then, he shrugged his shoulders, and his mouth hardened.

"I will beg pardon for my mother. I think we are all agreed she was at fault," he said. "But quite plainly, this is not good enough either, Hetta. I am aware you've been insulted, and I shall not allow it to occur again, but you've given me your promise to be wed on Midsummer Day and unless you are willing to be thought a vulgar jilt, I shall hold you to it!"

It was Hetta's turn now to stare in astonishment, a faint blush mounting her cheeks. "Do you say I am a jilt?" she cried, stung, but also secretly impressed by this evidence of his new-found determination.

"Not if you agree to marry me, as planned," he replied sharply.

"This past eight and forty hours I've listened to nothing but insults concerning my family from your mother, and now you finish it by calling me a jilt!" she cried angrily, her favourable feelings ousted by his arrogance. "I vow, I cannot believe my ears! I am to tolerate the intolerable, or be named a vulgar jilt! I say you may call me what you will, sir, but I'll see you in Hades before we are wed on Friday!"

With these last furious words, she turned her horse's head about and set off up the lane at a smacking pace. Will, his own face suddenly grim, stayed only to touch his hat to Cecily before cantering after her.

"Good heavens," said Cecily faintly, as Will drew alongside Hetta and pulled her horse to a halt. "Shouldn't we interfere? She's dreadfully angry!"

"Play with fire and you get burnt," Ned replied with a grin, as Hetta lashed out at her lover with her riding crop. "Ouch! That must have—yes I thought so, now he's really furious!"

"Ned, you'd best—oh!" she turned to stare at Ned in astonishment as Will snatched the crop from Hetta's grasp, threw it in the ditch, and pulled her bodily from her horse into his arms, kissing her soundly. Hetta applied two more buffets to his ears, but they lacked conviction, even to Cecily's inexperienced eyes, as she melted into his embrace.

"I rather think that's one matter settled," said Ned, with a laugh in his voice. "Was that exactly as she planned it do you think? No, no she was genuinely shocked when he called her a vulgar jilt, wasn't she?" He laughed out loud at Cecily's amazed expression, leaned across to steal a kiss on his own account, and then set his sights for Westwood.

❧

Chapter Seventeen

Justin, observing his quarry crossing the lawn in the direction of the yew walk made haste to follow her.

"Mistress Eustace, may I speak with you for a few moments?" he called, as he caught her up.

"But of course," she replied with her sad smile. "Only, we are brother and sister, you must call me Jane."

"Thank you, Jane," he smiled faintly. "I wanted to ask you about that note, if I may?"

"The one I gave Mr Hughes?" she asked. "Oh, how I wish I'd not, now. I feel so very foolish about it and it has made things worse for Hal."

"For Hal? How so?" asked Justin dismayed.

"Have you not heard? It seems it is written on a page pulled from one of his account books," she said. "And now the sheriff is trying to prove that Hal not only wrote it, but left it in my chamber in error for either his stepmother or Mistress Danvers."

"Well, as if Hal would do so!" exclaimed Justin in exasperation. "He of all people would know which people would be in which chamber."

"Well, he's talking to all the servants yet again, trying to get them to admit Hal has little to do with the running of the house and that Libby might have changed the rooms unbeknownst to him."

"The man's a fool," cried Justin.

"Aye, but a clever fool, with a grudge against Hal, it would seem," she replied sapiently.

"Hal and I worsted him last time, when your uncle was killed and your father accused. He feels Hal and I made him look a fool, and so this he time is determined to find one of us guilty," said Justin, looking worried.

"I heard him tell Ambrose—Mr Carver—that Hal has got the Westwood family off a murder charge twice now, but he'd get them the third time."

"That is slanderous—or very nearly," said Justin gloomily. The trouble is, on each previous occasion, the villains—you know, either Will Cuthbert or Mistress Soames—have killed themselves, too, and so have been unable to plead. Well, not that Mistress Soames would have been fit to plead—she was mad, as mad as can be!"

Jane shuddered. "Yes, I remember Bess writing to me about it in a letter. It must have been dreadful."

"It was," he replied. "Mistress Soames was, as I say, quite mad, and she dragged poor little Cecily Armstrong up out onto the crumbling leads of Sidworth Castle in the middle of a winter storm and locked us out. The only way to rescue Cecily was through a small casement window in my chamber. Hal went out there without a second thought and swung himself up onto the leads, but I'd seen his face as he dropped down onto his hands and realised his shoulder was still weak. He hung there, forty foot up over the narrow pit of a courtyard in agony until he got a foothold. Ned burst in—for he'd been trying to knock the door down with Guy and Soames—and immediately followed Hal.

"I felt such a useless fool! I felt sick even looking into the courtyard, but your brothers were both so courageous, I felt I had to go, too. I can't tell you how my knees were trembling and my head spinning, but I was some use in helping to hold the piece of cloth—which was all that stood between Mistress Soames and death —whilst Hal, Ned and Soames tried to catch hold of her hands. It was useless, the cloth split and she fell to her death, and in spite of the sort of confession she'd made about Sir Edward's death and that of the girl Meg, we had nothing on oath, and no proof. The justice of the peace listened to Hal's account and mine, and came to the same conclusion as we did, but many say he was a friend of Hal's—which he wasn't. They never met before that occasion and Geoffrey Soames—a knave if ever I met one—took great care that all should know of Mary and Guy's love affair in spite of his father, Sir Walter's promise. No, it was most unsatisfactory."

"And the earlier affair, with Will Cuthbert?" asked Jane. "I remember him well, a hard, ruthless man. I never liked him. He drowned my kitten, you know."

Justin smiled a little at that, for in that one sentence, she was very like his wife. "Yes, that was equally disappointing. It was my fault. I bungled it. I should have waited until Hughes was there to hear his confession, but I went ahead and accused him, challenged him, and he bolted. He took a nervous young filly he'd previously terrorised, and rode her full at a gate when pigeons were fluttering all around her. She took the gate, but stumbled on landing, and Will Cuthbert came off into a ditch, breaking his neck."

"So again, nobody to take to trial," said Jane thoughtfully.

"Exactly, so we must do better this time. So, if I may ask you some questions?"

"Please do," she paused and took a seat in the arbour, smiling up at him.

"You didn't recognise the writing, I suppose?" he asked doubtfully.

"Well, yes, I thought I did, you see, for I thought it like Mr Carver's hand."

Justin nodded, "Yet you believed him when he said he hadn't written it?"

"Yes, I did, for I realise now, that although I'd thought it like Ambrose's writing, I'd known truly it wasn't. Perhaps that's why I ignored the invitation," she smiled enigmatically.

"Can you think of anyone who might want to—well, to kill you?"

She laughed. "What a question, Justin, and how very rational you make it sound! No, I can't think of why anyone should want to kill me!"

"You don't own a lot of money that you've left someone heir to?" he suggested, coming to sit alongside her.

"I own nothing at all, but the clothes I have with me," she said, with a bitter laugh. "I won't even have my jointure by the time Philip dies!"

Justin nodded, frowning. "And plainly he cannot want to be rid of you to marry another, so I can see no reason for him sending you the note."

"Do you truly think I was the intended victim?" she asked, frowning in turn.

He shook his head. "I wish I knew. This affair is like an eel—there is nothing to grasp. Everybody in the house is well known, all members—save Mr Carver—of one family. I know they couldn't have killed in cold blood, yet one of them did."

She glanced to his shadowed face. "And you begin to fear it is Hal?" she suggested softly.

"No, no!" he cried violently, as if to refute the very suggestion. "And yet," he shook his head. "I can understand that reasoning you see! Jacqueline has always held this fascination for Hal. She is like the serpent in the Bible to my mind. She attracts and repels him! She seems to have some sort of hold over him. He hates her, avoids her as much as possible—yet when he's with her, she casts a spell over him, and it always leads to disaster! The despair he felt on Saturday evening when she arrived to tell him she carried his child was absolute. He didn't know what to do, he had to admit to me he'd been made a fool of in the spring, and the thought of telling Libby—who'd just lost another child of his—was a matter of great anguish. He was dazed when I told him she'd heard it all, and in that state, I can quite see that he might just think of Jacqueline falling down the stairs an answer to the problem! And yet, no—" he cried angrily, "now I'm beginning to think like Hughes! Hal is honour itself, he'd never do such a thing. He might be tempted, but his morals are too strong!"

She nodded her agreement, "Yes, Hal couldn't harm Jacqueline, even if he wanted—whatever the provocation. And he'd never have mistaken her for the other lady. He's a very acute observer."

"Yes, yes!" cried Justin. "Exactly, I've remarked it before, very little escapes Hal's eyes. Even in the dark, he'd have known that it wasn't Jacqueline!"

Jane gave a chuckle. "In fact, the more one thinks about it, the more impossible it becomes. Imagine Hal, lingering about the stairs waiting to ineptly push Jacqueline down! The whole idea is laughable."

Justin didn't laugh. "It wasn't necessary to do so, Jane," he said gently. "The note—allied to the length of cord—meant the murderer could even go to bed, or watch from a convenient place."

Jane shuddered. "Oh that's horrid! Yes, of course, I

see now and am even more convinced it can't be Hal. Hal in a fury, shaking Jacqueline at the head of the stairs and her falling down, that I could see. Although, he'd not run away from what happened had it been that. But Hal, stealing out in the dark to stretch a cord across the stairs, never!"

"And so back to the old question—who?" sighed Justin.

Jane sank her chin to her hand. "Indeed, who?" There was a silence whilst she thought. "One of the servants?" she suggested.

"Why?" he countered.

"Oh, I don't know, she'd slighted them in some way?"

"Most rarely see her. She's not popular, but they'd not think to murder her," he replied.

Another silence ensued. "What about that other fellow, the lawyer in Adamsholme?" she asked, "Didn't Libby say that he and her stepmother were lovers?"

"Libby thinks so. I don't know that they were," said Justin. "I must say, I'd not thought of him, but I suppose if he'd wanted, he could have got into the house. Nowhere is locked up. Well done, Jane! I'd never even considered an outside force, but it certainly bears investigation." He glanced to the sky. "In fact, if I set off now, I'll reach Adamsholme as he's closing up for the day. I can kill two birds with one stone, and see how the business goes, too! Will you tell Bess where I am gone, and Libby not to wait supper on me?"

"Right gladly, and may your errand prosper," she replied as he hurried away.

❧

Jane continued to sit on in the late afternoon sun, well-shaded from its burning properties by the thick yew hedges. She let her mind drift, thinking what a change it made for her to sit in peace like this. Usually, she was at Philip's beck and call, but the journey had spent even more of his slender resources of strength. These past days he'd been content to keep to his bed for the best part of the day, only dressing for the evening and dinner. The sense of relief was enormous—to be allowed to think, move, dream even—without his incessant cruelty gave her a foretaste of what was to come. It made even the prospect of a impending widowhood seem positively rosy.

She was lost in these dreams when footsteps approached.

"You are finally alone then," said Ambrose Carver sharply.

"Oh, Ambrose, you made me jump! Yes, Justin has gone to Adamsholme, to speak to this man his step-mother had called in to replace him," she replied, smiling up at him.

"He was with you a good while," he replied, and she stared to hear the note of jealousy in his voice.

"Yes, we were talking of this awful position Hal finds himself in," she agreed, wondering a little, but mostly flustered by his attitude.

"For almost an hour?" he asked incredulously.

"Yes," she replied adding, "Is there any reason why we shouldn't?"

"No, no," he snapped. "For myself, I wouldn't think so little of a lady's reputation as to sit by her half-hidden for best part of an afternoon, but then, perhaps, I am too nice in my notions."

She smiled faintly. "How could my reputation suffer? Justin is my sister's husband. He is a brother to me."

"Ha, sister's husbands have been known to stray before!" he cried. "Especially when their wives are huge with child."

"Bess isn't huge," she laughed, "and she and Justin are devoted to each other. I think you are being rather silly."

He knew it, and felt it, but took refuge in his stateliness. "Oh I beg pardon, Mistress, I didn't mean to interfere, but to warn you. However, 'tis plain my opinion is unwelcome, so I'll say no more."

"Your unbiased opinion is always welcome," she replied gently. "You need not chide me, Mr Carver, I have an active enough conscience as it is."

He reddened at this and lost some of his annoyance. "I beg pardon, Mistress Eustace, as you say, I have no right to censure your conduct."

"Save the right of friendship," she replied gently, wishing to soften the blow.

"No, not even that right," he returned, looking away down the length of the walk to the far vista. "For even in a few months hence, when you are free of Philip, I'll still not have anything to offer you, but my heart."

Her heart began to beat rather rapidly, for she'd never expected this, however much she might have hoped for it. "I shall be penniless myself, Ambrose," she said quietly. "Do you not think I know the value of what you offer?"

He turned to smile at her, his handsome face lit by it. "Oh yes, you value my love, sweet Jane," he whispered, "but your brother, your father, no."

"I am most like to be a charge on them," she said. "They'll not care for what I do."

"Oh, you dear fool," he cried, coming to stand with one foot on the bench so he could lean closer to her. "You are young, you are beautiful. They—your brother —is wealthy, he'll find you another dowry and another good match."

She looked up at him, her heart misgiving her as she realised the truth of this. It was exactly what they'd do. Oh, Hal would try his best to make sure it was a decent fellow, if Hal had the chance to do anything at all. There was but one chance, and Bess and Mary had shown her how.

"I doubt any would want to marry into this family now, Ambrose," she said ruefully. "The scandal which envelops us is too great."

"Any man who saw you wouldn't give a fig for that!" he declared. "A man with any spirit at all would insist you became his wife, and not care for the opinions of others."

"Are you such a man?" she asked daringly.

"I?" he cried. "I've told you, I have nothing."

"Yes," she laughed bitterly. "That's how they'll all be, Ambrose, most willing, but—"

He grew red-faced again. "Do you mock me?" he cried. "I tell you, I love you and would hold it an honour if you'd be my wife."

"And I'd be honoured to be your wife, Ambrose," she replied promptly. "Of course, there can be no official declaration, can there, until after Philip's death?"

"Wait, we cannot be married!" he cried in dismay.

"What, did you not just ask me to be your wife?" she asked, hiding a smile at his look of horror.

"Yes, no, yes, I did theoretically!" he cried wildly. "My dear love, you know I want nothing more, but I've no money!"

"Neither have I, so we'll have to be poor, like Bess and Justin," she replied. "Or is it that which makes your heart fail?"

"Being poor?" he cried. "God no, I've never been anything else!"

"Neither have I," she replied tranquilly. "My uncle was the one with the money—he left it to Hal—the rest of us are little better than paupers. Oh, except Guy Armstrong, he put some money in with Libby's father on a merchant venture, just before he died and the ship came back laden with gold and spices and precious things. That's why they think of buying Elmley Park."

"Yes, he was telling me of it the other morning and trying to persuade me to come in with him and his sea-captain on the next venture," he smiled bitterly. "He lost interest when I told him I had about forty pounds a year."

"I've even less," she replied. "Is that why you don't want to marry me?"

He looked down into her upturned face, his heart missing a beat. "You know I long to marry you," he said, and there could be no doubt of the look in his eyes, or the pain in his voice. "But I love you too well to do so. Your family will find you a decent man who'll hold you dear and whom you can love, too."

"Like last time?" she asked, meeting his eyes. "You've been with us for three months now, Ambrose, you know my life, and I tell you it is a hundred times better since your coming than it was before. You know of the evil men and boys who used to haunt my home, of how I was reviled and tormented by my husband! Do you not understand that my father cares nothing for us? That he used us as moves in his power game? That we were, in effect, sold to the highest bidder? Ask Mary of her life with Sir Edward Jolyon. Get Guy to tell you something of how she was when he first met her, hovering on the edge of madness because of Sir Edward's brutality! Ask Justin of what Bess's fate would have been if he hadn't married her. Do you think one so rational would lose his inheritance as he did, but that the need was so great?"

"I thought your father promised Justin Bess's hand for getting his name cleared," said Ambrose, frowning.

She shook her head, tears filling her eyes. "He did, in the first relief of it all, but my father is no honourable man, like Hal. Never trust his word in anything."

"Oh, my dear, don't weep," he said in dismay, as tears slid down her cheeks. "I beg you won't weep." Without thinking what he was doing, he sat down beside her and drew her into his arms, kissing away her tears. "In all these months, I've watched you be so brave—face everything with the same cheerful good humour, come what may. Don't break down now, I beg."

"I beg your pardon," hastily she mopped her eyes. "I've been holding on so tightly, never allowing myself to hope or dream, just existing for the next hour, and sitting here in peace I'd forgotten everything and began to plan for the future."

"Oh, my darling, I would that we could," he sighed, holding her fast to him. "But our future is so dim, I dare not."

She nestled closer to him, delighting in the feel of a strong arm about her, listening to the slow rhythm of his heartbeat. "Hold me close, Ambrose," she whispered. "Keep me safe. I care nothing for the future if I can but be in your arms now."

Chapter Eighteen

"Ned, you're back—and Cecily and Hetta, too!" said Hal in surprise. "Ah, hello there, Will, I thought Hetta and Cecily were to remain at your home until the wedding."

"That was before I and Mistress Shearsby quarrelled, Hal," said Ned bluntly.

"Quarrelled?" exclaimed Hal. "Oh, dear God, not more trouble!"

"No, no trouble, Hal," said Will firmly. "The wedding will go ahead as planned, my father will most certainly join us. My mother may do so."

"Nothing is yet certain," said Hetta sharply. "I've not yet agreed, Will Shearsby, to becoming your wife."

"Now wait one moment!" said Hal, looking harassed. "You agreed weeks ago, Hetta. You can't go—"

"Take no heed of her, Hal," interrupted Will. "She

is merely in a tantrum because of my mother's foolish words. We shall be married on Friday."

"I will do no such thing!" cried Hetta, only further irritated by Hal's attitude. "You seem to think, Will, that a few kisses and soft words alter the principle of the matter!"

"No, I don't, the principle remains the same, I merely say—"

"Dear God!" said Hal, looking appalled. "What has happened? Hetta is usually so pliable!"

"They've been like that all the way home," said Ned gloomily, as Hetta continued to scold, and Will to obstinately reiterate that they would be married, even if he had to carry her to church by force. Ned glanced to his brother, "You've not been arrested yet, then?"

"No," Hal passed a hand wearily across his face. "My father's threats are plainly not without effect! It seems Hughes dare not do anything until he has proof! You haven't seen Jane, have you? Philip Eustace is calling for her, or his cousin, and he is in no pretty temper, either."

"No, shall I go and look for her?" asked Ned, as the quarrel began to rapidly descend to nursery level.

"No," said Hal. "I'll go, I need the air. Cecily, take

Hetta away, I beg, and keep her from Will's company until suppertime. You, Ned, go and soothe Will's ruffled feathers, if you'll be so good."

❧

Without a backward glance, Hal left the hall and the house, going out into the garden, where dusk was rapidly approaching. He needed a period of calm reflection to try to bring some order to the chaos of his thoughts. Ever since his quarrel with Jacqueline on Saturday evening, it seemed he'd been precipitated from crisis to crisis with no time for thought or measured decision. He was sure in his mind he'd missed something, that somewhere along the way, something had been wrong. But he couldn't, try as he did, recollect what it was, or even when it was. It was just there, niggling in the background of his thoughts.

He turned his steps into the walled garden, gloomy now in the half-light as the sun dipped in the west, and turned aside at Libby's favourite seat, which backed onto the yew walk, to sit awhile and ponder. Perhaps, if he went over it all just again, he might remember.

He sat down and, as usual, his thoughts, instead of following the ordered pattern and training of these last few years, began to dart like a dragonfly from one subject to the next. He never fully got a hold on one problem before rushing off to the next. Then, just as he was wearily deciding there was no help for it but that he'd have to write it all down, the sound of a man's voice came softly to his ears.

"My darling, do say you have no regrets."

"I have no regrets," said a female voice promptly.

"Ah, that I could believe it true," he replied harshly. "I am a scoundrel, a villain, to use you so ill."

"I've not been used ill," said Jane, laughing.

"But sweetheart, I swore to you your reputation was the most precious thing to me. Yet, here I am, keeping you out in the garden while it grows dark."

"And I still hope it is," she replied, "but you are right, it is almost dark. I must return to the house. Philip will be waking now."

"Philip!" cried Ambrose. "In my joy, I never gave Philip a thought!"

"An excellent idea," she agreed with a sigh. "He seldom gives you one."

"I have betrayed him!" he said, dismay in his voice.

"As long as you don't betray me, too, I don't care," said Jane, a shade tartly. "This is Philip we are talking about, Ambrose, you know what a creature he is! How he betrayed me a hundred—nay, a thousand—times with those boys of his!"

"My darling, don't!" he said, as Hal gaped in horror on the other side of the wall and, quickly getting to his feet, stole away. "I know what you had to endure, I wasn't levelling any criticism at you! How could I, my angel, my darling, but all my vows, my intentions are in the dust!"

"The best place for them," laughed Jane. "How old are you, Ambrose?"

"Six and twenty," he replied.

"I'm four years the younger," she said. "And a hundred the older in experience! Three terrible years of marriage have taught me nothing if they've not taught me to take pleasure in full where one may. We'll be a long time dead, Ambrose."

"My darling, I promise you thirty years of happiness once we are wed, to blot out your dreadful three. What was it the old woman said to you? It sounded more like Mary's fortune than yours!"

"*No love, nor joy from man or boy, for your life will only begin when you let the lady in.* It makes no sense to me," she replied, shaking her head.

"It does to me, especially when coupled with mine: *Put aside the pretence, cast off the mask, happiness will await you, if you will but ask.*"

"What must you ask? What is the mask?" she replied, frowning.

"The mask is my name," he said. "I tell everyone I am called Ambrose, but in fact, that is my second name. My first is Marion."

"Marion?" repeated Jane, blankly.

"Yes," he said reddening. "It is the greatest curse ever. I was born on Lady Day, and my mother was a Catholic, so she called me Marion."

"The lady! Happiness will begin when I let the lady into my life," cried Jane, laughing.

"Exactly. As soon as she said it, I knew, and that I'd have to tell you. You will keep my secret, won't you? My mother died whilst I was still a baby, and my father always called me Ambrose, so none knew, save him and I."

"Yes, I'll keep your secret, provided you keep mine," she replied.

He kissed her tenderly. "I'm hardly likely to tell anyone, am I? It's too precious," he whispered. "Come, we must go, already we are late!"

❦

Hal, meanwhile, had walked round to the stables in no pretty mood, still shaking his head in dismay, to find Justin dismounting stiffly from a staid cob.

"Oh, I wish I'd listened to you, Hal!" he said, catching sight of him. "You said I'd need to take some exercise if I was to get back to riding again. I shall pay for my idleness in stiffness, I fear."

"I rather think it was weariness more than idleness," said Hal, realising that Justin was, in fact, looking better than when he arrived the previous week. For he had a good colour in his cheeks from the exercise, and the pinched look in his face, which had so worried him, had disappeared. "Why did you ride? Why not take the carriage?"

"I thought it nerve enough to help myself to one of your horses, let alone order your coach," he replied candidly. "But I was in a hurry, and didn't want to waste time looking for you to beg leave."

"There is no need to beg leave, Justin," he replied. "If you saw a need, you must know I'd not care."

"I wanted to talk to Robin Dwyer, the clerk at my father's office," he said, as Hal looked blank. "Jane suggested he might have been the one to have the assignation with Johanna. I mean, there had to be a reason for her going downstairs at night, don't you think?"

Hal nodded his agreement, but said sharply, "Don't talk to me of Jane! I vow, I don't understand women, do you Justin?"

"I don't think I'd care to do anything so rash as claim to do so," he replied candidly.

"Sometimes I wonder if Libby is the only sensible female left on earth," Hal sighed.

Justin frowned, "I must confess, I count my wife as such."

"Yes, yes of course," Hal agreed, "and little Cecily, too—and Hetta, I think. But oh, I don't know—what with Mary taking Guy as her lover—Jacqueline has a string of them—and now Jane and that fellow Ambrose!"

"Oh, are they lovers?" asked Justin. "I thought it was just admiration on his part."

"It sounded rather more than that to me when I inadvertently came across them in the garden some minutes ago!" Hal retorted, uncomfortable from the experience.

"Oh, dear me, how embarrassing," smiled Justin, understanding the cause of his ruffled feathers.

"Quite," said Hal, "but you don't say, how did you

fare with Dwyer? Do you think he could be our man?"

"No," said Justin. "No, he seems honest enough by his own rights. Which is to say, a pretty rogue who'd cheerfully cheat anybody, but not a murderer. He had too much to gain from Johanna remaining alive. He was very upset about Johanna, of course, but he'd plainly never been near this house."

"Damn!" said Hal. "So, it still looks as if I am chief suspect!"

"Mmmn!" said Justin. "What do you think of Guy Armstrong, Hal?"

"Guy?" said Hal blankly.

"Well, it was never proved Avis Soames killed Sir Edward Jolyon, was it? And you can't deny Sir Edward's removal was very opportune for Guy and your sister."

"True enough," said Hal, "but for what reason would he wish to be rid of Johanna Danvers?"

"None, of course, but say it was mistaken identity! What if he thought it was Jacqueline?"

"Why would he want to get rid of Jacqueline?" repeated Hal. "Admittedly, she irritates him—as she does most people—but not enough to plot to push her downstairs!"

"Perhaps she's tried her tricks on him, as she has on

you," he suggested. "He and Mary spent a few weeks in London in the spring, we don't know that she didn't try to fasten the paternity of her child on him, too! And, I couldn't see Mary being as forgiving as Libby, could you?"

Hal looked amazed at this suggestion, and somehow rather piqued, too. It wasn't that he enjoyed Jacqueline's attentions, far from it, but the idea that he was one of many, was rather humiliating. "Well, yes, I suppose it's a logical thought," he said, making a quick recover. "I mean, perhaps all men are a challenge to her? Especially those of her own family who appear happy. Has she made any advances to you?"

"Me?" Justin laughed. "No, Jacqueline is very French, and very well aware of her own worth. She'd not waste her time on one she sees as a tradesman. Besides, I don't admire her."

"No more do I!" protested Hal.

Justin threw him an indulgent look. "Not with your head, perhaps!"

"Nor with my heart!" he cried indignantly.

"No, nor with your heart," he agreed laughing. "Merely, perhaps, with your loins!"

Hal stared at him. "Not with any part of me!" he said, with cold emphasis.

"Have it as you will," agreed Justin, hiding his amusement hastily. "So, you don't think we could make out a case against Guy?"

"I'm appalled at the thought," he cried. "Mary would be torn apart by such a thing."

"But don't you see, Hal, it has to be one of us," said Justin sharply. "If not, you, me, Ned or Guy, who then?"

"That Ambrose Carver, or Philip Eustace!" he said quickly.

"Philip Eustace is a dying man," replied Justin wearily. "And you can't accuse Carver, because you don't approve of him being Jane's lover."

"Well, you tell me who then!" he cried. "Or perhaps Hughes is right, and it was me after all!"

"Don't be silly!" Justin replied reprovingly, as if speaking to an over-excited child. "Look, I know this is difficult, but we've got to go over it all again and think harder. The answer must be there. We just can't see it, that's all."

Hal's stomach gave a lurch as Sheriff Hughes and his man rode into the stables. Each time he arrived, Hal expected to be arrested. A grim foreboding that disaster was stalking him descended like a black cloud.

⚜

Chapter Nineteen

"Mr Westwood," said the sheriff, as he dismounted and approached. "I'm glad to find you here."

"We did agree, when you left here last, that I'd not leave Westwood," replied Hal, his face pale. "I am still justice of the peace, Hughes. I can be trusted to keep myself under house arrest."

"I wasn't suggesting any such thing, sir," he replied hastily. "I merely didn't want you going off to London again before we'd finished investigating Mistress Danvers's death."

"I've been to London three times in the past six months, on each occasion seeking my brother-in-law here," replied Hal coldly. "As he is now resident in Adamsholme, I am not likely to go to London again this side of Christmas."

"I'm glad to hear it, sir," said the sheriff. "For you

and your brother-in-law must agree, the quicker this is settled, the better for everyone."

"Provided it is settled, as you phrase it, by finding the guilty party," said Justin sharply, "not just a convenient scapegoat."

"I am confident of doing so, sir," he replied woodenly. "I merely require the assistance of those present."

"I'm glad you are confident of something," sighed Hal. "Who do you want to talk to this time?"

"The wives of you both, if I may," he said warily.

"You can have no objection to our being present?" asked Justin sharply.

"No, none, sir," said the man. "Although, I can assure you I'll not harm either."

"I'll be the judge of that!" said Justin.

"You might care to note, Sheriff," added Hal, as Justin began to lead him toward the house, "that my wife was lately delivered of a child, and has not yet fully recovered. Mistress Danvers is also heavily with child. Should either lady suffer any ill-effect from your interview, I'd have no hesitation in taking the matter up with your superiors."

"Your warning has been noted, sir," said the man icily.

Hal lingered in the yard a few moments longer,

giving his jangling nerves time to settle. Justin was right, of course, this was no time to panic or be woolly-minded. Somebody in the house had laid a trap for one of his guests, and that somebody had to be either one of the family, or a close associate. Once again, he thought back to last Christmas at Sidworth Castle. What did he really know of Guy Armstrong, save that he was Mary's lover before her husband was killed? And that Mary worshipped him?

Justin was correct. It had never been proved to satisfaction that poor, mad Avis Soames had killed brutal Sir Edward Jolyon. They'd just assumed it, in light of her madness. True, she'd confessed in a roundabout way, to clearing her husband's path to the lordship of Sidworth Castle, but, the testimony of an insane person was suspect at the best of times.

Had they been too eager, as Geoffrey Soames claimed, to find his mother guilty, that Mary and Guy might be proved innocent? True, Mary and Guy had both been under guard when the death of Mary's servant Meg, occurred, and so they assumed that had cleared both—but *had* it cleared them? Or had he just clutched at anything in an effort to clear Mary's name and that of the man who was the father of her child?

He had to confess, he liked Guy, who was a sound enough fellow on the face of things, not over-endowed with brainpower, perhaps, but good-natured. A little indulgent of his womenfolk, especially now he'd had the good luck to restore his fortune in some measure. He was eager to pay Cecily's dowry, and just as happy with an alliance between Ned and Cecily as he had been between himself and Mary. Could such an all-round family man also be a ruthless killer? And, much more to the point, what did he have to gain from it? The murder of Sir Edward Jolyon gave him a distinct advantage, but the murder of Johanna Danvers made no sense at all—any more than did the supposedly bungled murder of Jacqueline.

No, if it were to be looked at purely as a logical exercise, the murder of Johanna Danvers must implicate himself, Justin and possibly Libby. None other made sense. He knew he hadn't done it, and he could vouch for it being impossible for Libby. That left Justin, and he paused to consider him coldly.

True, Justin had been embittered by his father's reaction to his and Bess's marriage—and even more chagrined at his father leaving the business away from him—not to mention the pretty fortune he must have been hoping to inherit. But, if Justin did have the best of motives, he also had the most scrupulous of characters. True, he could appear cold and unbending when considering a matter of law, but Hal had seen how deep his love was for Bess, Libby and the children—and even for himself. Justin might be angry that he'd not inherited from his father, but that anger was more likely to fuel him to make a fortune on his own account, than to lead him to consider murder.

That left Ned, Philip Eustace and Ambrose Carver. Ned, he could dismiss at once, but Philip Eustace, was a different kettle of fish. He was a nasty fellow. Hal felt it was a disgrace for his family to be connected with him. Had he known one tenth of what he'd since discovered about the fellow, he'd have moved heaven and earth to convince his father not to allow the marriage of Philip Eustace and Jane. Here he paused, thinking back only six months, to when his father had been intent on marrying Bess to another far-from-reliable character. Could the rumours of Jack Petherbridge's wife's death be true? He knew to his cost how such gossip spread and was widely believed.

Resolutely, he considered the unsavoury Philip Eustace. He was a dying man, and so dismissed by Justin, but was he indeed incapable of killing? After all, no actual physical strength was required, more a malicious evil, unrepentant mind, and in that, Eustace fitted the bill entirely. But again, what could have been his motive? Unless—as with previous ideas—Johanna fell into a trap set for Jane? Would Eustace truly want to kill Jane? A dying man, this close to his Maker, surely he'd not dare contemplate such evil?

And it was a method which left so much to chance. A piece of cord stretched across a stair—why, any might fall, as indeed they had. Surely Eustace, if he were to think of killing, would choose a more certain method? Then Hal recollected how weak the fellow was, how these last few days he needed his cousin to support him across a room. When he'd arrived, Philip Eustace said he had but weeks to live. Hal rather thought he was being too optimistic, and that he'd be lucky to see Hetta's wedding.

That left only Ambrose Carver, who, on the face of things, appeared agreeable enough. He'd not had a great deal to say to him previously—his own thoughts being totally dominated by his problems with Jacqueline—but, he'd found him a pleasant-mannered guest, with more than a fair store of patience, to deal, as he did, with his cousin. He supposed he'd been inclined to dismiss him as an inferior, as he combined the duties of nurse and valet to Philip Eustace. Now, he considered him more intently. He recollected Libby telling him that Ambrose was of a good Royalist family, who'd lost virtually everything in the war. An orphan since he was a child, he'd been educated at the Eustace family's expense. Now like many another young Royalist gentleman who'd lost his estate, he had to find employment. Hal was thankful that his lot was different, as he tried to find a motive for the man. Surely, in that position, it would have made more sense for Ambrose to court Johanna Danvers. He was a personable young man, and had the connections Johanna so desired. To kill her served no purpose at all. Neither did it make sense if Johanna had been killed in error for Jacqueline or Jane. He could have no connection with Jacqueline, and as the conversation he'd overheard made clear, quite the opposite plans with regard to Jane.

That left only the women, of whom one was his wife, four his sisters, and one shortly to be his brother's wife. He would swear all were not only innocent, but also incapable of such wickedness. The only female he couldn't acquit was Jacqueline. He could quite see she might kill

Johanna—and for no more reason than that she'd worn the same gown—if the mood took her. Reluctantly, he realised that he'd run out of people, once again he'd run through all the suspects and come to the conclusion that none of them could have done it. He had to confess, on the face of it, he was the obvious choice for the murderer.

Chapter Twenty

"Good afternoon, Delia," said Cecily, as she crossed the drying ground to where the girl stood, collecting linen from the hedge, where it had bleached and dried.

"Good day, Miss Cecily," said the girl, casting Ned, who'd lingered in the yard, a dubious glance.

"I've come to thank you for washing all my linen," said Cecily, handing her a coin. "Only, you weren't by when I sent for it yesterday."

"No, Miss, neither were it all ready and ironed!" she replied. "I were right ashamed of that flighty Tilda taking it to you willy-nilly! If I'd been in the laundry, she'd never have left with it like that. If you'll leave it out, Mistress Cecily, I'll iron it all again, so it'll be aired proper. You never know what you are like to go down with, wearing un-ironed linen."

"I'm afraid I needed it in a hurry, so it wasn't truly

Tilda's fault," said Cecily peaceably, "but, thank you again, you are most kind."

"You're welcome, Miss," she said, dropping a curtsey.

"Delia, could I ask you a question?" asked Cecily, casting Ned a doubtful glance over her shoulder.

"Ay, Miss, though I doubt I can answer," replied the maid, looking bemused. "I ain't clever thy knows. I never had no book learning."

"But, you're not a fool like Tilda," said Cecily swiftly, "and I dare say you can remember something which happened only a few days ago."

"Oh, aye, Miss, that ain't no trouble to me," agreed Delia. "I just can't normally answer the parson's questions."

"Do you recollect the day I arrived, Delia?" asked Cecily, not wanting to let her digress.

"Indeed I do, Miss. Last Friday, it were. We were that run off our feet, with everyone arriving at once! And Mistress Jacqueline—Lady Westwood, I should say—demanding this and that within the hour of her coming—hot water for a bath, a tisane for her head, a cup of wine and herbs!"

"Yes, I remember. The men were yet struggling upstairs with pails of hot water," agreed Cecily. "And then

I was a nuisance, too, wanting all my linen washed."

"Well, that couldn't be helped, could it Miss?" smiled the girl. "I know what gentlemen are like when they get into a fury! My old da' now—but you'll not want to hear about him!"

"I expect he was as awful as mine was," smiled Cecily. "Not that I remember him very well, he died when I was a child, but I do remember being frightened of his shouting," Cecily sighed and then, catching sight of Ned, recollected her errand. "It's about my trunk, Delia. Do you remember it was bound by a piece of cord?"

"Why yes, Miss, didn't I struggle to undo the knots on it? Indeed, Mistress was going to get her scissors when the knots finally gave."

"Yes, and little Guy woke up, do you remember? And we all went to see him," said Cecily quickly.

"Indeed, Miss, and isn't he a sweeting?" said the maid, misty eyed. "He quite reminded me of Master Harry! Oh, the pity of the Mistress, losing her last baby like that!"

"Yes," agreed Cecily. "Poor Libby, but to get back to my trunk—do you recollect what happened to the cord?"

"The cord, Mistress? No, I left it there when I took the linen away," she replied, frowning. "I thought you might need it again when you left."

"Ned says he'll mend it for me," she replied, smiling over her shoulder at him. "But Justin—Mr Danvers, you know—is concerned as to what happened to the cord."

"Well, I'm blamed if I know," she said doubtfully, as Ned came closer. "It were there on the chest alongside of your trunk—Mercy upon us, Mistress Cecily! Never say it were the same piece of cord as tripped up that flibbertygibbet from Adamsholme!"

"We rather think it must have been," said Ned, fetching it from his doublet.

"Oh, you've found it, sir?" she cried, dropping a curtsey. "Miss Cecily were looking for it."

"No, Guy found it across the stairs," he reminded her. "We need to know where it went after leaving Miss Cecily's trunk."

"Oh, yes, how silly of me!" she said. "I told you I weren't clever, Miss. Well, I don't know. It were there when I left Mistress Hetta's chamber to take down the first lot of laundry."

"And when you came back?" he asked.

"Well, I didn't go into Miss Hetta's chamber again.

I was fetching the nursery linen," she said doubtfully, folding the garments.

"This was—when? Much later?"

"No, sir, perhaps ten, maybe fifteen minutes—for I'd stopped to put Mistress Cecily's linen to soak in buck water."

"Did you notice anything? Where was everyone?" asked Ned eagerly.

"Still with little Master Guy," replied Delia. "He were being passed round like good luck, he were, in the nursery, the darling."

"Still with the baby?" said Ned incredulously.

"Yes, Ned, for Harry had woken, and we were cuddling them and talking of Bess's confinement and how Mary's had gone," explained Cecily.

Ned looked amazed and turned back to Delia. "Do you remember if the door to Hetta's chamber was still open?"

Delia frowned as she filled her basket of clean, dry washing, hitching it onto her hip. "I can't say as I can remember, sir," she said blankly.

"Think, Delia! This is most important!" urged Ned.

"Aye, Master Ned, and so it is Thomas don't find me gossiping," she replied, glancing toward the house.

"Never you mind Thomas, I'll make it right with him," said Ned firmly. "Don't you understand your Master is accused of this murder? Nothing is as important as clearing his name!"

"Master Hal!" she cried. "No, never!"

"That fool Hughes is determined it shall be him," said Ned. "Now think—was the door closed or no?"

"Aye, sir, it were," she replied, nodding her head. "I remember now. I closed it myself when I left. It were the gentlemen's door as was just closing as I went up the stairs."

"The gentlemen's door—which one, which gentleman?" asked Ned quickly.

"The handsome gentleman as is on attendance to the sick one, on Mistress Jane's husband, I mean."

"Mr Carver, that gentleman?" asked Ned, frowning.

"Aye, as I came up the stairs, I heard the creak of the door, just across the stairwell it be from Mistress Hetta's chamber. And that door has creaked I don't know how many months—for Tilda has told Thomas near all spring about it. So I looked up, and I saw the door, just closing, quiet-like."

"Is there any reason it shouldn't?" asked Cecily.

"No, like as not," sighed Ned, "but when you

returned to the chamber, Cecily, the cord was no longer there."

"Well," said Cecily. "None of it was, you know. Someone had tidied away the trunk and everything."

"Oh, aye," said Delia. "Thomas did that, he took the trunk to the closet, sir, until such time as it's required again."

"Yes, so he would," nodded Ned, "possibly putting the cord inside. If he did so, only a member of the family would know where it was stored. I must speak to Thomas—and I'll mention that I've detained you."

"Thank you, Master Ned," she said, curtseying again and hitching up her basket.

⚜

Hal, meanwhile, had entered the house to find the sheriff waiting for him, with Justin plainly full of news.

"Is something amiss?" asked Hal, his heart sinking, wondering what had occurred now.

"Amiss, Mr Westwood, no. A matter requiring some explanation, perhaps," replied the man.

"How can I help?" asked Hal glancing at Justin.

"I don't know that you can, sir," he said. "My sergeant and I have been going through the dead woman's effects."

"Yes," said Hal.

"And we came upon this note, sir, which we feel deserves some explanation," continued the man. "So, I hoped you'd be so good as to summon everyone again, that I might find the author if it."

"It's not signed?" asked Hal wearily.

"No, nor can I swear to the handwriting," said Justin, with a small smile. "I've asked Thomas to call everyone, Hal. We are to meet in the Jericho parlour in ten minutes, and I've explained that Sir Francis and Lady Westwood are out for dinner."

"In that case, you'll forgive me, I hope, if I fetch myself a cup of wine," said Hal. "I hope my people have been tending to your needs, Sheriff Hughes?"

"Thank you, Mr Westwood, your man has taken good care of us," he replied politely.

"What is it?" asked Hal in an undertone, as Justin joined him at the court cupboard.

"I don't know, he's being very secretive," he replied.

"But we went though Johanna's things immediately, Justin. We found nothing," said Hal quietly.

"Quite," said Justin. "It's odd!"

"Do you think it's something he's manufactured?" hissed Hal.

"Good God no, he's not that intelligent and he has too much integrity," said Justin tartly. "Hush, here comes everyone."

When they were once again all seated in the Jericho parlour, the sheriff took up his stance by the table.

"This letter, or poem perhaps, was found in Mistress Danvers's linen," he said. "It was hidden between the garments, and it is proof of an attachment between herself and another in this household, where only yesterday you all claimed she was little better than a stranger to you. We have also found a half-finished note or letter to a friend or cousin of hers that she was plainly writing to on the evening she was killed," he added, "but more of that anon." He paused and coughed, continuing, "I shall now read you the letter:

'My darling love,

    You have just passed me by. The velvet of your gown brushed against my foot like the gentle kiss of the sun's first rays. That faint elusive perfume that is you, still lingers on the air, filling my nostrils and lungs, rising to entrance my brain. Oh, that I might bury my face in the silkened shadowy mass of your hair, inhale that perfume, and in that instant, breathe no more! That I might stroke the soft curve of your slender neck, touch the velvet down of your rose cheek, and in that second, feel no more! Trace with my eye the outline of your lid, taste the honey on your lips, and see and taste no more! That I might hear the dulcet tones of my name fall from your tongue, and then be deaf forever! Nay, I dream. Taste, touch, sight, hearing, smell, they are all mine, I would have it no other way. For, to see you across a room is food and drink to me. Without the sight of you, the sound of your sweet voice, I am nothing'

"Here the writer breaks off," said Sheriff Hughes.

"As well he might," said Guy. "What stuff and nonsense!"

"It was beautiful," said Mary, tears filling her eyes. "Poor man, did you not feel his pain?"

"Pain?" cried Guy, by no means pleased by this. "His pain? What of our pain listening to such rantings? The man's demented, whoever he is!"

"He certainly appears to be in the grip of a powerful emotion," said Hal, thoughtfully.

"Why should a man be demented because he chooses

to write of his love for a woman?" asked Mary of her husband.

"You can't tell me such maudlin moans would impress you, Mary?" he cried, in amazed exasperation.

"What woman couldn't but fail to be impressed by such devotion?" she retorted. "Can you doubt the depth of his love?"

Guy scratched his head. "Depths of love? A lot of silly sentiment! I thought women were more impressed by actions."

"If you'll excuse me, Mr Armstrong, may I take it from your words that you deny being the author of this poem?"

"Is it a poem? It doesn't rhyme!" said Guy. "Yes, yes, it's nothing to do with me, I assure you. I couldn't write such nonsense!"

"I can vouch for that," said Mary waspishly. "Nay, nor say it."

As Guy looked astounded, Justin hid a smile and said, "Surely the best way, Sheriff, would be for us all to write on a piece of paper, that we might compare hands?"

"Writing can be disguised, Mr Danvers," he said, "but I dare say, it'll make it easier."

"There is no need," said Ambrose Carver, his face very

red. "No need for the trouble, the letter, poem—call it what you will—is mine. I wrote it."

"You did?" asked Guy. "Out of your own head?" He eyed him, much as he might another species he'd not seen before.

"Yes, I believe so," said Ambrose.

"You thought all those things yourself?" asked Guy. "All those words came from your head?"

Ambrose looked nonplussed. "As far as I am aware," he said blankly.

"If you'll excuse me, Mr Armstrong, I am trying to establish the murderer of Mistress Danvers," said the sheriff.

"Sorry, sorry," said Guy hastily. "I just find it difficult to believe—and you think it beautiful, Mary? It was only words, you know. Nothing solid, just words, spoken, and then gone forever."

"The spoken word has more power than any engine of war," said Hal softly.

"Never," cried Guy. "Why, I saw cannons take down dozens of men when I was a lad at the Battle of Worcester."

"Aye, and a dozen more rise up to fill their places, such is the power of the spoken word, the communication of thought," replied Hal.

"Gentlemen, gentlemen, please. This is hardly the time for a philosophical discussion. Ambrose Carver, you have admitted freely this letter is by your hand. It was found amongst the effects of Mistress Johanna Danvers, proving you had more than a chance-met acquaintance with her. I therefore charge you with the murder of—"

"No, no!" cried Ambrose, quickly getting to his feet. "It wasn't written for her! I'd never met the woman before we all sat down to dinner together! I had no previous meetings with her. I never even spoke to her in my life!"

"Sit down, Mr Carver, or I'll have you restrained," warned the sheriff, as the sergeant stepped forward hastily. "You can't expect us to believe that sort of excuse."

"I fear you must, however, Sheriff Hughes," said Justin. "For Mr Westwood and I went through Mistress Danvers's effects immediately following her demise, with the same idea as you had, but we found nothing. I suggest this letter has been placed there since."

"Or you missed it," sneered the sheriff.

"I think not," said Justin. "Rather an obvious place, don't you think? Amongst her linen? Not the action of a sophisticated mind."

"Who would want to place such a thing amongst a

female's petticoats, anyway?" asked Ned. "I don't understand any of this!"

"Thank heavens for that," said Guy. "I was beginning to think I'd wandered into a mad house."

"The fact of the matter is, Sheriff Hughes," said Ambrose, "this is a letter I wrote some time ago about a married lady I hold in high esteem. As far as I was aware, it was in my writing case, along with odd poems and papers. How it came to be amongst Mistress Danvers's effects, I can have no idea."

"It was written for my wife, Hughes," said Philip Eustace harshly. "I am dying, and this fellow they have given me to assist my last moments, writes love poems to my wife. Has anyone taken the trouble to test my food for poison? I warn you, this man is a murderer who'll stop at nothing! Take heed, you'll have my corpse on your hands yet!"

"We'll have that anyway," said Hal sourly. He could not approve Jane's conduct, but her husband was a singularly unpleasant specimen. "I don't see that writing a poem or love letter inspired by a married woman is a capital offence. If so, the greatest of our poets would have ended on the scaffold! Mr Carver has made no secret of his unrequited love for Mistress Eustace. There is nothing to suggest it is a guilty love—more one of cerebral fancy."

"What could it have achieved by tripping Johanna Danvers down the stairs?" asked Justin hastily, backing him up. "Mr Carver is in attendance with his cousin, 'tis most unlikely he'd go wandering about the house at night."

"You've not heard this piece of corroborating evidence," said Sheriff Hughes, producing another letter and wrinkling his nose distastefully as he opened it to the accompaniment of a cloud of sickly perfume. "This is written by the deceased herself, plainly to a close friend, one she addresses as cousin:

Dear Cos,

  Here I am at the place itself. Didn't I tell you I'd storm its pure portals! Poor Philip had no idea as to further his own best interest. Hal Westwood, (Libby's husband) is as proud as Lucifer, and Philip's boy Justin nothing but a pompous prig, but I saw them off! Came to tell me my rights as if I didn't know them already—aye and made sure Philip gave them to me! A pity he couldn't have lasted a little longer until the baby is born, but once it's a boy they are less than nothing to me! Robin says we can have

Justin out of the house and business and run it ourselves as we planned. All I've got to do is stick tight until after the baby's born and trust me to do that! That precious pair think they are so clever, but I'll get my way round them, especially Libby, her husband, he is so handsome—"'

"Is this really to the point?" objected Hal loudly, who'd been sitting there seething, to hear Johanna's true feelings expressed so vulgarly.

"I do believe so, Mr Westwood," replied the sheriff, an amused glint in his eye, showing how he'd enjoyed reading the letter out loud, (parts of which he agreed with wholeheartedly), "I am very close to the point I am making, and all has so far been relevant, you'll agree?"

"Oh, get on with it!" snapped Justin, irritated by his manner.

"he is so handsome that when he smiles a poor woman's legs turn to water. A great pity he smiles so seldom, but I know I can change that if I decide to make the effort! Yet I might decide to try another old friend who is here instead and, if possible, is just as handsome and unattached as ever. You remember Master Ambrose Carver I'm sure, as well as I do—"'

"She lies!" cried Ambrose, jumping to his feet again. "I'd never met the woman before."

as well as I do from his days at Oxford. Does he still have his liking for clean linen? I wonder, this I'll surely discover—"

"Oxford?" cried Ambrose, amazed. "My God! Oxford! Johanna—the laundry maid!"

"Laundry maid!" cried Justin in disbelief, stunned that his father could have been so deceived.

"Yes, she used to wash fine linen," stammered Ambrose. "I used to swim, and she'd often be there washing for people, she was—was—"

"Your lover?" suggested the sheriff quickly.

"Well, hardly that," stammered Ambrose, crimson-cheeked. "I—I knew her for—for a short while, in one term."

"Is that 'knew her' in the Biblical sense, Carver?" asked Justin sharply.

Ambrose cast a fleeting glance at Jane, who sat calm and composed as ever. "Well, yes," he admitted, "but this—this was years ago. Nearly seven years ago, in my first year. She moved on to richer men and then, as far as I knew, married."

"But you must see, Mr Carver, taken with this information, your letter now assumes a far greater importance!" continued the sheriff. "You say it was written for a married woman long ago, and has lain in your writings ever since. I suggest you wrote it long ago to Mistress Danvers, and she's held it ever since, and now on meeting you again threatened, perhaps, to show it to Mistress Eustace."

Ambrose stared at him. "I sat down to dine with a woman I'd known seven years previously, but didn't recognise," he said. "After dinner, she sat in the Hall, as we all did. Later that night, she died. She had recognised me, it seemed, but where had been the time to try to threaten to show it to anybody? And why should Mistress Eustace care what I'd written—if indeed that were the case?"

"He's right, Hughes, you haven't a case," said Justin. "Carver may indeed have been her lover once, but what if he had? He's not a married man. If he had any sense at all, he'd have been trying to cultivate her acquaintance. She was a wealthy woman."

Hughes shrugged his shoulders. "Very well, I shall write my report as I see fit. It isn't for me to decide who may or may not be charged with this murder."

"Quite," said Justin calmly. "Then, may we take it this meeting is at an end?"

The sheriff looked rather put-out that these startling revelations had not had more results, but unable to press the matter more, gave way with bad grace.

"Yes, yes indeed, if none of you have anything more to add. However, I shall be back, and I'll keep coming back until I do find the murderer."

✤

Chapter
Twenty One

"Which means, he's back to thinking I am his man," said Hal sometime later, when the sheriff had departed and they were left alone.

"I don't think the poor fellow has any idea who did it," said Mary. "He seems to get more confused each time he visits."

"A good thing, too," said Guy. "What do you think of this Carver fellow, Hal? I mean, it's a bit strange that he didn't recognise Mistress Danvers, isn't it?"

"Would you recognise a doxy you'd been with ten years ago, Guy?" replied Hal, who was sitting, staring into space.

"I certainly recollect the young female who was the object of my affections in my youth, yes," he replied stiffly, not liking the inference.

"No, not your first love," said Justin. "A whore you

had one night when you were drunk—saving your presence, ladies."

"I think men are odd," said Mary, wrinkling her nose distastefully. "They appear to have no sense of the fitness of things! I do believe almost any female would do for most of them."

"We certainly are vile creatures," agreed Hal. "Not cast in the finer moulds of you ladies, especially if our affections haven't been fixed."

"'Tis a man's way," said Guy bluntly. "As Hal says, until he fixes his affections on the woman he wants to marry, he'll make do with second best."

"Luckily, not all men think so," said Mary icily. "Some appear to have higher thoughts."

"Why do you question Carver?" asked Justin, smiling at Guy's look of disgust. "Is it because he writes poetry?"

"No, although to my mind, it just shows you he's not normal," began Guy.

"I've written a few verses myself, Guy," said Hal pointedly.

"Exactly," agreed Justin. "Most men of education do, I believe, on occasion."

"Well, I've never!" said Guy with an air of defiance. "And I'll swear Ned hasn't either!"

Justin smiled. "What's your point, Guy?"

"Hal!" Ned came hurrying into the parlour with Cecily. "Hal, I've been talking to Thomas, but he'll tell you himself! Speak up, Thomas."

The servant glanced doubtfully to his master. "Master Ned were asking after this 'ere piece of cord," he said. "I told him I ain't never seen it! I mean, I saw it around the young lady's trunk, but when I went to fetch it to put it away, like, there weren't no piece of cord."

"Now, Thomas came upstairs as Delia went down, she passed him in the hall, so that means the cord was taken as soon as Delia left the room," explained Ned.

"Unless it fell to the floor, or down the back of the chest, Master Ned," suggested Thomas doubtfully.

"No, because you see, Delia came back up after you, Thomas, did she not?" said Ned. "Passing you on the stairs this time. She said she heard the door to Mr Carver's chamber softly closing as she got to it, and that is opposite Hetta's chamber."

Justin frowned. "So, you think Ambrose Carver nipped across the gallery and took this piece of cord from beside Cecily's trunk, already having it in his mind to trip Johanna Danvers, who he'd only just met, down the stairs later that night."

"Well, not when you put it like that," said Ned blankly.

"He couldn't possibly want to trip Jane, who he's devoted to. Nor yet Jacqueline, and in any case, how could he know they'd all wear the same gown?" confirmed Justin.

"Apart from which, Carver was with me, you know," said Guy. "I was talking to him in the stable not half an hour after we'd arrived."

"I've found out about the cord," said Ned huffily. "You told me to find out about it, and I did. You said if we discover who took it, then Hal would be cleared."

"So I believed, and I was wrong," said Justin. "I'm sorry, Ned, I've never come across such a confusing investigation! Everything leads nowhere!"

"Except to me!" said Hal, who'd been all this time staring blankly before him. "I begin to wonder if Hughes isn't right, and I did do it, you know." Then, as his companions stared at him in horror, he added, "You've all wondered, and so now do I. Perhaps, I was sleep walking—or in the grip of a night terror—who can tell?"

"Don't—don't even think it!" cried Justin. "And never, never allow Hughes to hear you make such a suggestion."

"You are weary, Hal," Libby came to stroke the tumbled hair from his face, much as she would have done for his son. "You've not slept in three nights. How can you expect to think straight?"

Hal leaned his head against her for a few seconds. "You are right, of course, my dear," he agreed, "but I can't seem to still my brain long enough for sleep."

"I'm afraid your father's right, Hal," said Guy. "Half a bottle of brandy is what you need to get you to sleep."

Hal smiled faintly and shook his head. "I've learned a hard lesson of going drunk to bed, Guy. I can't stand the headache the next morning brings."

Justin, looking from his sister's anguished face to Hal's one of strain, mentally shook himself. "Well, this just isn't good enough," he said firmly. "Somebody killed Johanna, and it wasn't one of us. So, we'll just have to keep going back over things until we find something which doesn't add up."

"I have—continuously," said Hal.

"No, not you, Hal," said Justin. "You need to sleep, or you'll drive yourself insane."

"Ambrose Carver has some drops he gives to Eustace to help him sleep," said Mary. "I'll go and ask if he'll let you have some, Hal. Justin's right, this affair must be settled quickly now."

Without waiting for his consent, Mary hurried away. She was, she had to admit, shaken to the core by Hal's words. For, she had begun to wonder about him, and now told herself crossly in reaction and guilt that, as his elder sister, she should have seen how close to collapse he was.

Hastily, she came up the stairs, shadowy now in the dusk, mentally taking Thomas to task for not yet lighting the candles. If Ambrose Carver hadn't any sleeping drops to spare, she'd brew Hal a posset of valerian and a little brandy that should surely make him sleep.

Softly, she tapped on the door, wondering where Ambrose Carver had gone. He rather impressed her, she had to admit, with his good looks and bookish air. Not but that she loved Guy dearly, but an occasional romantic remark wouldn't have gone amiss. Sometimes, she thought, he showed more devotion to his dogs, now that they were safely married and settled into domesticity.

She tapped again, and then, when there was no reply, hesitated. The catch of the door hadn't quite caught, and she could push it open, if she could be sure the room wasn't inhabited. She might admire the man, but she'd no desire to catch him in a compromising situation. On the other hand, Hal did need the drops, and if they were to hand, she might as well get them and explain to Ambrose later.

The silence from within decided her. Gently, she pushed the door open and then leapt back with a scream of pure agony and fear, as a heavy weight fell past her face, striking her arm before crashing to the floor.

Staggering back in pain and shock, she gave a sobbing gasp and looked up to see a shadowy figure observing her from the doorway of the chamber opposite, looking like a ghost in the dusk.

"You stupid woman!" he hissed, and as Guy's voice was heard from below, and he and Ned came thundering up the stairs, followed by Justin and Hal, he disappeared back whence he came.

"Mary, are you hurt?" cried Guy, seeing her clutch her forearm. "What happened?"

"What was that crash?" cried Ned.

"Why is it so dark on the stairs? Thomas, bring a light!" called Hal. "Mary, what has happened?"

"I—I hardly know," she cried, caught between shock and pain as she cradled her arm to her chest. "I went to —to open the door, Mr Carver isn't there, and—"

Justin, who was already examining the doorway, liberally littered with pieces of a Delft jug, glanced up in dismay as he picked a small cannonball from the ruins. "Look at this, Hal," he said quietly, as Libby and Bess appeared on the stairs with cries of surprise.

"What happened?" cried Guy, cradling Mary to him. "Did someone fire a cannon at Mary and hit a jug?"

"No," said Hal, looking grim as he dropped to his haunches beside Justin and looked to the top of the door. "No, Guy, our friend the murderer, who likes a jest, is back with a vengence! This time, he put a cannonball inside a jug, and balanced it above the doorway, so that when Mr Carver opened the door, it would kill him! You've been very lucky, Mary."

"I don't feel it," she cried. "My arm is broken!"

"Yes, it looks as if it might be," Hal replied, looking at it in dismay, as Guy tried to persuade her to flex her fingers. "Come, we must get Jack Codling to take a look at that arm."

"Jack Codling, he's the farrier!" cried Guy. "This needs a physician!"

"We can send to Adamsholme for one, if you wish," said Hal, "but I've seen Jack set a lame filly's leg after a fall, when we all thought we'd have to shoot it!"

"That's true, Guy," said Ned. "He's a capital fellow. He'll mend any animal as good as new."

"This is my wife, and your sister, not a beast of the field!" cried Guy. "We'll have a physician!"

"Whatever you say, Guy, only carry her downstairs, for I think she's going to faint," said Justin. "Ned, bring that cannonball, will you? Am I right in thinking, Hal, it's one of those from the fireplace in the gallery?"

"Yes, I imagine so," he replied. "I had picked them up from the west wing when we started to repair it, brought them to the gallery, arranging them by the fire to remind us all of what had gone before. Can you manage, Guy, or do you need a hand?"

"No, I can carry my own wife, thank you," he snapped.

"Bring her into the parlour, Guy, and lay her on the day bed," cried Bess. "Hetta has gone for some feathers to burn and Cecily for some water."

"Why is it so curst dark everywhere?" cried Guy, nearly slipping on the bottom stair. "You, man, for God's sake, light the way!"

As Thomas belatedly hastened to light the candles, Mary was tenderly laid out in the parlour, her relations clustering round her.

"Sit still, Mary, do," cried Guy, as Hal hastily handed him a glass of brandy. "Here, sip this."

"No, Guy, not brandy," she cried. "I hate the smell!"

"I'll brew you a soothing posset," said Libby. "Ned, go and send someone for the physician in Adamsholme!"

"Aye, Ned, send for the sheriff," called Justin, as Ned hastened away.

"I rather do think we should send for Jack Codling, too, Guy," said Hal, as the room cleared a little. "He's not five minutes away in the village, and could set Mary's arm in a trice. She'd have to endure less pain that way, and the physician wouldn't set it himself you know, but send for the barber surgeon."

"That's true, Guy," whispered Mary, as Bess smoothed back her hair from her brow. "Do let Hal at least send for the man."

"If you are agreeable, Mary," Guy said, squeezing her hand tightly. "I only want what is best for you."

❧

Chapter
Twenty Two

Ambrose looked in dismay at Mary's wan face and red eyes, for the setting of her arm, even by the deft hands of Jack Codling, had been a painful business, and she'd been more than glad of the drops Jane had brought to her. He felt guilty that he should have delayed Jane, initially to explain himself with regard to his early acquaintance with Johanna Danvers, and thereafter with more pleasant matters, so that poor Mary had only just taken the drops.

"I am sorry, Mistress Armstrong, that you suffered instead of me," he said apologetically.

"Don't be, Carver," said Justin. "For you'd not be nursing a broken arm, but laid out in the chapel."

"Are you serious?" he asked, staring.

"I don't imagine you push your door open tamely from the threshold, do you?" asked Hal.

"No," he replied blankly. "I walk in."

"Exactly," said Justin. "Almost everyone does and they, too, would be dead."

"Well, my sister—do correct me if I'm wrong, Mary —felt a degree of unease at entering the chamber of a young man, and so having knocked twice, she pushed the door—the lock of which wasn't caught—open to make sure you weren't there and hadn't heard her. She was wishing to borrow some of these sleeping drops from you for me," he added by way of explanation, as Ambrose looked amazed.

"I see," he nodded quickly. "And the jug fell on to your poor arm, ma'am?"

"The jug and cannonball," corrected Justin.

"Breaking the forearm," said Guy. "I think it wouldn't have done your head much good, Carver."

"No indeed," he said, suddenly pale. "But, why?"

"I can only assume you've got too close to the murderer," said Justin, "perhaps in our discussion earlier. This cousin of Johanna Danvers could be one of us." He looked hard at Guy Armstrong. "You are of an age with Mr Carver, Guy. You weren't at Oxford, were you?"

"Me? At Oxford, are you mad?" asked Guy blankly. "Seven years ago I hadn't even the money to feed my family. The house was in ruins after those Roundhead bastards had finished with it, and I'd scarcely a beast left on the farm! We lived on bread and Pease pudding that winter, with the occasional bit of bacon one of the villagers could spare us. There was no money for me to go dancing off to Oxford—even if I'd had the brains."

"Tell us a little more of what happened, Mary," said Hal quickly, as Guy glared at Justin and Ambrose. "Was there anything odd about things as you went up the stairs?"

"It was dusk, Hal," she said slowly, as the throbbing pain ebbed away from her arm, leaving her feeling strangely displaced. "And Thomas hadn't lit the candles, so the staircase was full of shadows."

"Was the door awkward, heavy, as you pushed it?" asked Justin.

"Yes," she said. "Yes, I remember thinking how odd it was. I'd knocked twice, you know, and then I saw the door was a little ajar, so I pushed, calling Mr Carver's name. For I didn't want to walk in on him in a state of undress, you understand—and it didn't swing open as I expected, so I pushed again harder. I was sure by then he wasn't there, and then something rushed past my cheek and hit my arm before falling to the floor!"

"You had such a lucky escape, Mary," said Guy, stroking back her tumbled hair.

"Do you realise this means none of us are safe?" said Hal. "I can't think why anyone should want to try to kill Carver here, but this is becoming deadly. Who knows what trap the killer might set for us next."

"Then, I looked up and saw the ghost," continued Mary, plainly sleepy from the effects of the drug. "And I was so afraid. He hissed at me, showing his teeth, and I felt certain I'd die. Then I heard your voice, Guy and the footsteps, so he melted away."

"A ghost?" said Hal, frowning. "You are confused, Mary, there is no ghost here."

"I saw him," she insisted. "Standing in the doorway of the chamber opposite."

"What did he look like, Mary?" asked Justin quickly.

"Like a ghost," she said simply. "He was pale, in a long gown, like a skeleton!" She shuddered. "Horrible, only his eyes were alive."

Justin glanced to Hal, trying to see if he was following his own train of thought. "A long white gown—like a nightshirt, perhaps?"

"Perhaps," she agreed. "It was dark, I didn't see—only his eyes in his skull-like head, and his teeth!"

Hal's head suddenly came up and he met Justin's eyes, his own awake and the fatigue gone. "Justin!" he cried. "Do you think?"

"It's Sheriff Hughes, Hal," announced Ned, bounding into the room. "And do you think it's safe for us to be going about the house alone? I do wish you'd call everyone together, where I can keep my eye on Cecily. She and Hetta are closeted together in their bedchamber because Hetta's cross with Will again."

"Yes, no, I mean—I dare say the sheriff will want everyone gathered, anyway," said Hal, his mind plainly full of a new thought.

"Is it true, as your man says, Mr Westwood?" demanded the sheriff, coming in, looking harassed. "Has there been another attempt on somebody's life?"

"Yes," said Hal. "My sister, Mistress Armstrong, was lucky only to sustain a broken arm when she went to call upon Mr Carver."

"Carver, ah?" said the sheriff in a satisfied tone.

"Yes, the trap was set for him," continued Justin. "A cannonball dropped inside a jug set atop of the door."

"Set *for* him?" asked the sheriff incredulously. "No, surely not."

"Well, how else would you see it?" asked Hal.

"A trick, mayhap, to protest his innocence, even to injure me or my man, should we think to search his chamber again," concluded the sheriff, looking more pleased as he decided this.

"But you weren't expected before the morning," protested Hal.

"Look here, Hughes, my wife has been injured by your inability to catch this murderer," said Guy, inpatient with this discussion. "Now, I'm not going to sit idly by and allow my family to become targets for a mad man. You are the sheriff of this county—it is your duty to protect us from danger, and, it seems to me, you are singularly lax in this matter!"

"I can assure you, Mr Armstrong—"

"Never mind that!" cried Hal. "Justin, don't you think—"

"No!" said Justin quickly. "No, don't say it, Hal. Remember, this murderer needs to be brought to justice. Say nothing!"

"What is this?" cried the sheriff. "What are you attempting to conceal from me?"

"Nothing," said Justin. "We'll conceal nothing from you, but we need to talk in private."

"No, I'll not have that!" cried Guy. "Why, you tantamount accused me of being Johanna Danvers's lover at Oxford, not half an hour ago! I'll not have you go off into a corner with this fool, and accuse me!"

"What?" cried the sheriff. "Armstrong was Johanna Danvers's lover!"

"No!" roared Guy. "I'd never seen her before in my life!"

"Have you proof of this, Mr Danvers?" demanded the sheriff, disregarding Guy.

"Will you all listen!" cried Hal. "Silence!"

The sheriff turned to him, annoyance on his face. "Mr Westwood?" he asked icily.

"Too many are talking at once," said Hal. "There is no order or method. We must establish the truth calmly and quietly. I suggest we do so by assembling in the Hall formally, and allowing you to conduct another series of questions."

"But Hal, this fool now thinks I knew that trollop!" cried Guy infuriated.

"Hughes, my brother-in-law has never met Johanna Danvers before Saturday. He has never been to Oxford in his life, and never had a lady of ill-repute," said Hal wearily.

"Well, I'd not say that, Hal," said Guy hastily, glancing to his wife who was dozing lightly. "But, I'd certainly never met her before."

"What's all this?" cried Sir Francis Westwood's voice. "Are you all still from your beds? I thought you'd long be asleep and we'd have to let ourselves in to a darkened house." He appeared in the doorway, his face clouding over as he caught sight of the sheriff. "Oh, 'tis you!" he said coldly. "Have you taken to hounding us into the night now?"

"I was sent for, Sir Francis, by your son, Mr Westwood," he replied curtly. "There has been another development."

"Yes, sir, another attempt," said Hal quickly. "And your arrival is timely, for you can take control of the proceedings. You can have no objection, I take it, Sheriff, as my father hasn't been present for either the murder, or this last attempt?"

❖

Chapter

Twenty Three

It was plain Sheriff Hughes was most unhappy to have Sir Francis Westwood running the proceedings, but he had little choice but to comply, and quarter of an hour later found them all assembled once again in the Hall with the sheriff talking.

"In conclusion, none of you need me to tell you how serious this latest development is," he said. "It would seem the murderer is intent on fresh quarry, and will lay any trap that occurs to him or her."

"Then why is not the arrest made?" demanded Jacqueline.

"Because in this country, madam, proof is required to be laid before a magistrate before an arrest can take place," he replied coldly.

"But you do have a person in mind?" asked Hal.

"I do, Mr Westwood," he replied. "It was my intention

to arrest Mr Carver tomorrow morning."

"Mr Carver?" asked Hal, as Jane's hand flew to her mouth and Philip Eustace directed a long, unsmiling look at her. "But Mr Carver was the object of this last attack."

"So you say, Mr Westwood," returned the sheriff with irony. "It is my opinion that this trap was set up by Mr Carver, to throw suspicion away from himself."

"Don't you find that rather far-fetched, sheriff?" suggested Justin.

"I find the whole thing, nay, this entire family, far-fetched!" retorted the man. "But, I know to my cost, they are true!"

"Ask your questions, Hughes, and keep your opinions of your betters to yourself," said Sir Francis.

"I don't have any further questions," said the man sullenly. "I simply intend to arrest Mr Carver. Mr Westwood asked for this gathering."

"If I may say something?" said Justin. "Mr Carver, from my observation, you came directly from the garden to the meeting earlier this evening?"

"Yes," agreed Ambrose, his face, which had been deathly pale, reddening.

"And you'll agree, sheriff, that as you'd just left

Mr Carver's chamber after searching it, he couldn't possibly have set the trap. Either with deadly intent, or to clear himself, at this point."

"Obviously not," snapped the sheriff, irritated.

"We were with you, what? Perhaps an hour. Then, you departed, and the rest of us either followed or stayed to discuss the matter," confirmed Justin. "Where did you go, Mr Carver?"

"I went back out into the garden," he replied. "I was somewhat ruffled in spirit and needed a few moments of reflection."

"That's true," said Will Shearsby. "For I followed him from the house. He went to the yew walk."

"You both went out immediately?" said Justin quickly. "You did not stay to fetch a hat, or set a trap?"

"Will was in a tantrum," said Hetta, her eyes cold. "He stayed for nothing."

"Then, neither could Mr Carver have done so," said Justin, satisfied. "How long did you remain outside Will, Mr Carver?"

"I was out there until it began to get dark," said Will huffily. "I finished up in the stables with my groom, so I didn't see Mr Carver again."

"A fitting place, with your manners," remarked Hetta.

"That will do Hetta," said Hal, whose attention was fixed on his sister Jane. "Were you alone in the garden, Carver?"

"Yes," he replied promptly. "I wasn't fit company for anybody."

"Then he could have just as easily turned about and come back to set the trap!" cried the sheriff quickly.

"No!" cried Jane. "No, tell the truth, Ambrose! We met outside in the garden and remained out there until well after dusk fell."

"Why, you abandoned hussy!" cried her father, as Philip Eustace drew his breath in harshly. Mary looked up, her senses still dimmed, and gave a cry of fear.

"'Tis he! 'Tis the ghost, Guy! Oh God, help me, that's the ghost I saw!"

"I beg pardon for my wife, Eustace, but she's in some confusion and shock," said Guy awkwardly, reddening.

"Nay!" said Justin. "Don't apologise, Guy! Mr Eustace, were you standing at the door to your chamber when Mistress Armstrong nearly met her death?"

He sighed heavily. "The only things in life one can't predict, it seems, are the actions of foolish women! Yes, I set the trap for Ambrose, the same as I left his letter out for this idiot sheriff to see! He never sent it to

Jane—or that trollop of Saturday night. He never had the courage to do anything, but lust after my wife! Yes, I killed that silly, vulgar jade!"

"Why?" asked Justin, rather amazed at his attitude and off-hand confession.

"I'm dying," he replied, drawing his teeth back in a grimace that was ghastly enough to make Cecily shrink closer to Ned. "I'm three and twenty, and I'm dying! Why should you all go on living? Yet I'll be worm's meat in a few weeks!"

"Revenge?" asked Hal incredulously, as the sheriff sank wordlessly to a stool.

"Yes, revenge, Hal Westwood," Philip Eustace cried with a sneer. "I've given you a few nasty days, aye, and ruined your credit with your kin! You'll not hold your head up again and preach, will you? And you, my fine lawyer, the best in the land! Pshaw! I had you running in circles."

"You killed that unfortunate woman to make your brother-in-law look foolish?" asked the sheriff blankly.

"No," he replied, getting to his feet. "No, not even to make you look inept—you do that yourself. No, I killed her, as you two guessed, in error." He walked slowly around the room and came to stand before Jane.

"You shouldn't have shown me how relieved you were by it, Jane!" he said bitterly.

"What else could she be!" cried Ambrose, finally getting back the power of speech. "She's had a life of misery with you. Isn't it natural to feel a lifting of spirits if oppression is about to be removed? Don't you dare reproach her."

"And you should have hidden your feelings better, Ambrose," he said. "I'd never even looked at her until your dog-like eyes followed her everywhere. She was nothing to me, until you made her your goddess! Then, when she might finally have been some use to me, you filled her head with your devotion, and suddenly she found me repulsive. She couldn't even bring herself to touch me."

"I always thought you repulsive, Philip," she said quietly. "Only, you never cared until Ambrose loved me."

"Mr Eustace, did you stretch a piece of cord across the top of the stairs?" asked the sheriff, recovering from his stupefaction and getting to his feet.

"Yes," he replied, "yes, I left my bed after I heard everyone settle! I already put a note to my wife in her jewellery case from Ambrose, telling her to meet me. Then, I stretched a cord across the stairs. If she were true to her vows, she need have no fear. I wasn't to know that fool of a slut would go walking about in the night. Anyway, I forgot about it, and after Janey gave me the drops, fell asleep."

"You left a deadly trap for your wife and then fell asleep?" asked Hal, horrified.

"I've told you, if she were true, she'd be safe," he snarled.

"But what of Ned, next morning?" asked Hal angrily.

Eustace shrugged, "I'm dying, why shouldn't he? He risks his neck near everyday in the hunt."

"Your callousness is horrifying," said Justin. "Don't you fear for your immortal soul?"

Eustace threw back his head and laughed and laughed. The laugh progressed into a racking cough, which shook his frail frame. A drink was hastily procured for him, and a chair to support him. After a few moments, all attention was focused on him as Ambrose, with Hal's help, tended the dying man. Then, they stepped aside leaving him to continue.

"You know, this has been probably the most interesting few days of my life," he said hoarsely, wiping his blood-flecked mouth. "Watching you all growing increasingly suspicious of each other. Listening to your wild theories, seeing you running round and round in circles, and thinking that you were oh, so clever!" he smiled wolfishly as they all looked stunned. "Once Janey, for whatever obscure reason, hadn't taken the bait, I was left in a quandary, but with such entertainment! To see you, Hal Westwood, impaled on your own nobility! That was something indeed, and to watch all your kin try to convince themselves they believed in you!

"Then, I hit upon the idea of making it look like Ambrose had done it! If I couldn't kill Janey, then I could make her life unendurable by getting this fool she'd fallen in love with charged with murder. That would have been even more exquisite enjoyment for the last few weeks of my life, if he'd been imprisoned and I could have taken him into death with me, leaving her as she should be, grief-stricken."

"Don't you feel even the smallest degree of compassion?" cried Libby, tears filling her eyes.

"Strangely enough, I felt it for you," he said. "I'd never felt it before, but I thought it unfair you had to suffer for your pompous husband, for you've probably never had a wicked thought in your life."

"That's where you are wrong!" said Libby angrily. "I've

had many evil thoughts. Most people do, I believe, but with the help of the Lord and their friends and loved ones, they conquer them."

"Oh, don't talk religion at me!" he cried impatiently. "I know you devout people, you imagine your own evil!"

"You are wrong," she said. "On Sunday, I went into my garden and collected seeds to kill Jacqueline. I intended to make a tisane for her and poison her so that she'd cause no more trouble for me or my loved ones."

"Libby, hold your tongue!" cried Justin. "Sheriff, you must pay no heed to Mistress Westwood, she is but lately delivered of a dead baby, and her mind is a little uncertain. She knows not what she says."

Jacqueline, who'd been staring at Libby in horror, suddenly clutched her husband's arm. "You hear that, Francis? You hear what your prim Mistress Libby says! She was going to poison me! To poison my tisane and let me drink it!"

"Yes, I heard her, rather a case of tit-for-tat, isn't it?" he said coldly. "I'm only surprised, Jacqueline, she hasn't shown you animosity before."

"Sheriff," said Hal quickly. "My brother-in-law is correct, my wife has been ill and—"

"I didn't do it," interrupted Libby, as the sheriff stared at her, his mouth open. "Because, my brother came to find me and sat with me talking, convincing me of the love which surrounds me. He made me realise that I am but a humble petitioner, and that I must leave it to the good Lord to decide upon the fate of evil ones. I was never more thankful than when I realised what I'd been thinking of doing. Did it never occur to you, Mr Eustace, that Mr Carver has been a good and faithful friend to you? That he has nursed you like a mother? That Jane has never once opened her mouth to criticize you, but stayed at your side, waiting to help you in the next big task?"

"I'm all admiration!" he replied, disregarding the latter part. "Not only is your husband a red-blooded lecher, but you are a would-be poisoner! I never dreamt there were such depths to people!"

"Eustace," cried Justin angrily, "everyone here has known that instinct to harm another. It is inherent in us all! We strive daily to keep it under control. Only monsters like you allow their evil to bubble to the surface. Most of us kill the thought on the instant."

"What? You, too, Mr Clerk?" he chuckled. "Why, the roll gets larger! Are any of you the innocents you seem?"

"I could cheerfully strangle you now, Eustace, and think it a task well-served," said Guy contemptuously.

"Amen to that," cried Ned. "One kills a dog or a horse turned ill, the same should be done to men!"

"As the law allows, Mr Westwood," said the sheriff sharply. "Mr Philip Eustace, I charge you with the murder of Johanna Danvers on Saturday, June the eighteenth, or the following Sunday, June the nineteenth, in this county."

"Charge me with what you will, my good man, you'll never bring me to trial," sneered Eustace. "I'm dying, I've nothing to lose."

There was an abrupt silence, as the truth of this sank in. "You can't, even in humanity, throw him in prison," said Hal bitterly.

"He'll not even make it to trial," agreed Justin blankly.

"I'll have a deposition, though," snapped the sheriff. "I'll have my man out here tomorrow to write out his confession, and he'll sign it—or I'll throw him in the darkest cell in my prison!"

"Stay for that," said Justin. "I'll fetch quill and ink and do it for you."

"Indeed, Master Clerk," sneered Philip Eustace. "And what if I don't choose to sign?"

"Then, I'll take the deposition of each and every one present," he cried. "This time, there shall be no doubt as to who murdered Johanna Danvers."

❧

Chapter
Twenty Four

"Sheriff Hughes!" Justin hastened after him across the moonlit stableyard, as the man was about to mount his horse.

"Mr Danvers?" he replied with a sigh, halting.

"About my sister, Mistress Westwood," he began.

"I've already had the speech from Hal Westwood," the sheriff interrupted. "I am fully aware of how she's just lost her second child in a year, and that you both fear her brain is a little turned by grief." Something that might have been the beginnings of a smile hovered over his hard mouth. "I am not unfamiliar with the situation, you know," he added his voice gentler. "My own sister is barren, and prays daily to whatever graven image she can find to assist her."

"Oh," said Justin blankly, for he'd never imagined the man to have a family.

"Whereas, my brother's wife has just been delivered of her ninth," he continued. "Life can be a mixed blessing at times! By the by, I didn't tell your brother-in-law that, it would be like rubbing salt in the wound." He put his toe into his stirrup and heaved himself wearily into the saddle.

"Yes," agreed Justin. "But to get back to my sister—"

"As I said," he interrupted firmly again. "My own sister and I are close, and I am used to every female fancy, so you need have no fear for your sister's foolish ravings. I have heard like things from the lips of Polly, each time she loses her babies. Life can be very cruel, Mr Danvers, for some."

"Yes," agreed Justin hollowly.

"Do, for everyone's sake, make sure that wicked fellow Eustace is kept under strict lock and key, won't you?" he continued, anxiety returning with a frown for a moment. "I'm not sure I shouldn't take him with me. I could probably house him decently enough, if I put my mind to it."

"I don't think Hal's conscience would allow that," said Justin, "but you may be sure, he'll keep Eustace secure. He has a horror of him and his evilness."

"With just cause," agreed the sheriff. "I just hope Hal

Westwood doesn't live to regret his high-handed ways! Well, Mr Danvers, I hope I won't have dealings with you and your family again."

"You have all the depositions safe, and Eustace's confession?" asked Justin anxiously, as the man gathered up the reins.

"Especially Eustace's confession," he replied. "This murder will not be hung round any Westwood neck, Mr Danvers, I assure you. Good night!"

❧

Meanwhile, back in the house, Hal's mind, relieved of one care, had sought out his sister Hetta.

"Henrietta!" he said sharply, coming to where she sat gazing from the window in the small parlour into the moonlit garden.

"Oh, Hal," she visibly jumped and looked up into his face.

He sat down close to her. "Now this is all cleared up, your wedding can go forward as planned on Friday."

"Oh, yes," she said dully.

He waited a few seconds and then said carefully, "Hetta, I've witnessed the despair of two of my sisters tied to wicked men in marriage, and whilst I've no such thoughts about young Will, if this marriage is not to your taste, better to speak now than to risk years of misery such as Jane and Mary had to endure."

She was silent for a space, then she said softly: "Have you noticed, Hal, when you pray for something really hard, often the Lord gives it to you, only it's not how you think it will be?"

Hal sighed, thinking of Libby praying constantly for another baby. "I don't think that can be the Lord's fault, Hetta," he said mildly, "more like your misinterpretation."

"Oh, yes, I realise that," she said tearfully. "Only—only it's well—almost unfair! I'd been asking God to make Will more—well, more manly in his dealings with his mother—more decisive, less dependant, if you understand. And finally earlier today he took a stand against her and her outrageous demands. I was thankful at first, only now, well now—"

"Now?" prompted Hal.

"Now he's treating me in a similar manner!" she cried indignantly.

"I see," said Hal gravely.

"I'm not a vulgar jilt—am I, Hal?" she asked tearfully.

"You are certainly not vulgar," he agreed. "And it depends

whether you intend to marry him on Friday or no."

"I don't see that I should be hectored and bullied into it!" she cried defiantly.

"Hetta," he said, trying hard not to let the weariness creep into his voice. "Do you love Will?"

"I don't know," she sniffed. "I used to, but he is so changed! He keeps shouting at me and saying I must do this and I shall do that! Do you think he could become as dreadful as Sir Edward, Mary's first husband?"

Hal laughed. "Never in a thousand years! My dear Hetta, you've forced your poor Will to flex his muscles. Now you must take the consequences!"

"What! Have him lecture me forever?" she cried indignantly.

"No, you little fool," he said, shaking her a little. "You must learn how to manage him better."

She frowned. "Manage him?" she queried.

"Yes," he shook his head. "I had thought you the clever one. Tell me, how does Will react to a kiss?"

"Hal!" she blushed rosily. "You shouldn't ask such things of me!"

"Heaven forbid," he replied, smiling. "Am I to assume you never kissed him?"

She glanced away, all maidenly confusion. "He has

kissed me," she admitted.

"Very right and proper," he agreed. "Now, you go to him and beg his pardon for being such a crosspatch and kiss him."

"Beg his pardon!" she cried. "Never, he is in the wrong!"

"No, Hetta, there is no right and wrong, only love," he replied, quoting his wife. "What matters it if you are right or he is right, beg his pardon and kiss him."

She eyed him uncertainly. "But then he has won," she muttered.

"No, you have both won, if that should be important," he replied. "Trust me, once you have stopped being so stubborn, and both surrender, you'll see how foolish you are being."

She eyed him uncertainly. "Are you sure, Hal?" she asked.

"Being married to Libby has made me certain," he replied. He glanced up as a step was heard in the Hall. "Hello, isn't that Will now? Will!"

"Sir?" Will's head came about the door. "I was looking for—oh, you are here Hetta! Your sister, Mistress Armstrong, says you should be abed." He hesitated, looking miserable and then added: "I'll also, if I may, take my leave, sir. 'Tis plain I am not wanted here. No doubt, you'll be discussing the matter further with my father."

Hal squeezed Hetta's arm. "Discussing the matter with your father? I see no reason to," he said quickly. "Hetta, you've something to say to Will, I believe."

Slowly Hetta got to her feet. "I've—I've to beg your pardon, Will," she said reluctantly, a little dismayed and angered that he was thinking of going.

"Oh," he said, looking surprised.

Hetta glanced to Hal reproachfully, expecting a better response than this.

"Try the second part first, Hetta, and put a lot more love into it," he advised, smiling faintly.

She looked scandalised. "What, here, before you?" she asked in a horrified whisper.

"I've seen a couple embrace before," he hissed. "Be quick about it before he leaves!"

Will, who was staring in blank amazement at this low-toned exchange, almost backed warily from his love as she came to him.

"Hal says I must kiss you, Will," she said blushing hotly. "He says there is no right nor wrong, only love." She bit her plump lip and looked into his bewildered eyes, timidly slipping her arm about his waist. Will, meeting Hal's eyes in amazement, saw him nod before surrendering to her embrace and, if her kiss was a little uncertain, his left no room for any doubt.

"Oh Hetta, Hetta, I'm sorry," he whispered into her flaxen curls. "Do you forgive me for being such a bear?"

"Yes," she replied, hugging him hard.

"I got so confused," he admitted. "First, quarrelling with mother like that—for I'll not have her say such things about you. Then, when I came after you, quarrelling with you, it was like a night horror. I couldn't seem to make it right, however much I tried."

She snuggled into his arms. "It doesn't matter now," she said, glad to be back on terms with him.

"And you will marry me on Friday?" he asked anxiously. "I've not given you a complete dislike of the idea?"

"Of course she'll marry you on Friday," said Hal. "She's given you her word and we Westwoods don't go back on our word."

"No, indeed," she agreed docilely.

"But come, 'tis late, and you should be abed, Hetta," added Hal, stifling a yawn.

"Are you sure that horrid Philip Eustace is safely locked up, Hal?," she asked with a shudder as they dowsed the candles.

"Yes, indeed," he said grimly, "of that I am very certain. He'll not escape us!"

❧

Whilst Hal was seeing his sister to bed and making sure one last time that Philip Eustace was safely under lock and key, Libby, in her chamber, had a visitor.

"Oh, Sir Francis," she said as he knocked on the door and looked round it, to see her sitting up in bed, braiding her hair.

"Libby," he said urbanely. "I was wanting Hal, is he not come to bed yet? It is very late."

"Not yet, sir," she replied blushing. "Can I be of any assistance? He has gone to see if Mr Carver requires any help in guarding Philip Eustace."

"No, not really. I only came to say that it looks as if I won't be able to remain for Hetta's wedding, after all. I've had a summons from the King and must hasten to Hampton Court tomorrow, but I know Hal will deal with everything as he should."

"A summons?" she asked frowning. "When, sir?"

"It came by post this morn," he replied.

"There was no post this morn, sir," she said quickly.

"A special messenger was sent," he amended hastily, recollecting that she was more astute than she looked.

"Strange that none of my servants should have mentioned it," she remarked blandly.

"No, for I work for the secret service," he replied rapier-like, then, changing his tone, he added: "Believe me, my dear, 'tis better if we go quickly."

"I cannot deny that," she agreed.

"No," he glanced to her, his gaze considering. "I feel I must beg your pardon, Libby, for the trouble I've brought upon you. I've been remiss in the past, but I'll attend to the matter now so that no further damage is done!"

"Sir?" she said sharply, doubtful of his meaning.

"We go back to France, Jacqueline and I," he said deliberately. "I'm pretty certain to be sent there, and if it should happen that my wife takes sick and dies on the road, few will be surprised."

Libby stared. "I would, sir. Jacqueline is very robust."

"No female's neck is robust, my dear," he replied softly.

"You cannot," she whispered, horrified, unable to stop a shudder.

"I not only can, I will," he smiled faintly. "It won't be the first life I've taken, child, and she deserves it, if ever a woman did. She is a jade, and a whore, and will forever haunt Hal unless I can free him of her."

"But the baby, sir, Jacqueline's child!" she cried in dismay.

"The offspring of a strumpet and a courtier, none will weep for its fate," he shrugged harshly.

"No, sir, the child of your wife—and perhaps Hal," she cried, tears filling her eyes. "Don't you see, if it's a boy, and anything should happen to dear little Harry, it could be Hal's heir."

"My dear, you'll give him many more heirs. Harry will grow big and strong and sit at the table at your three score and tenth birthday to toast you," he said. "No, no more now. Just give Hal my message for me and I am for my bed."

"But, sir, I beg of you," she cried, getting from the bed and coming to clutch at his sleeve. "It could be Hal's child, and even if it is not—it is a child, a baby— give it at least a chance!"

He stared down at her, his expression difficult to read. "What? You'd plead for the life of your rival?" he asked.

"I'll beg for it on my knees, if need be," she cried.

"No, no don't do that!" He caught both her arms, supporting her weight. "By heaven, I begin to see how Hal gets to be so principled." He smiled faintly as she, her face flushed with emotion, her hair all tumbled about her shoulders, and her eyes raised beseeching, looked up at him. "And indeed, perhaps even the power you have over him. I'd never even considered the effect a virtuous woman could have on a man. Hal is to be congratulated."

"Sir, Jacqueline shall be safe with you?" she asked, clutching at him.

"My dear, twice you've held her life in your palm and have turned from temptation. Rest assured, she is safe from harm," he replied smoothly.

"I have your word on it, sir?" she asked, as he made as if to turn from her.

"My word," he smiled. "Child, I've told you already, I've killed men—aye, and women too—in the course of my life. What use is my word to you?"

"The word of my husband's father will be of much note to me," she said simply.

He stared, becoming irritated by her insistence. "My word I cannot give—my intention, I will vouch for."

"The road to Hell is paved with good intentions," she replied.

His face darkened. "By God, woman, you go too far. Allow me to be a better judge than you!" Then, as she continued to hold his gaze calmly, not moved by the flash of anger, he added sharply: "Very well, I shall do nothing and see how well virtue is rewarded! My word, Libby Westwood, Jacqueline shall take no harm of me!"

"Thank you, sir, and good night," she replied.

"Don't thank me," he snapped. "You've probably given yourself a few more years of misery from tonight's stupidity!" He stalked from the room and Libby got back into bed, carefully re-braiding her hair.

Hal entered a few moments later, yawning. "Was that my father I just saw leaving?" he said anxiously.

"Yes," she replied. "He came to say he's been summoned by the King to Hampton Court and cannot remain for Hetta's wedding."

"That's nonsense," said Hal. "He has received no message."

She veiled her eyes. "Nevertheless, that's the one he gave me."

He was silent as he quickly undressed and got into

bed. Then, as he slipped his arm about her shoulders, he said: "He's going away again and taking Jacqueline away so she can do no more harm."

"That is, I believe, his intention," she agreed with a sigh.

He heard it and hugged her closer. "Do you see the need?" he asked tentatively.

"No, and so I told him, but he was adamant that the King needs him to be in France," she replied, trying not to sound glad.

"Surely, the King cannot require him to spend his life in exile," said Hal. "And what of Jacqueline and—"

"Her child?" suggested Libby, as he hesitated.

"No, no, I was merely thinking it a little unfair that she is never allowed to settle—but he is probably right," he added hastily. There was an awkward silence between them before he continued quietly, "My father seems to think the father of her child is her courtier lover, and that I should dismiss her claims from my mind."

"But?" said Libby, after the silence lengthened.

"I just fear for the child's fate," he said, almost in a whisper. "Be it mine—or any man's—as a pawn in my father's and Jacqueline's hands."

"He gave me assurance of their safety," she said gently.

"I don't doubt it," he replied, his tone weary.

"And his word upon it. He called me a fool, but I have his word," she added.

"Much good may it do us," he said with a sigh. "But I don't see—short of keeping Jacqueline safe here— what else we can do." He hugged her closer. "By heavens, I am weary. I'll speak further with my father tomorrow. He can hardly be gone before first light, can he?"

"Mmmmn," she agreed sleepily. "We'll talk to him at breakfast."

⚜

Chapter
Twenty Five

Ned bounced cheerfully into the Hall the next morning, his ruddy cheeks flushed with exercise, a broad smile on his freckled face.

"Father has gone then," he announced.

All eyes turned on him at once.

"Father? Gone?" Hal cried incredulously.

"Gone? I had thought them both still abed," said Libby, in dismay.

"Indeed," Mary replied tartly. "I can't imagine Jacqueline leaving her bed much before noon."

Ned looked adoringly at Cecily as he took a seat opposite her, then he grinned again. "Jacqueline was spitting fury and that woman of hers, Marie, was as sullen as a winter's day—but there they all were in the stables, at five o'clock this morn when I went to saddle up a horse to take out my hounds. Which reminds me, Hal, there's a vixen in cub over at—"

"Oh, never mind your hunting, Ned!" Bess interrupted impatiently. "Tell us do! What did father say? Why, if he has left us Hetta can't be married!"

"Aunt Margery and Aunt Kate are due back tomorrow. They'll be so cross, for Cousin Tom can ill-spare them at the moment," cried Mary.

"Most of what father was saying isn't repeatable," said Ned. "His horse had thrown a shoe and he was forced to travel in the coach with Jacqueline, which plainly wasn't part of his plan. He said the King had recalled him, and that they were for France."

"Don't fret, Hetta," soothed Hal, as she and Will looked at each other in dismay. "Father told Libby the same tale last night. It seems I am to give you away as was planned earlier. There will be no need to cancel the wedding."

All the women immediately relaxed, as Hetta replied prettily: "I'd sooner it was you anyway, Hal."

"When you say 'tale' Hal, is one to assume you are not convinced by it?" Justin asked, frowning.

Hal smiled grimly. "It sounded a little thin to my mind, Justin. It had been my intention to discuss the matter further this morning. I know I should have pursued it last night—late as it was—but I must confess by the time Carver, Jane and I had settled that monstrous husband of hers into bed, I was sore weary and not in need of another quarrel."

"You thought there would be a quarrel?" asked Mary doubtfully.

"Jacqueline seems determined on most occasions to promote one," replied Hal wearily.

"I've never known a female like your stepmother, Hal," agreed Guy. "She's nothing but trouble, that woman. I tell you what, we're better off without her."

There was a pause as everyone, who had previously been considering the state of their affairs and wandering what could be done, thought about Guy's statement.

"Certainly Aunt Margery and Aunt Kate will be happier if Jacqueline is no longer one of our number," said Hal, who'd been dreading explaining all the shocking events to his aunts.

"Yes, you and Libby must be greatly relieved, too," said Mary tactlessly.

"I don't think anyone of us will miss Jacqueline's unkind remarks," said Bess quickly. "And if Hetta's wedding can go ahead after all, perhaps Jacqueline and Father's departure is for the best."

"At least Jacqueline won't be here to recount the more recent events with great relish to our wedding guests," said Libby with an inward shudder, as she thought of how it might have been.

All around the table brightened visibly. "Indeed," said Justin thoughtfully. "Once our stepmother's funeral is over later today, Libby, there should be no further occasion to discuss the matter."

"Hughes said last evening at his departure, that he thought his report would take a few days before becoming common knowledge," remarked Hal.

"So we can easily pass it off as a tragic accident for now," said Mary. Then as they all looked askance at her, she added sharply: "Well, we can, you know! Oh, yes, there will be talk, it's true, but if we just try to remember that it was a sad accident by one who didn't know the house, I think we might get by. After all," she added as Hal opened his mouth to dispute this, "we don't want to ruin Hetta's wedding, do we?"

"No!" agreed Hetta, Will, Libby, Bess and Cecily in unison.

"All we want to do, Hal," said Mary sweetly as he fell silent, "is to stand firm as a family and that is something we Westwoods are very good at!" ❧ THE END ❧

Refresh your memory by reading the last chapter of the previous book:

A Storm in the Wassail Bowl

It was a grim-faced and subdued party that gathered before the roaring fire in the Great Hall a little later. The bloodied, broken body of Avis Soames had been picked up by the servants and put upon a hurdle awaiting laying-out, with her victims, in the chapel.

The remainder of the guests sat, exhausted by events, sipping mulled wine, and allowing the women to minister salves and bandages to their hurts.

Ned and Justin had cuts and bruises to both hands and legs from their struggles with the frozen stones. Guy Armstrong's shoulders were aching from the attack on the tower door, which now hung drunkenly on its hinges, but Hal was in the worst case. Now all sense of urgency was over, his injured shoulder was screaming in agony, which showed in the greyness of his face, and tautness of his mouth.

"What a dreadful, horrible end, " faltered Sir Walter, ashen-faced and twitching. "Oh, my poor dear wife! Oh, that sweet, sainted lady!"

"Sweet, sainted lady be damned!" cried Guy Armstrong hotly. "She was a dangerous lunatic, who killed your cousin, and his whore, and tried to kill my innocent little sister! Sweet, sainted Lady? She was an evil, old harridan, who deserved to die. A pity she had so easy an end, I say."

"Aye, we noted your reluctance to assist!" snarled Geoffrey Soames. "And your hurry to smear her name with murder. It's you that profit from her death, you, and your strumpet. Don't think I'll allow all this to be swept aside, and the blame put at my mother's door, now she's dead and can't defend herself. You had the most to gain, and I'll make sure all the details of this day are known far and wide. You are not going to get away with this piece of infamy, Armstrong."

"Gentlemen, less heat, if you please," said Hal. His pale face was etched with pain, as he sipped at a cup containing a noisome-looking brew, which his sister Mary had handed him.

"Less heat!" Soames rounded on the injured man, his teeth drawn back in a snarl. "Don't try to come the Justice over me, Westwood! I'll not be deterred by you all closing ranks, although you might not live to see the day out, sitting there drinking that Borgia's brew."

"My son, my son, I comprehend your grief," Sir Walter remonstrated gently. "But try, I beg, for a little civility, if you please. Hal Westwood is a hero, but for whose intrepid head, and quick wits, we'd be facing a greater disaster! He tried his best to save both ladies, you know, at not in inconsiderable risk to his own life."

"More risk than you realise, Sir Walter," cried Libby. She was endeavouring to fashion, with hands that she couldn't stop shaking, a sling for her husband. "He dangled a hundred feet above that courtyard by an already injured shoulder, in an effort to stop Lady Soames! What could you have been thinking of, Hal, to take such a risk?"

"I didn't think about my shoulder, until it was too late," he replied. He drunk off Mary's brew defiantly and sat up with a low groan, submitting to his wife and sister's ministrations, as they settled a sling about his neck, and tenderly lifted his useless arm into it. "Until I let go of that casement, I never gave it a thought. Then, I was in such agony, that I knew if I didn't move swiftly, I'd be splattered across that courtyard!"

There was an abrupt silence, as all seemed to see again, the figure of Lady Soames, flattened against the bloody snow. Then as he began a halting apology, Cecily interrupted hastily, "I'm so very glad you were not, Mr Westwood, and I thank you from my heart for rescuing me. Are you still in great pain?"

"I'm afraid I was all too aware of the risk," shuddered Justin. He was still extremely pale himself, and smiled uncertainly at Bess as Hal assured Cecily he hardly felt his shoulder now. "I fear I have no head for heights at all."

"Then you were doubly brave," soothed Bess. "For you went onto the battlements, in spite of your fear."

"Even if he did have to spew his guts in the privy after!" sneered Soames. "God, you Westwoods sicken me, with your heroism and nobility!"

"We Westwoods don't greatly care for you, either, Soames!" snapped Ned. He had Cecily's hand clasped fast in his own, and looked as if he'd never let it go again, "You're full of nothing, but threats and bluster. Don't think to throw us from the scent that way! Lady Soames was mad, and you both knew it!"

"Not knew it," bleated Sir Walter, as Soames turned from Ned's determined glare. "I had begun recently, I must confess to—to entertain the—the gravest of doubts— as to her sanity. Hadn't we, Geoff?"

"No!" Geoffrey snapped curtly. "No, my mother

was as sane as any of you. She may have been a little over zealous, mayhap, in matters of religion, but that is hardly a fault in these godless days. I shall take my affidavit she was sane enough, until literally tipped over the edge, by you mad pack of Westwood dogs, baying for her blood!"

"Come, Soames! I can understand your horror and grief," said Justin. "But to try to whiten your mother's actions thus, is criminal! Sir Walter, I shall require a deposition from you, stating that your wife's sanity had recently become suspect. I shall hand that, along with my report of findings into this matter, to the sheriff and crowner, as soon as this snow thaws. I imagine the case will rest there."

"Yes, yes indeed," said Sir Walter hastily. "No, Geoff, leave it. I beg— no more this night—I beg you. Let us both retire with our grief."

Surprisingly, Soames made no further protest, but got up abruptly and left the hall. Sir Walter got to his feet hesitantly. "Do you think the findings will preclude a Christian burial, Mr Danvers?" he asked piteously.

Justin glanced blankly to Hal, who stared at the wine in his cup. "I can't see why, Sir Walter," he replied at last. "The lady slipped, did she not?"

He bowed his head. "Thank you gentlemen, thank you," he said quietly and followed his son from the room.

"Do you truly believe so, Hal?" asked Ned.

Then, as Hal shrugged and drank off the mulled wine, Libby said gently, "It seemed to me, she wanted to die. She made no effort to help herself, in fact, quite the reverse, poor woman."

Ned nodded. "Yes, she was screaming foul abuse at me, and trying to pull off the cord about her waist, all the time we were struggling to haul her back." He gave a sudden shudder, as he recollected her mad eyes. "But she deserved to die, trying to kill Cecily as she did!"

"Will that be the end, do you think, Danvers?" Guy Armstrong asked anxiously, as he refilled Hal's wine cup, "Do you truly think she killed Sir Edward, and the girl Meg?"

Justin sighed. "I don't think we could have got a conviction on her confession," he admitted. "She was quite clearly mad, yet if not her, who?"

"I thought it was Soames," said Ned.

"Perhaps, in which case, she'd have gladly died for him," replied Justin. "I don't know about Sir Edward, but I think she killed the wench. Most certainly she would have happily taken Mistress Cecily to her death. In truth, Armstrong, it was a better end perhaps, than the horror of a trial, and either hanging, or being shut up in Bedlam for life."

Guy Armstrong shrugged. "This result doesn't clear either Mary, or I, from suspicion. And in the future we've still Soames, and his dissatisfaction and complaints to contend with. He'll not let matters rest."

"Oh, I think he will," said Hal, grimacing in pain, as he moved slightly. "I think Sir Walter will find a way of persuading him." He met the others blank eyes. "Sir Walter was rather concerned over the burial, don't you think?"

"You mean, we can always threaten to tell the authorities she took her own life?" Guy said, enlightenment breaking on his puzzlement. "Of course, if she's a suicide, she wouldn't be allowed a Christian burial."

"I don't think we need be quite that crass." Hal frowned at this spelling out in words that which he would much rather have left unspoken. He drunk deeply of the wine, and felt the warmth finally coming back into his bones, with some relief.

"Yes," said Justin thoughtfully, "I think we'll tell Sir Walter, we'd best leave justice to the Lord, who sees so much more than we do, and knows well the secrets of our hearts."

"Speaking of secrets," said Guy, observing how Bess sat beside her husband, with her head on his shoulder, and gazed adoringly at him. "Are we to gather that your wedding is no longer to be concealed Mistress Bess?"

"Well, of course, it isn't," said Mary firmly. "Fill Hal's cup again Guy, We'll all drink a toast to their happiness! Hal knows there is little point in continuing a senseless quarrel."

Hal felt a curious lassitude stealing over him. The pain was still in his shoulder, but not quite so fierce, and a pleasant warmth and muzziness surrounded him. "Indeed, I do Mary," he said, his words a little slurred. "I know, of all the people in the world I can trust, my new brother-in-law must rate highly. I merely hope the next brother-in-law you mean to present me with, won't try to get me drunk each occasion we meet. You are prepared to carry me to bed, are you, Armstrong?"

"Both you and your sister," he replied with a grin. "But if you are enquiring as to when we mean to be married, the answer is at once, privately, as soon as the rector can get here. My son won't be born a bastard, never fear."

"But the scandal, Guy," protested Fanny, looking horrified. "I beg you won't involve Tom in it."

"Tom is involved up to his neck," he replied. "He married Bess and Justin on Christmas Eve. If there's going to be one great scandal anyway, we may as well give the gossips something to really get their teeth into."

Hal gave a tipsy laugh, "I rather fear, Mistress Armstrong, you are destined to a life of disappointment, if you cannot live with scandal. It appears you will probably be related to the Westwood family twice over. And we Westwoods cannot, it would seem, exist without scandal."

"Hal!" Ned's ruddy face flushed deeper with gratification, "Does that mean you'll back me with father, in my desire to marry Cecily?"

"Having gone to such lengths to rescue her, should we lose her to another?" Hal asked with a lazy laugh. "In truth, beside the furore that will be caused by Bess and Justin, and Mary and Guy, I think your betrothal and a marriage will be a shining example of the normal. Apart from that, if we can get you settled, Ned, that only leaves Hetta for our father to find an unpleasant surprise for. It seems, after all, he must be satisfied with one of us wedding an heiress!"

"I rather think, my dear, you've had too much of Guy's wine. I fear it might take two, or three, to get you to bed," said Libby, smiling, but with a faint air of disapproval.

"No, my dear," he returned her smile. "On the contrary, I've had just enough wine to see clearly, how lucky we are to be here this night. I raise my cup—A health to us all!"

Enjoy the first chapter of the next book in the Hal Westwood Series of Restoration Mysteries:

Dancing with Fire

The face of the blonde giant of an innkeeper changed at the question.

"Sir Henry Westwood?" He repeated the words, and if he didn't spit, the sense of it was in the tone of his voice, "Yes, he's here."

"Good, then I shall require lodgings, too," said Justin Danvers, "and a hot supper, if you'll be so good."

"'Tis lateish!" muttered the innkeeper sullenly.

"Indeed it is," agreed Justin. "I've travelled thirty miles to get here. I am weary and I'd appreciate a hot meal at once."

"At once, your honour," an older woman said, as she came hurrying to them. She cast the innkeeper a frowning look and continued, "I've a rabbit pie as will go down a treat, aye, and just the last portion of a baron of beef that Sir Henry himself complimented me upon! Will your honour be a friend of Sir Henry?"

"I am married to his sister," replied Justin, as the inn-keeper returned to serving ale with sour grace.

"Then I've no doubt he'll be glad to see you, for a man powerful for his family they do say Sir Henry be! Will you be pleased to follow me, Mr—"

"Danvers," he replied, "Justin Danvers."

"I'll put you up here, near Sir Henry." She led the way up a creaking set of stairs and along a low-beamed corridor. "Sir Henry being justice at the Sessions, he has his own private parlour. Alas, I have only the one to offer, your honour."

"No matter," said Justin pleasantly, following her over the threshold, down two steps into another low room with a large casement window. He cast his hat and gloves to the comfortable looking bed, noting the linen looked spotless. "Someone will bring up my bags?"

"At once your honour, and if you are wanting to visit Sir Henry, I could serve your supper in his parlour, sir. You'll find it a deal more comfortable than the coffee room which is overfull—it being market day."

"Was it market day? Justin asked. "Yes, I never thought, but thank you Mistress—?"

"Blackwell, your honour," She replied with a dimpled smile and the suggestion of a curtsy. "Susanna Blackwell."

"Thank you, Mistress Blackwell, I'll do just that," he replied, realising that she wasn't, in fact, much older than her husband.

She bustled away, whilst Justin, staying only to wash off the dust of the road, walked along the corridor and down two steps to the private parlour.

He entered on command and paused in the doorway, rapidly scanning his brother-in-law's face in the candle-light, for any confirmation of his sister's fears.

"Justin?" Hal said blankly. "What do you—?" Then in quick fear, he added, "Libby? The children?"

"All alive and well, not three hours since," he replied swiftly. "Especially the baby, young Francis. By heavens, what a pair of lungs! It seemed my lord was a hungered and would not wait. He is most definitely your father again, Hal."

Hal's face, relieved of care, relaxed into a slight smile. "Yes, he is, isn't he?" he agreed. "And doesn't he like the admiration, too?"

"I'd have not thought it possible in one but a month old, but yes," Justin agreed with a smile. "So I've left my brood with Libby and Jane for a few days and thought to come to join you here," he added.

Hal's handsome face took on a sardonic look. "By

whose order?" he enquired tartly.

"No order," replied Justin, with an air of innocence. "But folk go on pilgrimages in April, you know, and I've had word through my cousin Eunice about a possible client who feels he has a matter of some concern to put before me. So I thought, why not? Hal can bear the company, I am sure."

"Yes, you and your sister are so very transparent," Hal replied with a satirical glance. "I know she sent you to watch over me."

"Are you a child then to need watching?" Justin asked mildly.

"No indeed!" he retorted robustly, "but I know Libby when she gets herself into one of her fusses."

Justin smiled innocently. "Hal, in truth, I had to come to Chawcester, and the Greyhound is the best inn."

"Run by the surliest innkeeper," replied Hal.

"Yes, indeed," laughed Justin. "What a welcome! How does he get trade—but of course, his wife is very comely."

"Not his wife—his step-mother," replied Hal. "Mistress Blackwell was married to his father, a ruined King's man—or so she tells me—who lost vast estates in the last war. Did not everyone? It would seem the

Greyhound Inn was all that remained to them. I am given to understand that Master Blackwell senior drank himself into oblivion fairly quickly, but his son has decided to hold a grudge against the world."

"The whole world, or just you personally?" Justin asked smiling.

"I am doubly in his bad books for I sent a friend of his off to the Assizes yesterday where I devoutly trust he'll be transported to the colonies and bad luck to them as far as I can see," he replied, with a return to his former gloom.

"May I help myself to a cup of your wine?" Justin asked as he darted him a sharp glance.

"Do and be welcome," he replied, drinking off his own.

"I've further imposed upon your good nature, by telling Mistress Blackwell to serve me my supper here," Justin continued, pouring wine for them both.

Hal shrugged his acceptance, and returned to his chair, yawning prodigiously. "Bess is well" he asked after a space, "and the baby?"

"Both are very well," he replied. "I'd not have left them else, but we think Bess is with child again, so we thought a little country air would be best for them both through the heat of the summer. There are cases of plague in Adamsholme."

"Are there?" Hal asked sharply. "That's bad news. You must take care upon your return, Justin. I know there are always a few cases, but I live in dread of a bad attack!"

"I think we all do," agreed Justin, "and we were lucky last summer. No more than twenty taken in all, Hal. I must admit I was never more thankful that you made us stay at Westwood, and that you got us from London, for there were a good few cases there, as ever. Both Jack Steene and Will Johnson were killed you know, and their clerk—not to mention the people in Rankin's Court."

"Yes, it must have been a prime area," agreed Hal. "But many towns and villages suffer every year. We were lucky at Westwood."

"Especially lucky when you consider Hughes's man, Hoskins died not a month after he visited us," said Justin.

"Yes," agreed Hal, his thoughts going back to the previous summer. "Yes, very lucky in many ways, even poor Will survived with Hetta's nursing, though he is but a shadow of his former self."

"He's gaining ground," soothed Justin. "He'll do better now the warm weather is here. Not much of a start to married life for poor Hetta, though. Little more than a month a bride and her groom was at death's door."

"Not to mention Will's mother going as she did within a few hours," said Hal. "Such grief for the poor lad."

"Yet a blessing in some ways for Hetta, you can't deny," said Justin. "It would have been a difficult life with Mistress Shearsby as her mother-in-law."

"Yes, especially after the scandal broke about Eustace's death," said Hal. "I must say Isaac Hughes stood by us in a magnificent manner."

"Mmmn," said Justin. "He's improved enormously since he doesn't personally hold you and I responsible for every murder locally."

Hal chuckled as a knock came upon the door. "Ah, Mistress Blackwell, is that my brother's supper? He is obliged to you," he said, the laughter still in his voice.

"Nay then, your honour, I'm obliged to him," she replied, her eyes bright, "Ah, but his coming has banished your melancholy, and for that you must be doubly thankful! Such a time as he's been having at the Sessions, your honour," she continued, turning to Justin. "Such dreadful long pleas, and his honour forced to sit best part of the day, listening to a lot of lies told by lawyers."

"Nay, you must not say so," said Hal gently. "Lies they are not, merely differing versions of the truth. Especially you must not say so before this gentleman, for he, too, is a lawyer."

"Nay, then!" she cried indignantly. "As if we've not enough of the rascals of our own, without more coming. For that Jonas Capel now—he's a rogue as anyone who lives in Chawcester will tell you."

"No, ma'am, you must not tell me," Hal replied patiently.

"I assure you, Mistress Blackwell, I've been sent for," said Justin, in some amusement, hungrily attacking his supper, "by a Mr Benton, a maltster?"

"Edmund Benton has sent for you?," the woman cried, opening her deep-blue eyes wide.

"Well," amended Justin, "my cousin, Eunice Latham recommended me to her sister-in-law, Dorothy Palmer —and is not Master Benton her brother?"

"Only by marriage," she replied, but she was obviously impressed by this pedigree. "Oh, aye, I never said Edmund Benton wasn't well-connected. That's what makes it all the more shocking, I suppose."

"Shocking?" asked Hal succumbing to her lure.

"It'll be about the lad, I suppose," she continued, and a faint smile curved her lips, for she'd been trying to remove the blank look from her important visitor's eyes for the last few days. Why, she didn't know, but he stirred something within her. Yes, he was handsome, very handsome, but it was more than that. The air of melancholy that hung about him had wrung her heart many a time, bringing out all her motherly instincts. "Poor thing! Ah, but he was a golden lad, if you know what I mean."

"Was?" asked Hal.

"An apprentice of Mr Benton was killed last month," said Justin. "Robin Tripp, his name was, just finished his time—and was universally popular."

"Not universally so," replied Hal dryly.

"Well, perhaps not," agreed Justin. "Although it may only have been an accident."

"Pooh, that was no accident," Mistress Blackwell replied tartly. "Robin were the best fire dancer we've ever seen! This were the third year that he leapt the flames at Beltane for luck and none able to go higher."

"Leapt the flames for luck?" Hal repeated the words incredulously.

"Tis a custom, Hal, going back to ancient times when a young lad was, indeed, a sacrifice to the forthcoming season," explained Justin.

"As it would appear this poor fellow was," said Hal in disgust. "I trust the town does well out of his blood."

"Nay then, Sir Henry, 'tis nowt but a bit of fun on a fair day," she cried, sensing his disapproval. "The local lads train for it they do, for weeks, and generally, it be safer than football that they play at Chipping Barbury on Easter Day! Over in Chipping Barbury there is always a death, at least—and I don't know how many broken heads besides."

"These sports and games take place in most towns and villages at this time of the year, Hal," said Justin in explanation, as Hal looked appalled at this description. "Did they not do a like thing in France when you were there?"

"Not that I recall," he replied frowning, "but then we were seldom in one place for any length of time. I certainly don't recall them occurring in England, when I was a child."

"They died out a lot in the war," said the landlady preparing to leave. "I guess there were enough killing to satisfy the blood-lust of most men then."

"She's right," said Hal thoughtfully, as she closed the door behind herself. "That's what it amounts to, isn't it?"

"I don't know until I've investigated it," said Justin. "I shall begin by interviewing Mr Benton tomorrow. Have you seen much of Mary and Guy?"

"No," he replied. "I've been too busy and they have been taken up with these cousins of Guy's who are staying with them." He grinned suddenly. "I gather Guy's not best pleased with the elder of them. It seems he has some land in Hereford and Guy and Mary make a convenient stopping off place in his journey. Guy said to me, that he never knew he had cousins from Hampshire until he made a fortune, now suddenly he has a whole host of kin there."

Justin smiled faintly. "Is Ned still with them?"

"Aye, and still bemoaning fate and his put off marriage." Hal agreed.

"Both him and Ambrose," said Justin. "He wrote to me only last week saying that he thought this year would never be done with, but I wrote saying that by the time he'd eaten his dinners at the Inns and qualified enough to help me, it would almost be next January." He paused, choosing his words carefully. "That's when you agreed upon for the weddings, isn't it?"

"Well, my father will only have been dead just over the year, but Ned insists he won't wait a day longer," replied Hal sourly.

"Well, Ned is very much in love," said Justin gently.

"Aye, but—oh well, there's no point in going over it again. Tell me instead about this boy Robin Tripp. Do they suspect foul play?"

"Presumably so, or I'd not have been sent for," Justin replied. "I know little more than the barest facts, but if you care to accompany me tomorrow, perhaps we can discover more. You don't sit again until Monday, do you?"

"No, no, I don't," he said thoughtfully. "And yes, it might be pleasant to bend my mind about different problems. I'll gladly accompany you tomorrow to visit your worthy maltster."

www.ingramcontent.com/pod-product-compliance
Lightning Source LLC
Chambersburg PA
CBHW031424240626
47154CB00001B/189